REGISTER
OF
ROYAL AND BARONIAL DOMESTIC MINSTRELS
1272–1327

REGISTER OF ROYAL AND BARONIAL DOMESTIC MINSTRELS 1272–1327

Constance Bullock-Davies

THE BOYDELL PRESS

First published in 1986 by
The Boydell Press
an imprint of Boydell & Brewer Ltd
PO Box 9, Woodbridge, Suffolk IP12 3DF and
51 Washington Street, Dover, New Hampshire 03820, USA

ISBN 0 85115 431 X

British Library Cataloguing in Publication Data

Register of Royal and baronial domestic minstrels
1272–1327.
1. Minstrels – England – History
I. Bullock-Davies, Constance
780'.942 ML182

Library of Congress Cataloging in Publication Data

Bullock-Davies, Constance
Register of royal and baronial domestic minstrels, 1272–1327

Bibliography: p.
1. Minstrels – Great Britain – History.
2. Great Britain – Royal household – History.
3. Great Britain – History – Edward I–II, 1272–1327.
4. Great Britain – Social life and customs – Medieval period, 1066–1485.
I. Title.
GT3650.5.G7B84 1986 784.5'00942 85–29073

Printed in Great Britain by
St Edmundsbury Press, Bury St Edmunds, Suffolk

CONTENTS

ACKNOWLEDGEMENTS

The publication of this book has been assisted by a grant from the Twenty-Seven Foundation

It is with sincere pleasure that I express my thanks to the Twenty-Seven Foundation for the generous grant awarded me. To Professor Martin Smith and Dr Richard Barber I am deeply indebted. Their most kind consideration and help in seeing to my correspondence concerning the production of the book while I was incapacitated by illness relieved me of great anxiety. Mrs Nerys Hague has been responsible for the typing and processing of the whole script, a task she has accomplished with admirable expertise; to her and to Messers Boydell and Brewer, who have gone out of their way to overcome practical difficulties caused by my illness, I offer my warmest appreciation and thanks.

C. B–D.

ABBREVIATIONS AND SOURCES

References prefaced by E101 and C are to the Exchequer accounts in the Public Record Office.

Abbrevatio Rotulorum Originalium in Curia Scaccarii London, 1805–10
Add.MSS. Additional Manuscripts in the British Museum/Library
Archaeolgia
Bain *Calendar of Documents relating to Scotland*. ed. Joseph Bain. 4 vols. Edinburgh, 1881–88
Bodley MSS. Manuscripts in the Bodleian Library
Book of Fees
Botfield *Manners and Household Expenses of England in the Thirteenth and Fifteenth Centuries*. Beriah Botfield. London, 1841
CCR *Calendar of Close Rolls*
CPR *Calendar of Patent Rolls*
CLL *Calendar of Letter-books of the City of London*
Calendar of Ancient Deeds
Calendar of Chancery Warrants
Calendar of Fine Rolls
Calendar of Inquisitions Post Mortem
Cartularium Monasterii de Rameseia Rolls Ser. 1884–93
Cartulary of Holy Trinity, Aldgate London Record Society. 1971
Cheshire in the Pipe Rolls edd. M. H. Mills and R. Stewart Brown. Record Society of Lancashire and Cheshire
MSS.Cott. The Cottonian Manuscripts in the British Library
Foedera ed. Thomas Rymer. Record Commission. London, 1816–69
Fryde *Book of Prests of the King's Wardrobe for 1294–5*. ed. E. B. Fryde. Oxford, 1962
Giraldus Cambrensis *Opera. De rebus a se gestis*. Rolls Ser. 1861–91
Gough *Scotland in 1298*. H. Gough. Edinburgh, 1888
Itinerary of Edward I. 1272–1307. Paisley, 1900
Green *Lives of the princesses of England from the Conquest*. Mrs M. A. Green. 6 vols. London, 1849–55

MS.Harley The Harleian manuscripts in the British Library

The Issue Rolls

LQC *Liber Quotidianus Contrarotulatoris Garderobae Anno Regni Regis Edwardi Primi Vicesimo Octavo*. ed. for the Society of Antiquaries by Lort, Gough, Topham and Brand. London, 1787

PW *The Parliamentary Writs and Writs of Military Summons*. ed. Sir Francis Palgrave. Record Commission. London, 1827–34

The Pipe Roll

The Red Book of the Exchequer Rolls Ser. 1896

Rotuli de Liberate ac de Misis et Praestitis and *Rotulus de Praestito* ed T. Duffus Hardy. Record Commission. London, 1844

Rotuli Scotiae edd. D. Macpherson, J. Caley and W. Illingworth. Record Commission. London, 1814–19

Records of the Wardrobe and Household 1285–1286 edd. B. F. and C. R. Byerly. London, HMSO, 1977

MS.Soc. of Antiq. Manuscripts in the Library of the Society of Antiquaries of London

Swinfield *A Roll of the Household Expenses of Richard Swinfield, bishop of Hereford, 1289–90*. ed. John Webb. Camden Soc. 1854–5

Ward *Romances in the Department of Manuscripts in the British Museum*. H. L. D. Ward. London, 1883–93

Warton *History of English Poetry*. Thomas Warton. 1778/81

Wenlok *Documents illustrating the Rule of Walter de Wenlock*. ed. Barbara F. Harvey. Camden Soc. London.
Walter de Wenlok. ed. E. H. Pearce. London, 1920

INTRODUCTION

I was in the Round Room in the Public Record Office, reading manuscript E101/369/6, the small parchment roll containing the names of a number of minstrels who had been given largesse for their performances at the banquet held on Whitsunday, 22 May 1306, to celebrate the knighting of the then Prince of Wales, 'Edward of Carnarvon', later to become King Edward II. It is an unimpressive roll, some twenty-four inches long by eight inches wide, containing no more than the names of the minstrels and the amount of money each one received. Only two laconic, explanatory statements by the recording clerks are to be found on it: the heading, 'Payment made to various minstrels on the day of Pentecost in the thirty-fourth year' and, written on the outside of the roll to serve as a shelf or reference mark, 'Cash given to minstrels'.

I was reading it because I had set myself the task of identifying as many as possible of the minstrels named on it, and, although I had fingered, transcribed, translated and written about many medieval manuscripts before, this was the first document belonging to the royal household it had fallen to my lot to examine. Insignificant as it is it made an immediate, vivid impression on my mind, for, as I gazed at the list of the names I became aware of what lay, so to speak, behind them: music, song, dance, laughter, silks, gold tissue, scarlet, ermine ... in other words, these names were the faint reminders of people who, over six hundred years ago, had been walking about London and entertaining the royal family and the nobility in the palace of Westminster. Who were they? What kind of people? What were their daily lives like? Questions such as these came thick and fast. Within minutes I was sending for other manuscripts from the Exchequer Accounts which might provide me with the information I was seeking, and when I had some of the Wardrobe Books in front of me, time past and time present rushed to meet with startling rapidity. These ancient volumes were the cash-books of King Edward I. I tried to imagine their modern equivalents in Buckingham Palace. Here was one, with the caramel-coloured hair of the calf which had supplied the vellum still smooth to the touch on its cover; in another the clerk had had such a wretched, sputtering quill that his handwriting had gone awry and there were inkspots spattered across the folios; there were erasures, crossings-out, insertions, corrections, marginalia, names spelled in a variety of ways with all the happy inconsistency of medieval scribes; little tag-labels of parchment were sewn on the tops of the folios to indicate the different categories of entries. These and all the others I eventually went on to read were intensely human documents. No hint of fiction pervades them; they are filled with plodding, down-to-earth details of money spent on all kinds of transactions relative to the running of the royal household. And the people? There they were; the names on the Payroll suddenly stirred into life; out of the folios walked the king's and barons' heralds and harpers, their trumpeters and nakerers, their waferers and psaltery-players, their acrobats and jugglers. I was able to identify nearly all of the minstrels named on the Payroll, and in process of doing so found scores and scores more; which is why this Register has come into being.

The minstrels on the Payroll were just a minority; they were the chosen few, the lucky ones who were the recipients of the 200 marks the King had ordered to be distributed among them in his son's name. I soon discovered that several of the most important royal minstrels, for example, the King's personal trumpeters, were not mentioned. No one now knows who was ultimately responsible for selecting the ones who were given the money, but, as the other manuscripts proved, it was plain that, taken by itself, as it has been in the past, the Payroll offers a quite distorted view of the minstrels' status and their work. I hope that the entries I have collected here will help to put matters right.

Just as our own daily lives constitute a microcosm within the macrocosm of the political and economic life of the nation, so these Wardrobe and Exchequer Accounts provide us with a microcosmic view of what was going on during the reigns of Edward I and Edward II. More often than not our history is painted for us on the larger canvas; the past is described and discussed in terms of decades and centuries; chronology is made the handmaiden to duration of wars or the course of social and economic uprising and change; yet we all know that the lives of all men are ruled by 'the sly, slow hours'. What goes on in the world at large impinges upon and moulds our existence but we are, perforce, constrained to accommodate what we do to the demands of each passing moment; the sand has to run down the glass grain by grain. It is precisely because the Wardrobe Books are day-books that we are able to catch this priceless if fleeting picture of intimate life in the royal households. It is as if we were being allowed to step over the threshold and become one with Master John Drake, who is making wafers for dinner or with King Robert the herald who is busy organizing the performance of a miracle play for the queen and court while the king is in bed, ill. Hundreds of vignettes of this sort are to be found among the entries: Nicholas le Blund and Adam de Clitheroe, two of the royal harpers, with their beds packed on a sumpter horse, at Bures St Mary, ready to set off with the King to Flanders; Walter Woodstock, the messenger, going out one June day in Worcester to catch fish for the kitchen, because William the court fisherman was sick; Richard Rounlo, the vielle-player, being given the pleasant duty of presenting on behalf of the king a silver-gilt cup to the famous King Adam, Adinet le Roy, King Minstrel and vielle-player of the Count of Flanders, at Ghent; Janin, John Warenne's organist, mending the Prince's organ at Langley, in readiness for the visit of the king and queen. These were the little importances of the moment. Priorities are reversed; Edward's wars in Wales, Gascony, Flanders and Scotland seem to be no more than a shadowy backcloth. So, too, the ever-deepening tragedy of Edward II's reign appears almost non-existent. When, in the summer of 1312, the hated Gaveston had been executed and the Lords Ordainers had issued their harsh reprimands and conditions to the king, when tension must have been terrific and the repercussions in Court, baronial hall and ordinary household seething, the only reference to the mounting political feud one finds in the Wardrobe Book is one which nevertheless speaks volumes to the alert and shrewd reader who happens to be knowledgeable in the history of the reign: on the anniversary of the execution of his favourite, 19 June 1313, Edward II was enjoying himself at Pontoise, watching a show of Bernard le Fol and his 54 naked dancers. He had slipped over to France to get away from it all. The entry is an unconscious confirmation of the waywardness of humanity, common to all men at all times; yet it cannot fail to raise a smile of amusement. *Plus ça change, plus la même chose*. The *Folies Bergères* has a long pedigree.

To be a minstrel was to be a minor Court servant. That was the original meaning of *menestrellus* and that is one of the reasons why people whom we would not now regard as minstels were designated as such in the Household Ordinances. Music was an integral part of the daily routine; not necessarily music as entertainment. It is virtually impossible to discover exactly in what official light the *menestrellus* was regarded, because his duties varied considerably according to his 'office'. He announced the arrival of the king and other members of the royal family with fanfares; he blew the reveille; he called everyone to meals; he told the hours and the watch on his horn; he worked with the hunt; when necessary, he sounded the alarm for fire; yet these seem to have been only part of their duties; the king's trumpeters were professional musicians but they were also professional soldiers; so were his nakerers, taborers and pipers; so were his heralds. At the same time, the royal household and every baronial hall was full of what we would call amateur musicians, young men and old, who played an instrument of one kind or another and had a repertory of songs at their command. These were the ones who augmented the professionals whenever occasion demanded, people like Roger the Naperer, John the Hairdresser, or Philip de Windsor and John de Dorchester, two young grooms of the Chamber. Like Chaucer's young squire, like our young people today, they were 'syngynge or floytynge al the daye.' The professional 'string men' however appear to have been in a class apart. They were the élite. All were squires and gentlemen of the Court; sometimes very arrogant, litigious and murderous gentlemen. The references to them in the Wardrobe Accounts testify to their status and importance. It is possible to piece together a good deal of their lives, except, of course, the music they played and the songs they sang. It was not the business of the clerks to enter such details; they probably did not know what went on in Hall and Chamber; what mattered to them was how much money had been paid out; all performances were, as a general rule, entered under the covering phrase, 'making his/their minstrelsy.' Historians of medieval music have to search elsewhere for the tunes and the songs current at the time; the ones which saturated the walls of the royal palace cannot be recaptured. We have to console ourselves for the loss by remembering the lines of Keats:

> Heard melodies are sweet but those unheard are sweeter.

Nevertheless we have in the Wardrobe Accounts that which no

contemporary melody or song of itself could give us; that is, an unpretentious, impartial record of real medieval domestic minstrels. In following their activities, their lives, even to a certain extent their personalities, can be reconstructed; not entirely, of course, but in sufficient detail to convince us of their actuality; indeed, the cumulative effect of reading the Wardrobe Books is to make one conscious of that eternal vitality exhaled by ancient documents dealing directly with people who lived long ago. All kinds of facts, relevant, incidental and miscellaneous, are revealed; facts which throw light on individuals or the contemporary scene; we get to know the minstrels by name, what wages they received, how often they were paid, how they were appointed by contract, how often they stayed or were absent from duty at Court, how they travelled everywhere with the king and queen, where they went, what clothes and furs they wore, how often they received new outfits, how long they were in the king's service, what happened to them when they became too old to work, even what horses they rode and how they behaved themselves. With the help of Stowe's invaluable *Survey* we can today visit the places where some of them lived; such as Upper Thames Street and Cannon Street, Fenchurch Street and Hart Street. On these very spots, near Ebbe Gate, Swan Lane and St Olave's church two of the most notable royal minstrels once lived: John Drake the Waferer in Hart Street and William le Sautreour in Upper Thames Street. Just outside Aldgate, where Holy Trinity Priory used to stand, poor Simon, the royal mounted messenger who went blind, received his daily commons. Not far away, in Cripplegate, there were once two tenements and ten shops that William le Sautreour acquired in lieu of a debt owed him by John Lung the goldsmith. There is so much information packed into these entries that it would be foolish to attempt to categorize it. Each reader will approach it from his or her own angle of interest and draw whatever conclusions seem appropriate. One thing is certain: unlike the researcher into fiction, who can be beguiled into hazardous speculation, anyone who reads this compilation can feel perfectly safe on one score: it is a register of facts.

I think I ought to point out that this register is not the result of systematic research. I collected the entries incidentally, while I was prosecuting other research work. The book is, therefore, a step towards a definitive register of medieval minstrels, because a wealth of additional information awaits discovery and recording.

In my translation of the manuscripts I have kept closely to the Latin, for the formulaic nature of the entries gives the flavour of the time; but, on occasion, I have allowed myself a slight measure of freedom when I felt that the Latin might contain a degree of ambiguity; for example, *per vices* seems to mean sometimes 'in turn' or 'by turns' and sometimes 'on various occasions', according to what the clerk apparently had in mind. Similarly, with *roba*; it does not appear to mean invariably the complete medieval gown, pelisse and hood, but at times a single garment. Where there has been doubt in my mind I have differentiated between the possible meanings. 'Robe' and 'gown' carry such particular connotations nowadays that neither seems to me to indicate what *roba* meant in the thirteenth and fourteenth centuries. I decided to use the general term 'outfit' which approaches the original meaning more nearly.

The inconsistencies of the clerks are a delight; I have let them stand; but the habit is infectious; I hope I have eliminated my own. In one respect I may be called to book. It will be seen that there are a few entries outside the stated chronological limits, 1271–1326. They are chance references I came across in my casual reading, to minstrels of note: such as Walter Vyolet, the vielle-player of King John, Perinus Teutonicus, a favourite of Henry III and John Teyssaunt, King Herald of Edward III. It seemed a pity not to include them.

ADAM

1285 E101/351/17.
One of the King's Watchmen.
Probably Adam de Skyrewith, father of the Adam who was King's Watchman later in the reign.

ADAM (LE BOSCU)

1306 E101/369/6.
Present at the Whitsun Feast. Styled 'Maistre'.
Received 20s.
See BOSCU

ADAM (le Vilur)

1212 Book of Fees. I. 207. (Inquisition of the County of Lancaster)
Payn de Vilers gave to Adam le Vielur one carucate of land and Robert fitz Robert now holds it by the aforesaid military service.

ADAM [OF LONDON]

1284/5 C. 47: Bundle, 91 No.4 pp. 23, 25, 37
Harper of Bogo de Clare
1. 2s. 5d. for 'Adekin the harper.'
2. 7 ells of striped burnet, one fur and one hood of budge for a 'parti-coloured gown for Adam le Harpeur.'

ADAM THE MESSENGER

1316/17 MS. Soc. of Antiq. 120 f. 181[r]
Mounted messenger of Aymer de Valence, earl of Pembroke. A gold cup, with four silver-gilt knobs, with a foot and cover. Valued at 38s. 8d.
Given, on behalf of the lord King to Adam, *nuncius* of the earl of Pembroke, for bringing news to the lord King about his master's counsel (*deliberatio*).
Westminster. 17 June.

ADAM THE TRUMPETER

1322 *Foedera*, II. 375
Pardon, concerning the death of Thomas of Lancaster, to Adam le Trompour of Burton.

ADAM THE WAFERER

1316/17 MS.Soc. of Antiq. 120
King's (Ed. II) Waferer.
f. 69[r] 4s. 8d. to Adam le Waffrer for his shoes, for the whole year.
f. 175 Paid, 1 mark. (for what, not specified)

1319/20 E101/378/4. f. 1r
2s. 4d. to Adam the Waferer, for his summer shoes.

1319/20 Add. MSS. 17632 f. 21r
2s. 4d. to Adam the Waferer, for his winter shoes.

ADINET LE HARPOUR

1306 E101/369/6
One of the minstrels present at the feast held at Westminster, on Whitsunday, 26 May, when Edward, Prince of Wales, was knighted.
Paid, 40d.
Perhaps, Adam of Clitheroe King's Harper, who is sometimes called 'Adekin'.

ALAN THE HARPER

1298 CPR. 390
Pardon to Ralph, son of Alan le Harpour of Swynton, by reason of his good service in Scotland, for the death of John Goldesone.

ALAN THE TRUMPETER

1301 E101/359/5. ff. 4v, 5r, 6r
To Alan le Trumpour, carrying the King's letters.
(payment not specified)
Warwick. 18 May.

ALEMANNUS

1247 CCR. 18
A German minstrel of Geoffrey de Lusignan.
Order by the King (Hen. III) for a gown to be made for 'Alemannus, the minstrel(istrio) of Galfridus de Lezinan.
Clarendon. 18 December.

1248 CCR. 56
It seems that by this time Alemannus had become King's minstrel.
An order from the King for a gown to be made for Alemannus, King's minstrel, by gift of the King, for the approaching feast of Whitsun.
Faringdon. 1 June (which was a Monday; and Pentecost was the following Sunday)

See PERINUS TEUTONICUS.

ALEXANDER THE HARPER

1203/4 Rotuli de Liberate. (ed. Duffus Hardy. 1844) p. 92
Perhaps a King's harper.
A mandate from the King (John) to the sheriff of Buckingham, to give Alexander le Harpur a prebend which Passemer had.

ALKIN

1305/6 E101/369/11. f. 103^v
100s. to Alkin, the minstrel, for himself and his wife, in cash, by gift of the King.
Given to him at the Exchequer, on 16 June, by order of the Treasurer.
(The King, Ed. I, was at Watford, Herts. on this day).

AMANDUS

1302/3 E101/363/18. f. 21^v
Minstrel of Arnold de Gardin(?)
20s. to Amandus, minstrel '*domini Ernaldi de Gardinis*' for making his minstrelsy in the presence of the lord Prince. By gift of the Prince.
Straddle. 7 April.

AMEKYN

1306 E101/369/6
Harper of Edward, Prince of Wales.
(*Amekyn Citharista Principis*)
Present at the Whitsun Feast.
Received 5s.

ANDREAS

1306 E101/369/6
Andrew, vielle-player of Hor'
(*Andreas vidulator de Hor'*)
Present at the Whitsun Feast
Received 2s.
Perhaps one of Prince Edward's minstrels. (see next.)

1303 E101/363/18 f. 13^v
24s. 6d. to 'brother Andrew the little' (or, Andrew Petit) his (i.e. the Prince's) minstrel, to buy himself a tunic.

ARNALD THE TRUMPETER

1314/15 E101/376/7 f. 40^r
King's (Ed. II) Trumpeter
Given the price of cloth and fur to make a gown.

See ROGER THE TRUMPETER

1316/17 MS. Soc. of Antiq. 120 f. 97^r
40s. to Arnald le Trumpour, in compensation for his iron-grey dapple horse, returned to the Almonry at Clipstone on 17 December. Paid into his own hands there on 21 December.

ARNULET

1303/4 Add.MSS. 8835 f. 44^v
Court vielle-player.

See DRUET.

ARNULPH THE TRUMPETER

1314/15 E101/376/7 f. 43^r
Probably King's (Ed. II) Trumpeter and perhaps the same as Arnald (?)
12s. 6d. to Arnulph the Trumpeter, by gift of the King, in the form of the price of 5 ells of cloth to have a gown made for himself.
Denne 5 October.

1317/18 MS. Soc. of Antiq. 121 f. 57^r
40s. to Arnald le trumpour, by gift of the King, in compensation for a black and white piebald horse of his, which was killed in the King's service, at Westminster in the month of November. Paid into his own hands at Westminster on 16 November.

1320/21 MS. Soc. of Antiq. 121 f. 130^r
[1 mark] for his summer outfit.
London. 20 October.

ARTISIEN

1306 E101/369/6
Present at the Whitsun Feast.
Received 30s. by the hand of King Caupenny.

ARTOYS

1290 C47/4/5 f.48^r
Court Fool of the Count of Artoys, who came to the wedding of Princes Margaret and then returned to 'his own country'.
Received 40s. by gift of the King (Ed. I).
Westminster. 12 July

AUDOENUS LE CROUTHERE

1306 E101/369/6
Owen the Crowder.
Present at the Whitsun Feast.
Received 12d.

AYLESHAM (William de)

1310/11 E101/374/7
p. 9 ? Court Trumpeter
10s. to Willelmus de Aylesham, trumpator, for his wages.

B

BAGGEPIPER

1332/3 E101/386/7 f. 7^{v}
12d. to a certain minstrel called Baggepiper, meeting with the Lady Alienor on her journey; fcr making his minstrelsy in her presence.
By gift of the lady, into his own hands.

BAISESCU

1306 E101/369/6
Le Roy Baisescu: A King Herald. so far unidentified.
Present at the Whitsun Feast.
Received 5 marks.
One of the minstrels deputed to share out the remainder of the 200 marks among 'les autres'.

BALDEWYN THE SKIRMISHER

1290 C47/4/5 f. 49^{r}
Magister Baldewyn the Skirmishour; a fencer from Brabant, who was in the household of John de Brabant for 3 years.
20s. by gift of the King (Ed. I) on his returning to Brabant.
Northampton. 28 August.

1290 E101/352/21
as above, with the addition, 'to Brabant by licence of Lord John.

BARBER (JOHN)

1306 E101/369/6
Johannes le Barbor.
Present at the Whitsun Feast. Received 5s.

1316/17 MS. Soc. of Antiq. 120 f. 69^{r}
4s. 8d. to Johannes le Barber, groom of the King's (Ed. II) Chamber, for his shoes for the whole year.

BARBER (ROBERT)

1300/1 E101/359/6 On back cover of MS.
To Robert le Barber, groom/squire of Lord Hugh le Despenser.

BARBER (ROBERT)

1305/6 E101/368/27 f. 61v
Called Robert Barbitonsor by the clerk, in the margin, but Robertus le Barber in the body of the account.
Prests, for his wages:

1/2 mark	Meryntone	3 August

13s. 4d. for going toward London with Sir Simon Fresel, prisoner, of Scotland, conducting him there.

	Carlisle	25 August
13s. 4d.	Westminster	9 June
5s.	Lanercost	2 October
5s.	Grantham	13 July
1/2 mark	Thrapston	5 July
1 mark	Lanercost	1 November

BARBER (ROBERT)

1314/17 MS. Cott. Nero. C viii f. 192v
A royal trumpeter.
8s. 4d. by the hand of Robert Barber, trumpeter, in part payment of 28s. 4d. owing to him for his wages and outfit.
3 February

BARBER (ROGER)

1319/20 Add. MSS. 17632 (Wardrobe Acct. Remainder of E101/378/4) f. 8v
Roger le Barber, King's Sergeant-at-arms. He, with 8 companions, was carrying 1000 marks from London to the King (Ed. II) who was at Fenham, in Northumberland.

BARKING (JOHN)

1285 E101/351/17 (Counteroll of Domestic Payments to members of the King's Household). John de Berking. King's minstrel/watchman.

1290 C47/4/5 f. 38r
Johann de Berking, Vigilator Regis.
2 marks for his outfits for the whole year.
5 February.

1294/5 Fryde, 53 (Book of Prests)
Johann de Berkingg.
57s. 9d. for his wages (4 1/2d. per day) from 20 November to 23 April, on which day he finished, because he died. 154 days (last day not included); paid into the hands of his fellow-watchman, John de Windsor.

BARRY (LUCAS)

c.1300 E101/371/8 (Part I) fragment 16
Lucas de Barry. 1/2 mark.
This name occurs directly with those of the King's Harpers and the King's Trumpeter. It is difficult not to draw the conclusion that he was a minstrel of some kind. The clerks grouped men together according to their position in the royal household. Perhaps Lucas was the Lucat of the Payroll? (and not John de Luke)

BARTHOLOMEW

1253 CPR. 231.
King's (Hen. III) Trumpeter.
Protection for Bartholomew le Trumpur, going with the King to Gascony, for so long as he is in his service in those parts, with the King.

BARTHOLOMEW

1312 Bain. (Doc^{s} rel. Scotland) III, 418. (Roll of Horses)
Bartholomew the Vielle-player. (le Viler). Had a bay, piebald horse, valued at 100s.

BAUDET

1296/7 Add.MSS. 7965. f. 52^{r}
Taborer of the Royal Household.
20s. for performing at the wedding of Princess Elizabeth

1300/1 E101/360/10. Membrane 1.
Baudettus Taborarius; one of the minstrels accompanying Prince Edward, when he and the Queen left Langley, in January 1301, to join the King at Lincoln.

1306 E101/369/6.
Present at the Whitsun Feast. Received 40s.

1307 E101/357/15. f. 25^{r}
Baudettus le Tanbourer.
3s. 10 1/2d. owing to him at the end of Ed. I's reign.

BAUDET THE TRUMPETER

1312 Bain, III. 418
Probably the same as Baudet the Taborer, since minstrels often played more than one instrument.
Baudettus le trompour has a black horse, valued at 8 marks.

BENEDICT

1284/5 C47 Bundle 91 No.4
Vielle-player of Bogo de Clare.
7 ells of striped burnet, one fur and one budge hood for a parti-coloured gown for Benedict le Vylour.

BENET

1289/90 Swinfield, 148
Vielle-player of London.

BENNYNG (ROGER)

1325 CPR 168/9
Probably a court trumpeter.
Letters of protection for Roger Bennying, trumpur, going with the King (Ed. II) to France.

LE BER (GUILLOT)

1290 C47/4/5. f. 49r and E101/352/21
Psaltery-player of Lord Edmund (Crouchback), the King's (Ed. I) brother.
40s. to Guillot le Ber, for playing in the presence of the King at Northampton; by gift of the King.
23 August. Northampton.

BERDU...

1310/11 E101/374/7. p. 24
Apparently a Court Lutenist.
7s. to the Clerk of the Marshalcy, by the hand of Berdu... le Leutour, for the expenses of 2 Gascon sumpters.

BERKHAMPSTEAD (RICARD)

1306 Add.MSS. 22923 f. 3v; and MS. Harley 5001
squire/groom of the Prince's Wardrobe.
5s. 5d. to Ricard de Bercamstede, vallettus Ganderobe, for lawn and silk (sindon et sericus) bought by him at Dover, in the month of May, for tunics made in the Gascon fashion, for the Prince's plays.

BERNARD LE FOL

1312/13 E101/375/8. f. 32^r
A French minstrel/dancer (menestrallus Francie) 40s. to Bernard le Fol and 54 of his fellow actors, coming naked into the presence of the King (Ed. II), and dancing (cum tripudio). By gift of the King, in 4 florins 'de Cathedra', a florin 'cum Regina and 9d. in sterling.
Pontoise. 19 June

BERNEVILLE (ROBERT)

1289 Add. MSS. 35294. f. 9^v
Minstrel of the King of France.
given 40s.

1290 C47/4/5. f. 47^r
Present at the wedding of Princess Joanna.
50s. By gift of the King (Ed. I)

1290 E101/352/21
50s. to Robertus de Berneville, minstrel of the King of France, for making his minstrelsy in the presence of the King.
By gift of the King.
1 June.

BERTIN

1285 E101/351/17
King's (Ed. I) Trumpeter.
His fellow-trumpeter was John.
Bertin et Johannes Trumpatores (Regis).

BERTRUD

1302/3 E101/364/13. f. 44^v
Trumpeter of the earl of Lincoln:
20s. paid to Gerard de Albercuque, for carrying a letter of the earl of Lincoln, under seal; paid to him by the hand of Bertrud le trumpour.

BERTRUCH

1305/6 E101/369/11. f. 96^r
A minstrel from Geneva.

See BETULPH

BERUCHE (see below)
BESTRUDE/BETRUCHE

1302/3 E101/363/18. ff. 22, 23
A vielle-player from Geneva.
f. 22^r 20s. to Bestrudus vidulator Geneuensis, for making his minstrelsy, with his fellow, BERUCHE, in the presence of the Prince at Newcastle and Durham, for 2 days in May, and returning thence to the 'aforesaid parts'.
By gift of the Prince, for their expenses in returning.
Newcastle-on-Tyne. 9 May.
f.23^r
76s. to Bestrude, minstrel of Geneva, for remaining in London after the return of the Prince to Scottish parts, by order of the lord Prince, for 102 days, in the months of July, August, September and October. By gift of the Prince, in cash, given to him by a merchant of the Friscobaldi Society, for his expenses during the said time.

BERUCHE
A Swiss vielle-player, companion of Bestrude/Bestruche.

BETULPH

1305/6 E101/369/11. f. 96^r
A minstrel from Geneva.
f. 96^r 30s. to Betulph and Betruch (Betulphus et Bertruchus), minstrels from Geneva, staying in London, awaiting the arrival of the Lord Edward, the King's son, Prince of Wales, from Scotland in August(1303/4). By gift of the Prince for their expenses while remaining in London for 15 days in the aforesaid month; by hand of Mathew Clarissimus, merchant of the Spini Society of Florence; given to them, in cash, there by order of Master John de Drokenesford, who [re]paid the merchant at Darlington.
3 August.

1306 Add. MSS. 3766. f. 5^v
30s. to Betulph and Bertruch, minstrels of Geneva, staying in London, awaiting the arrival of the Lord Edward, the King's son, by gift of the same Lord Edward, for their expenses in so waiting for 15 days, in the month of August, 32 Ed. I (1303/4); by the hand of Mathew Clarissimus, merchant of the Spini Society. Paid in cash, at Darlington.

BERMINGHAM (MELIOR)

1296/7 Add. MSS. 7965. f. 126r
Court Minstrel.
Receiving his winter outfit.

BLACKBURN (JOHN)

1305/6 E101/369/11. f. 100v
Henry de Lacy's harper.
40s. to Johannes de Blackburn, citharista Comitis Lincolnie, for playing his harp before the King on St. Gregory's Day (12 March). By gift of the King.
[Winchester] 14 March

BLIDA/BLYTH (ADAM)

1296/7 Add. MSS. 7965. f. 127r
Sergeant-at-arms of the Marshal.
Included in a list of minstrels receiving their winter outfits: Adam de Blida.

BLIDA/BLYTH (JOHN)

1306 MS. Harley 5001. f. 49r
Valet of the Prince's [and later, King's (Ed. II)] Household.

BLUND (NICHOLAS)

1296/7 Add. MSS. 7965
Nicholas le Blund; King's Harper.
f. 52r. 40s. to Nicholas le Blund and his fellow-harper, Adam de Clitheroe, to pay for a sumpter horse, carrying their bedding. On behalf of the King (Ed. I).
Bures St. Mary (Suffolk). 9 December.
f. 126v. 20s. to Nicholas and Adam, King's Harpers, for their winter outfits. At Harwich.
f. 131r. 20s. to Nicholas and Adam, for their summer outfits.

1299 E101/357/15. f. 2r (Debts of the Wardrobe, 25-35 Ed. I. John de Drokenesford's Account.)
Owing to Nicholas the Harper, (1299) - £7 10s. 1½d.

1299/1300 Add. MSS. 35291. f. 155^r

To Nicholaus le Blund, on account, for his wages:

10s. 29 November. York.
13s. 4d. 18 December. York.
20s. 29 December. York.

f. 158^r. To Nicholas, Citharista Regis, on account, for his wages: [A most valuable entry, for it provides not only details of the work, pay, and mobility of a King's Harper, but a picture of his travels. Nicholas accompanied the King to Scotland, and was present at the seige of Caerlaverock:

The Court left St. Albans on:
14 April. Nicholas was given a prest of 21d.
16 April. Dunstable. 3s
23 April. Pitchley (Northants). 3s.
30 April. Stamford (Lincs.). 3s.
5 May. Peterborough. 12d.
8 May. Chippenham (Cambs.) 5s.
10 May. Bury St. Edmunds. 10s.
17 May. Gaywood (Norfolk). 10s.
26 May. Coythorp (Lincs.) 10s.
15 June. York. 6s. 8d.
3 July. Carlisle. 4s.
12 July. Caerlaverock 5s.
14 July. Caerlaverock (day of Victory) 6s. 8d.
22 July. Kirkcudbright. 5s.
4 August. Twyndholme (K'cudbright). 5s.
30 August. Dornoch (Dumfries). 10s.
Money owing to him for a horse. 108s. 6d.

Sum total: £10 2s. 7d.

1300/1 Add. MSS. 7966A.

Several payments to Nicholas, King's Harper;; prest, including 3s. 4d. for the price of 10 ells of canvas (canabus) given to him.

c. 1300 E101/371/8. (Pt. I) frag. 101. [a page from a Wardrobe Account which has been entered elsewhere, and therefore crossed out]

Nicholas Cytharista

See Adam de Cliderhou.

1300/1 E101/359/5. f. 8^r

1 mark to Nicholas the Harper, for his wages.
Berwick-on-Tweed. 16 July.

1302/3 Add. MSS.35292.
f. 7^{v} 10s. to Nicholas the Harper, for his wages.
Brechin (Forfarshire) 11 August.
f. 9^{v}
10s for his wages, at Brechin.
f. 12^{r} 1/2 mark for his wages, at Dundee. 17 October.

1302/3 E101/364/13.

f. 75^{r} Prests, for his wages: 10s. at Wherwell (Hants) 21 December. 1 mark at Odiham 31 December. 1/2 mark at Roxburgh. 29 May. 10s at (?)Towete. 1 September.
40s. per Thomas de London, in cash, which he owed to him for a horse bought from him, on recognizance, in the Wardrobe, at Westminster. 12 March. 10s. at London. 17 March. 10s. at Brechin. 11 August.

f. 81^{v} Prests for his wages: 20s. at York. 22 April. 13s. 4d. by the hand of Ricard de Wodhull, being money which he owed him at York, on recognizance, there. 2 April. 10s. for his wages; St. John de Perth. 28 June.

f. 82^{r} 6s. 8d. for his wages at Dundee. 17 October, per John de Newentone.

f. 98^{v} 1/2 mark (prest) for his wages at Banff. 3 September.

BLYTHE/BLIDA (HENRY)

1299 Henry de Blythe, King's Minstrel.

E101/356/13. (Issues of Bread and Wine to those staying in Court)
Blithe: 1 pennyworth of wine per day.

1302/3 E101/363/18. f. 22^{r}
Henricus de Blide, menestrallus Senioris Regis
6s. 8d. for making his minstrelsy in the presence of the Prince. By gift of the Prince, to buy himself a tunic.
Newcastle-on-Tyne. 8 May.

1302/3 E101/364/13. f. 22^{r}
Henricus de Blida admitted for the first time on King's wages, in the Marshal's Roll at 4 1/2d. per day. 17 August. 24s. for his wages from that day to 19 October, both days included. 64 days, because he was never absent.
Dundee. 30 October.

1306/7 Add. MSS. 22923. f. 11^r (and MS. Harley 5001. f. 48)
39s. to Peter le Guitarer and Henry de Blida, minstrels, who were staying in the Prince's Household, by order of the Prince, for making their minstrelsy, by turns, (or, on various occasions) in his presence, during 52 days (of the present year).
By gift of the Prince, as for wages - 4 1/2d. per day each during the aforesaid period; in cash, given to them at Ringwood.

1311/12 E101/373/26. f. 18^r. (Acct. of John de Pelham, Clerk of the Marshalcy)
7s. paid to Henry de Blida for his groom's wages.
Westminster. 8 September.

1312 Bain, III. 413 (Horses valued at Berwick)
Henry de Blythe has a bay horse, valued at 10 marks.

BLYTHE/BLIDA (RICARD)

1302/3 King's Trumpeter.

Add. MSS. 35292.
f. 7^v To Ricard de Blida, trumpator Regis
5s. for his wages.
f. 9^v 1/2 mark for his wages at Brechin
f. 12^r 5s. to Ricard the trumpeter, at Gask (Perthshire)
25 October.

1302/3 E101/364/13 f. 80^v
Prests to Ricard de Blythe, King's Trumpeter, for his wages:
1 mark 9 July, at St. John de Perth
10s. 8 August, at Brechin, per Robert of York, trumpeter.
1/2 mark. 2 September at 'Kyndeward' [Scotland]
5s. 17 October, at Dundee.

1314/15 E101/376/7 f. 43^v
40s. to Ricard the Trumpeter of Blyth, first appointed on King's (Ed. II) wages, on 2 November of the present ninth year (1315).
By gift of the King; the gift being made to him at Tickhill, in the same month, for him to buy a horse for himself.
3 April.
By contract drawn up at Stratford.

1314/15 E101/376/7

f. 90v. 20s. to Ricard le Trumpour, for his outfit. 3 April (1317/18). Stratford.

1318/19/20 MS. Soc. of Antiq. 120

f. 165r. 20s. for his winter outfit. 20 June. London.

f. 174v. no issue of winter outfit (1318/19), because he was out of Court.

1319/20 MS. Soc. of Antiq. 121

f. 129r. Nothing for his summer outfit, because he was not in Court on Whitsunday.

1310/11 E101/374/7.

p. 23. 40s. to the Clerk of the [kitchen], by the hand of Ricard le Trumpour, for fish. 20 November.

BOISTOUS (ROBERT LE)

1306 E101/369/6.

Present at the Whitsun Feast. Received 4 marks by the hand of King Caupenny. Perhaps a visiting minstrel from France.

BOLOIGNE (GERARD)

1306 E101/369/6.

Probably a visiting French minstrel. Present at the Whitsun Feast. Received 4 marks, by the hand of King Caupenny. May have been a minstrel of Sir Brankalo de Boloigne, who was knighted with the Prince.

BOLTHED

1306 E101/369/6.

Present at the Whitsun Feast. Received 5s.

BONE VYE

1289 Add. MSS. 35294. f. 11r

20s. to a certain minstrel called Bone Vye, by gift of the Queen.

BOONE (GERARD) [BOHUN]

1299 Add. MSS. 24509. f. 61r

A minstrel of the Earl of Gloucester.

20s./10s. to Gerard le Boone, a minstrel of the Earl of Gloucester for performing, with Gressyl, in the presence of the King. By gift of the King. (20s. to each/or/both).

BORENGE (JOHN)

1290 C. 47/4/5. f. 48r
Waferer of Lord William de Fenes.
Present at the wedding of Princes Margaret: received 40s. by gift of the King and 20s. by gift of Prince Edward.
Westminster.

BOSCU (ADAM LE)

1306 E101/369/6
Present at the Whitsun Feast. Styled 'Maistre' Received 20s. by the hand of Monsire Bruant, herald.

BOTILLER (JOHN LE)

1311/12 MS. Cott. Nero. C.viii. f. 85v
10s to Johannes le Botiller, groom (garcio) of Peter Duzedeys, for making his minstrelsy in the presence of the King. (Ed.II). By gift of the King.
York. 28 March.

BOYESE (JOHN DE)

1285/6 Minstrel of the Count of Burgundy.

E101/352/4. (Counter-roll of Jewels)
Membrane 1.
No. 1990 [By the merchants of Lucca] 1 cup (silver-gilt, with foot and cover) of 3 marks 22d. weight, value 59s. 2d. given on behalf of the King to John Boyese, minstrel of the Count of Burgundy.

BOYS (PRINCE'S CHORISTERS)

See NEWENTON (ROBERT)

BRABANT (JANIN)

1306 Vielle-player of Hugh le Despenser the Younger.

E101/369/6.
Present at the Whitsun Feast. Received 40s.

Add. MSS. 22923. f. 6r (and MS. Harley 5001 f. 37r)
40s. to Johannes de Brabant, vielle-player of Hugh le Despenser, who came in his master's train to the Prince's court and made his minstrelsy in the presence of the same Lord(Prince) and other nobles there present, in the month of February at Wetherhall. By gift of the Prince, by the hand of Master W. de Boudon, who gave him the cash there on 18 February.

BRAYLES (WALTER)

1306 E101/369/6.
Present at the Whitsun Feast. Received 12d.
Perhaps a minstrel in the household of Guy, earl of Warwick, since Brailes was in the hundred of Kington, Warwicks.

BRIAN (LE WAFERER)

King's or Court Waferer.

1317/18 MS. Soc. of Antiq. 121.
f. 113r. Nothing to Brian the Waferer for his winter outfit, because he was not in Court on Christmas Day.

1319/20 f. 129r. 20s. to Brian the Waferer for his summer outfit.
London. 11 December. (1320/21)

1319/ E101/378/4. f. 30r
15s. to Brian the Waferer, for his wages in the Scottish war: from 13 September, on which day his horse was valued at Berwick-on-Tweed, for the aforesaid war, to 27 of the same mouth, both days included. 15 days at 12d per day.
London. 13 November.

BRIDE (GILBERT)

1303/4 Add. MSS. 8835. f. 43v
Gilbert Bride; Scottish trumpeter.
1/2 mark each to Nigel Seymour, Andrew Clydesdale and Gilbert Bride, Scottish trumpeters, accompanying the King from Stirling to Northam; by gift of the King as a help toward their expenses on returning to their own parts. Paid into their own hands at Northam, 22 August. [Clerk has added, 20s. at end].

BROMLEY (WILLIAM)

1311//12 E101/373/26. f. 93v
40s. to Robert de Clough, King's Harper, by the hand of William de Bromley, harper, in compensation for a horse of his.
8 February.

1325/6 E101/381/11.
In a list of the King's (Ed. II) household minstrels:
Willelmus de Bromle.

BRYE/BRIE (JOHN)

King's (Ed. II), later, Queen's Waferer.

1310/11 E101/373/10. f. 6v
5s. to the Clerk of the Pantry, by the hand of Janot de Brye, Waffrarius Regis. (N.D.)

1311/12 MS. Cott. Nero. C.viii. (Debts of the Queen's Household)
f. 15v 39s. 9d. owing to John de Brye, Waferer.
f. 41v Owing to John de Brye, Waffrarius domine Regine, for his expenses in the household of the said Lady Queen for 1309-1310, by two bills of the Clerk of the Pantry and Buttery; given in the Wardrobe of the Lord King, at Westminster. 16 June 1315, £12 7s. 7 1/2d. He has a bill.

1311/12 f. 136v
To John de Brye, Waferer of the Queen's Household; paid 4 1/2d. per day for his wages from 8 July, the beginning of the 5th (regnal) year (1311/12) to 7 July, the end of the same year, both days included, for 366 days, because it was leap year, except 22 days, during which time he was absent. According to the contract drawn up with him in the Wardrobe, at York, 13 July of the 6th year (1312/13) - £6 15s. 9d.

1316/17 E101/376/7.
f. 93r. 2 marks to John de Brie, for his winter outfit.
London. 21 December.
f. 124r. £12 12s. owing to John de Brye, Queen's Waferer, for his outfit for 9 Ed. II (1315/16) and for money owing to him for his office.

BRUANT (JOHN)

John Butler, alias Bruant, herald. Perhaps, King's Herald.

1305/6 E101/369/11. f. 100v
20s. to Johannes Butiler, Roger Macheys and Thomas de Norffolk, heralds, for their expenses on their journey between Winchester and London.
Winchester. 6 April.

1306 E101/369/6.
Present at the Whitsun Feast. Received 40s.
Styled 'Monsire Bruant'.
After the death of Edward I, he appears to have become King Herald in the household of Thomas of Lancaster.

1322 P.W. II, div. 3, 604; MS. Fragmenta Cott. Cat. Cleop. D ix ff. 83r–85r;
CPR (1324-7)153; Foedera II. pars I. 498; CCR (1323-7) 424.
Named among those who fought against the King at Boroughbridge (1322).
Imprisoned successively at York, Berkhamsted and Berkeley castles.

1322 CPR. 210. Foedera II pars I 498
Grant for life, to William de Morley, King's minstrel, called Roi de North, of the houses in Pontefract which belonged to the rebel John de Boteller, called Roi Bruant, and which, by forfeiture, came into the King's hands.

York. 28 October.

1322 Cal. of Inquisitions, II. 134
Horses and armour of Roy Bruant and his fellows found at Merston (Yorks).

BRUN (LE VILUR)

1242/3 Book of Fees. II, 1124.
Brun le Vilur holds 48 acres in Molston for 6d.

BURGHARDESLE (RICARD)

1306 Add. MSS. 22923. f. 6v (and MS. Harley 5001)
Prince's Watchman.
10s. to Ricard de Burghardesle, Vigil Principis, for helping to evacuate people from burning buildings at Windsor.
see RICARD (VIGIL)

BUSSARD (ROBERT)

1302/3 E101/363/18. f. 21r
4s. to Robert Bussard, the Fool, for the hurt he sustained through the Prince's fault, on 25 February, in the water, at Windsor.
By gift of the Prince.

BUTLER (JOHN)

Herald; alias Bruant (see ante).

1306 E101/369/6.
Carletone, Herald. Present at the Whitsun Feast. Received two gifts of cash:
5s. (Latin list) 20s. (French list) the latter being delivered to him by the hand of Monsire Bruant.

1305/6 E101/369/11. f. 67^{v}
60s. to Robert Foun and William Carleton, sergeants-at-arms, for bringing armour from London to Carlisle, to the Lord Edward, Prince of Wales; for their expenses in household and army; for their wages and expenses, in going, staying and returning; and also for bringing money delivered to them from the Exchequer.
Carlisle. 16 June.

1307 E101/373/15. f. 9^{r}
10s. to William de Carleton, sergeant-at-arms, coming from London to Carlisle, with £40 for the expenses of the King's Household; for his wages and his expenses for 8 days, during which he stayed at Carlisle and returned to London in the month of July.

CARLISLE (HUGH)

1306/7 E101/370/16. f. 10^{v} (p. 60)
Hugo de Karliola. Apparently a King's Harper, for he occurs here with John de Newenton and William de Morley. He may have been Hugh de la Rose.
Received 1 mark at Carlisle, on 21 April.

CARLISLE (JOHN)

1305 Add. MSS. 37656. f. 1^{r}
5s. to John de Carlisle, trumpeter, for making his minstrelsy in the presence of the two Princes, Thomas and Edmund, and for coming to them to beg for alms *pro subsidio implorando de Elemosina*.

CATALONIA (JOHN DE)

Prince's Trumpeter.

1302/3 E101/363/18.
f. 21^{v}
12s. to John de Catalonia, for making his minstrelsy, with Thomasin, John Garsie and John the Nakerer, in the presence of the Prince on Trinity Sunday, at Newbattle (Edinburgh). By gift of the Prince, to buy himself a black silk cloak.
Newbattle. 2 June.

f. 22^{v}
13s. 4d. to Janin de Cateloyne, Trumpator Principis, to buy himself a bronze trumpet. By gift of the Prince.
Dunfermline. 7 November.

f. 23^{r}
A gift of thc pricc of a habergeon and iron collaret to John de Catalonia, trumpeter, Prince's minstrel, from the Prince. 11s.

See GARSIE (JOHN)

CATALONIA (JAKEMIN DE)

Prince's Nakerer.

1302/3 E101/363/18. f. 21^{r}
13s. 4d. to Jakemin de Cateloyn, le Nakerer, menestrallus Principis, on his returning to his own country; to help with his expenses on his journey. By gift of the Prince.
Windsor. 7 February.

CAUPENY

1290 King Herald, of Scotland

Rex Caupeny de Scotia
C. 47/4/5. f. 45^{v}
Present at the wedding of Princess Joanna. Received 50s. by gift of the King.

1290 E101/352/21. (MS. in fragments, stuck on to a roll of new vellum) Rex Caupen de Scocie, 'who came to the King...'

1300 E101/371/8. Part I, frag. 41.
Rex Capainy - 1 mark.

1305/6 E101/369/11.
f. 103^{v} Capaignus Rex heraldorum.
73s. 4d. to Capigny, King of heralds, being the price of a bay horse bought from Brother Thomas de Waterwonge per Brother Geoffrey le Duy. Receiving the money at the Exchequer. By gift of the King.
Grantham (Lincs.) 16 July.
f. 172^{r} (Jocalia)
A gold clasp/brooch, worth £4. 10s. given by the King to King Copyn, herald, at Sheen (Surrey), 30 September (1305).
f. 203^{V} 1 mark to King Capini; prest for his wages.
Lanercost. 4 November.

1305/6 <u>E101/368/27</u>. f. 65r
1 mark to King Capiny; prest for his wages.
Lanercost. 4 November.

1306/7 <u>E101/369/16</u>
f. 9v <u>Rex Capyn</u> (in margin)
27s. 6d. prest, being the price of 3 1/2 ells of bluett, 3 1/2 ells of striped (silk/cloth) and 1 lamb's fur; given to him by Ralph de Stokes, Clerk of the Great Wardrobe.
f. 10v <u>Rex Capyny</u>.
24s. 6d. prest, being the price of 7 ells of blue and green cloths, 3 1/2 ells of each, given to him by Ralph de Stokes, Clerk of the Great Wardrobe.
f. 26r Prests to King Capigny, <u>Rex Heraldorum de Scocia</u>, for his wages:

2 marks	22 November	Lanercost.
20s.	30 December	Lanercost.
13s. 4d.	1 February	Lanercost.
13s. 4d.	26 April	Carlisle.
15s.	13 June	Carlisle.

1306/7 <u>E101/370/16</u>
f. 1r (p. 47) 2 marks to King Capiny for his wages.
Lanercost. 22 November.
f. 4r (p. 47) 20s. to King Capiny.
Lanercost. 30 December.
f. 6r (p. 51) 1 mark to King Capiny.
Lanercost. 1 February.
f. 13v (p. 65)
40s. given to King Capiny, John de Cressy and other minstrels, for performing plays and making their minstrelsies in the presence of the Queen.
By gift of the King, by the hand of Guillot the Psaltery-player.
Carlisle. 29 May.
f. 15r 20s. to King Capiny, for his wages.
Carlisle. 13 June.

1306 <u>E101/369/6</u>
Present at the Whitsun Feast. Received 5 marks. Was responsible for delivering their gifts in money to Le Roy de Champagne, Philippe de Caumbereye, Robert le Boistous, Gerard de Bologne, Artisien, Lucat, Henver and the minstrel of Monsire de Montmorency.

CAIARK (PONCE) CAIARK (WILLIAM)

1290 C47/4/4. ff. 19^v 24^v

King's (Ed. I) Trumpeters.

61s. to Poncius de Caiark and Guilleme de Caiark, for their wages from 1 May to 16 July.

CAMBRAI (JAKEMIN DE)

1300/1 Add. MSS. 7966A. f. 69^r and E101/359/6. f. 21^r

Minstrel of Lord Robert Daunget.

20s. to Jakemin de Caumbray, menestrallus domini Roberti Daunget, for making his minstrelsy in the presence of the King. By gift of the King.

Peebles. 9 August.

CAMBRAI (PHILIP DE)

1305/6 Vielle-player of the King of France.

E101/369/6.

Present at the Whitsun Feast: Received 60s.

E101/369/11. f. 101^r

10 marks to Philippus de Caumbray, vidulator Regis Francie, when he came from his country to these parts (London) into England at the knighting of the Lord Edward, the King's son, on the feast of Pentecost, at Westminster. By gift of the King.

Westminster. 28 May.

CARDENAL (WILLIAM)

Minstrel of Ed. III

1332/3 E101/386/7. f. 7^v.

7s. 6d. to William Cardenal, parvus menestrallus domini Regis Anglie, for coming from England to the parts of ...erl... By gift of the Lady Eleanor at Boscum ducis. By the hand of the Treasurer. 17 May.

CARLETON (WILLIAM)

King's (Ed. I) Sergeant-at-arms and King's Herald.

1302/3 Add. MSS. 35292. f. 26^v

With the King, at Dunfermline.

1303/4 Add. MSS. 8835. f. 64^r

£8 19s. 0d. to Willelmus de Carleton, squire, with a furnished horse, from York, for his wages from 19 November to 20 July (1305) both days included: 264 days, bar 65, during which time he was in England, on his own business.

Stonewell (? near Dover). 15 July (1305)

CELLING (JOHN DE)

1290 C47/4/5. f. 49r
Minstrel of Count Florence of Holland.
40s. to John de Celling, on returning to his own country in the train of his lord.
By gift of the King; by the hand of Walter de Sturton.
Silverston (Northants). 11 August.

CENE (MERLIN DE)

1311/12 Perhaps a minstrel of Ed. II.

See WILLIAM THE ACROBAT.

E101/375/8.
f. 14v delivering money to William the Acrobat.
f. 31r 40s. to Merlin de Cene, in compensation for a black hackney, returned to the Almonry, at Westminster, on 28 April.
13 March of 7th Ed. II (1313/14)

CHACEPORC (JOHN)

A Royal Herald.

1300 Add. MSS. 7966. f. 66r
10s. to John Chaceporc, for making the same proclamation (i.e. prohibiting the holding of tournaments in England) on behalf of the King (Ed. I) in the aforesaid hall (Northampton Castle) on the day and in the place aforesaid (Christmas Day).
By gift of the King, by the hand of Walter le Marchis there on the same day.
Northampton. 25 December.

See MARCHIS (WALTER LE)

CHAMPAGNE (LE ROY DE)

A French King Minstrel/or/King Herald.

1291 Botfield. 110
The executors of the will of Queen Eleanor gave a stemmed gold cup (bought for the purpose) "to a certain minstrel Regis Campanie, who brought news from France."

See POVRET

1306 E101/369/6
Present at the Whitsun Feast. Received 5 marks, by the hand of King Caupeny.
According to Botfield he was menestrallus Regis Campanie, which does not make sense, for there was no King of Champagne; perhaps it should read, menestrallus, Rex Campanie. The cup cost 39s.

CHAT (JOHN DU)

1306 E101/369/6
An envoy from the King of France, called 'Catskin', (dit Piau de Chat). Came to the Whitsun Feast with John de Bar. Perhaps one of his minstrels or a minstrel of the French King.
Received 1/2 mark.

CHAUNCELER (ROBERT)

Queen's Watchman.

1311/12 MS. Cott. Nero C.viii
f. 137^v
£6 9s. 0d. to Robert Chaunceler, Watchman, receiving 4 1/2d. per day for his wages, from 8 July of the 5th year (1311/12) to 7 July of the same year, both days included, 366 days, because it was leap year, bar 22 days, during which time he was absent. According to the contract drawn up with him in the Queen's Wardrobe at Westminster.
16 September (1312/13).

1313/14 E101/375/9, f. 16^v
£6 16s. 10 1/2d. to Robert Chaunceler, Watchman, for his wages for 365 days (7th year, 1313). At York.
10 August (1314/15).

CITOLER (JANYN LE)

Probably the Prince's citole-player.

1306 E101/369/6.
Present at the Whitsun Feast. Received 1 mark.

CITOLER (WILLIAM LE)

1269 CPR 359, 364
Pardon, at the instance of Edmund, the King's (Hen. III) son, to William le Citoler, for the death of Simon, son of Walter de Balebuck.
Westminster. 20 and 24 July.

Pardon, at the instance of Guy de Luzignan, the King's (half-) brother, to William le Citoler, for the death of Simon, son of Walter; and of any consequent outlawry.
Winchester. 25 August.

CLAY (LAMBYN)

Court Minstrel.

1296/7 Add. MSS. 7965. f. 52^{r}
20s. to Lambin Clay, for performing at the wedding of Princess Elizabeth.

1299 CLL. Letter-book C. 87.
Arnold Guillim de Mauveysin debtor to Lambin Clay and his wife.

1307 Add. MSS. 22923. f. 7^{v} (and MS. Harley 5001. f. 43^{r}
6s. 8d. to Lambin Claye and Ricard the vielle-player, Prince's minstrels, going in his train between London and Dover, in the month of May of the present year. By gift and grace of the Prince, for payment of 2 hackneys carrying them between the two aforesaid places. By the hand of Robert de Hurle, who paid them the money at London, in the same month.

MS. Harley 5001 f. 32^{v}
5s. to Lambin Clay, minstrel, ill, at London. By gift of the Prince, to support him in his illness. Paid into his own hands.
Ringwood. 21 December.

1306 E101/369/6
Present at the Whitsun Feast. Received 1 mark.

1307 E101/373/15. f. 21^{v}
13s. 4d. to Lambin Clay, King's Minstrel, ill at London and staying there after the departure of the King (Ed. II) thence.
By gift of the King, as a help toward his expenses while remaining there.
London. 18 July.

1328 E101/383/4. (pp. 375/6)
Clay(s) le Taburer listed among the squire minstrels of the Household of Ed. III.

1330 E101/385/4. (p. 381)
As above; Cley le Taborer.

CLITHEROE (ADAM)

King's (Ed. I) Harper.

1296 Bain II. 189
Adam the King's Harper, accused Gregory de Twyseton of possessing his sword, which was stolen by Adam's groom, Hugh. Gregory said he had bought it in open market, and was acquitted.
Berwick-on-Tweed. 12 April.

1296/7 Add. MSS. 7965.

f. 52^r 40s. to Nicolas and Adam, King's Harpers, as a gift from the King to buy themselves a sumpter-horse for carrying their bedding. By the hand of Master Nicholas, at Bures St. Mary (Suffolk).
9 December

f. 58^v 40s. to Adam, King's Harper, in compensation for a black rouncy of his, returned to the Almonry at Canterbury on 1 June by the hand of Adam, at Canterbury.

f. 77^r 33s. to Adam the Harper, Citharista Regis, receiving 4½d. per day for a horse, valued in addition to his wages, which he received on the Marshalcy Roll, for his wages from 20 August, on which day his horse was valued to 19 November, the end of the present year, both days included. 92 days, bar 4, on which he was paid in victuals.
Caen/Ghent.

f. 126^v 20s. to Nicholas and Adam, King's Harpers, for their winter outfits.
Harwich.

f. 131^r 20s. to Nicholas and Adam, for their summer outfits.

1299/1300 LQG 330.
20s. to Adam the Harper for his summer outfit.

1299/1300 E101/357/14. f.14^{r}
100s. to Adam, King's Harper, prest, for money owing to him. By the hand of Thomas Querle.
Windsor. 22 February.

c.1300 E101/371/8. (Part 1) frag. 16
5s. to Adam, harpator.
frag. 101 (a page from a Wardrobe account, which has been entered and so crossed out. Name only occurs: Adam Citharista.

1300/1 E101/359/5.
f. 8^{r} 46s. 8d. for his wages.

1300/1 E101/359/6.
f. 13^{v} 6s. 8d. prest for his wages; money owing to him on recognizance made in the Wardrobe.
Linlithgow. 14 October.

1301 Add. MSS. 7966.
f. 142^{v} 20s. for his summer outfit.
London. 1 March.
f. 178^{v} 6s. 8d. to Adam Citharista, by the hand of Master John de la More, chaplain of Master John de Bensted, for money which was owing to him on recognizance, drawn up in the Wardrobe at Linlithgow. 14 October.

1302/3 Add. MSS. 35292. f. 7^{v}
10s. for his wages; by the hand of Nicholas (le Blund).
Brechin (Forfarshire). 11 August (Sunday).

1302/3 E101/364/13. f. 75^{r}
Prests, for his wages:
1/2 mark. 20 December. Laverstock (Wilts) or Lavestoke (Herts).
1 mark. 31 December. Odiham (per Nicholas Citharista)
10s. 11 August. Brechin (per Nicholas Citharista)
10s. 22 April. York.
1/2 mark. 29 May. Roxburgh.
10s. 28 June. St. John de Perth.

1302 E101/364/13. f. 25^v
£4 13s. 9d. for his wages, at 7^1/2d. per day; for the whole of 1302, during which time he was in Court 150 days.
Paid, at London, 1 March 1307.
N.B. In this account it seems certain that the King's (Ed. I) old servants were being paid up; and were probably being dismissed from office under the new King, Ed. II. The PRO dates the MS. (Liber de unde Respondebit) as 1302/3, but this year refers to the period for which the money was being paid. As the above entry proves, actual payment was made 5 years later.

1305 E101/368/6.
f. 11^r Prests for his wages:
4s. 23 November. Wallingford.
5s. 5 December. Kempsford.
3s. 19 December. Ringwood.
f. 13^r Prests for his wages.
20s. by the hand of Master Gilbert. 8 January. Kingston Lacy.
N.B. In this entry the 4 King's Harpers are being paid together; which establishes who the current King's Harpers were in 1305: they were: William de Morley; John de Neweton; Hugh de la Rose; Adam de Clitheroe. They received 20s. each.

See MORLEY (WILLIAM); NEWENTON (JOHN); HUGHETHUN.

1306 E101/369/6.
Present, with his fellow-harpers, Hugh, William and John, at the Whitsun Feast.
Adekin - received 2 marks.

1306/7 E101/368/27.
f. 21^r £6 9s. 4^1/2d. to Adam de Cliderhou, Citharista, for his wages, at 7^1/2d. per day, for the whole of the current year. 315 days minus 158, during which time he was absent from Court.
London. 1 March (1307 I. Ed. II)
f. 39^r prests for his wages.
1 mark. 17 June. Westminster.
10s. 1 November. Lanercost.
f. 62^v 20s. prest, for his wages.
Newborough in Tyndale. 4 September.
f. 63^v 5s. prest, for his wages.
Newborough in Tyndale. 24 August.

f. 65v Prests for his wages (1305):
4s. 23 November. Wallingford.
5s. 5 December. [Kempsford].
3s. 19 December. Ringwood.

f. 67r 20s. to Adam de Cliderow, prest, for his wages; by the hand of William de Morley. Kingston Lacy. 2 January.

E101/369/16.

f. 9v 27s. 6d. prest, to Adam, the King's Harper, being the price of 3 1/2 ells of bluet cloth, 3 1/2 ells of striped, and one lamb's fur; given to him by Ralph de Stokes, Clerk of the Great Wardrobe.

f. 10v 24s. 6d. prest, to Adam de Cliderhou, being the price of 7 ells of blue and green cloths (3 1/2 ells of each); given him by Ralph de Stokes, Clerk of the Great Wardrobe.

E101/370/16

f. 1v (p. 42) 10s. (for his wages). 26 November. Lanercost.

f. 3v (p. 46) 1 mark; by the hand of John de Newenton. 24 December. Lanercost.

f. 6r (p. 51) 1 mark. 1 February. Lanercost.

f. 9r (p. 57) 1/2 mark. 26 March [Easter Day]. Carlisle.

E101/369/11

f. 165v £7 to Adam de Cliderhou, for his winter and summer outfits for the years 1302/3, 1303/4, 1304/5, and 1305/6,
40s. for each year, except his winter outfit for 1303/4, because he was absent from Court on Christmas Day of that year.
The account drawn up at the Exchequer on 1 March 1307.

1306/7 E101/357/15 (Debts of the Wardrobe at the end of reign of Ed. I).

f. 21r £8 9s. 6d. owing to Adam de Cliderhou, harper.

1310 CPR. 288
Pardon, on account of his good service in Scotland, to Adam de Cliderhou, for divers offences.
[May or may not be Adam the harper].

CLOUGH (ROBERT)

Prince's and later King's (Ed. II) Harper.

1306 E101/369/6

Present at the Whitsun Feast. Received 2 marks.

1307 E101/373/15

f. 5v To Magister Robertus de Clou, Citharista; prests, for his wages:

20s.	30 August	'Tynewald in Scocia'.
13s. 4d.	3 October	Nottingham.
20s.	20 October	Leighton Buzzard.

f. 20v 20s. to Magister Robertus de Clough, citharista domini Regis, for making his minstrelsy in the presence of the King (Ed. II) at Nottingham on 5 October. By gift of the King.

1311/12 E101/373/26.

f. 93v 40s. paid to Robert de Clough, King's Harper, by the hand of William de Bromley, harper, in compensation for a horse of his. 8 February.

CLYDESDALE (ANDREW)

1303/4 Add.MSS. 8835

f. 43v Andreas de Clidesdale, one of 3 Scottish trumpeters, who accompanied the King (Ed. I) from Sterling to Northam. Given 1/2 mark toward his expenses on returning to his home. Northam. 22 August.

See BRIDE (GILBERT); SEYMOUR (NIGEL)

COC (JANYN LE)

1290 C47/4/5 f. 48r

10s. each to Bastin Noblet of Liege, Saltator and Janyn le Coc de Dowayto, menestrallus, by gift of the King. Westminster. 18 July.

They had come to perform at the wedding of Princess Margaret.

see NOBLET (BASTIN)

COGHIN

1312/13 A Welsh minstrel of Aymer de Valence, earl of Pembroke.

E101/375/8

f. 25r 40s. to Coghin, minstrel of the earl of Pembroke for making his minstrelsy in the presence of the King (Ed. II) in Windsor Castle.

By gift of the King, by the hand of Oliver de Burgedala.

Windsor. 12 October.

[Coghin < W. coch. ? "Redhead"]

COLCHESTER (ROBERT)

1306 E101/369/6

Present at the Whitsun Feast. Received 3s.

CONRAD

See PEFER (CONRAD LE)

COLON (JOHN)

1312/13 E101/375/8 A snake-charmer.

f. 27v 3s. to John de Colon, a Lombard minstrel, for making his minstrelsy, with snakes, in the presence of the King (Ed. II).

By gift of the King.

Canterbury. 16 August.

COMPAR (PETER)

1325/6 E101/381/11

In a list of the King's Household Minstrels:

Piers Compar.

CORBET (WILLIAM)

One of the trumpeters of the Earl of Arundel.

1319/20 Add. MSS. 17632

f. 31r 40s. to William Corbet and his companion (Walter), trumpeters of the Earl of Arundel, for making their minstrelsy in the presence of the King, in his private room, in the house of the Friars Minors at York. From the Lord King, by the hand of Master Gilbert Wygeton, at York.

24 October.

1320/21 Add. MSS.9951

f. 21r 20s. to William Corbet and Walter the Trumpeter, minstrels of the Earl of Arundel, for making their minstresly in the presence of the King, in his private room, in the Castle of Devizes.
By gift of the Lord King, into their own hands. 10s. each.
Devizes. 26 April.

CORLEY (ROGER)

1306 Royal Trumpeter

E101/369/6
Present at the Whitsun Feast. Received 2s.

See ROGER (the Trumpeter)

COSYN/CUSSIN (JOHN)

Court Minstrel.

1297 Add. MSS. 7965

f. 52r One of the minstrels performing at the wedding of Princess Elizabeth.
20s. to John de Cussin.

1306 E101/369/6
Although present at the Whitsun Feast, he was not one of the minstrels receiving a specific gratuity. He is noted on the Payroll as one of the 2 minstrels responsible for giving the 3 anonymous minstrels of Sir Robert de Hastings their rewards.

1311/12 MS. Cott. Nero C viii

f. 3r A Cosyn *menestrallus* occurs in an entry concerning payment of wages to Reymund Arnald, one of the sergeants of the Royal Household. The clerk has entered his name in the margin. It looks as though he was dotting down a reminder that Cosyn the minstrel was the one who collected Reymund's money.
Compare the following entry:

f. 4r Cusin, the minstrel, collected the wages of Grillo, another minstrel, 13 March 1312.

See GRILLO

1312 BAIN III, 423
John Cosyn has a black horse, valued at 5 marks.
[N.B. 423 Ricard Cosyn has a black horse, valued at £9].

CRACKSTRINGS (ROBERT)

One of the trumpeters of Earl Warenne.

1303/4 Add. MSS. 8835 f. 42^v
13s. 4d. to Robert Crackstrings for his equitatura/chevaucie/riding out.
Dunfermline. 14 May.

See DONCASTER (NICHOLAS)

CRADDOCK (WILLIAM)

A crowder: and singer.

1312/13 E101/375/8. f. 30^v
20s. to William Craddock, the crowder, for making his minstrelsy in the presence of the King (Ed. II).
By gift of the King. The equivalent of 2 florins...and 4 shillings, sterling, given to him.
6 June.

See FOX (WILLIAM)

CRESSIN/CRESSY (JOHN)

1296/7 Add. MSS. 7965. f. 52^r
20s. for performing at the wedding of Princess Elizabeth.

1300/1 Add. MSS. 7966A. f. 66^v
20s. to John de Cressy, minstrel, for making his minstrelsy, with Janin, Earl Warenne's organist and Martinet, by turns, or, on various occasions, in the presence of the King and Queen.
By gift of the Queen.
Lincoln. February.

1306/7 E101/370/16. f. 13^v (p. 65)
John de Cressy received a portion of 40s. for performing miracle plays and making his minstrelsy before the Queen at Carlisle.
29 May.

CRETING (NICHOLAS)

Foedera II pars. I. 230
Among those pardoned for supporting Thomas of Lancaster, re. the death of Gaveston:
Nichol(as) de Cretingg, Taborer

CROWDER (JOHN)

John, the Crowder, of Salop.

1299/1300 LOG. 248
18s. 4d. to John le Crowder, *vintenarius*, for his wages and those of 20 archers on foot from the county of Shropshire, admitted to King's wages for the first time on 11 July, from which day up to 15 of the same month, both days included (i.e. 5 days).

1306 E101/369/6.
Present at the Whitsun feast. Received 12d.

CROWDER (ROGER)

1306 Minstrel of the Countess of Hereford.

Add. MSS. 22923. f. 6^v and MS. Harley 5001 f. 39^v
20s. to Roger the Crowder, minstrel of the Countess of Hereford, for coming to the Prince's Court at Wetheral (Cumbria) and making his minstrelsy in the presence of the same Lord (Prince) and other nobles there in his entourage.
By gift of the Prince, on his return from thence, by the hand of Master William de Boudon. Given to him, in cash, at Wetheral, on 3 April.

1317/18 MS. Soc. of Antiq. 121. f. 117^v
Under payments to various squires in Court on Christmas Day one to Roger le Croudere, who may be the quondam minstrel of the Countess of Hereford, the King's sister.

CROWDER (THOMAS)

Royal minstrel and standard-bearer.

1294 Cal. Fine Rolls. I. 305.
Ratification of the demise by Robert Tibetot, Justice of West Wales, to Thomas le Crouthere of a burgage and 2 acres of land in the town of Dryslwyn, Carmarthen.
Amesbury. 27 August.

1303/4 Add. MSS. 8835. f. 80^v
6s. to Stephen de Felton, Constable, for the wages of Thomas le Croudere, standard-bearer of the company of 157 archers on foot, remaining in the train of Lord Aymer de Valence in the parts of Lothian, from 6-23 July, both days included, receiving for that time 4d. per day.

1304 CPR. 256. 531
Pardon, in consideration of services in the Scottish war, to Thomas le Crouther of Whitchurch, for homicide.
Stirling. 20 July.
Pardon to Thomas le Crouthere of Whitchurch, of his outlawry, during his absence on the King's service in Scotland, for non-appearance before William Martyn and his fellow justices of oyer and terminer in the County of Salop; the King having, long since, in consideration of his service in Scotland, pardoned him all homicides etc. and any consequent outlawry.
Carlisle. 27 May.

1306 E101/369/6.
Present at the Whitsun Feast. Received 2s.

1306/7 E101/369/16. f. 17^v
3d. per day, prest for his wages, to Thomas le Crouthere, going into Scotland in the train of Sir John de Bourtetourte, for making a cavalry raid upon the Earl of Carrick (Robert Bruce). By order of Sir Robert de Cotyngham per P. de Colingbourne.
Lanercost. 12 February.

1306/7 E101/370/16. f. 13^v (p. 65)
David de Percy and Llewelyn Treblerth were detailed by the King (Ed. I) to go to the Prince of Wales and thence to Wales to press/choose foot soldiers to join the Prince and proceed to Scotland.
They were given 10s. each and then a further 5s. each, the latter by the hand of Thomas le Croudere.
Carlisle. 27 May.

1307 CPR. 492
Pardon for outlawry, on condition that he surrender immediately to gaol, to Thomas le Crouther of Whitchurch, for the death of Richard, bailiff of 'Luddesdone'.
[N.B. uncertain whether Thomas of Whitchurch is the same person as the other Thomas].

CUNRAD/CONRAD

One of two German geige-players at the Court of Edward I.

1300/1 Add. MSS. 7966

f. 66^{v} 13s. to Conrad [the clerk has written 'Girard'] German geige-player, King's minstrel. By gift of the King.
Kempsey (Worcs.). 29 April (1301).

f. 67^{r} 20s. to Cunrad, for certain necessaries bought for him. By gift of the King.
Burton. 14 January.

6s. 8d. for a sumpter-saddle and girth bought for him for his use. By gift of the King.
Eston. 19 January.

8s. 2d. for litter during the months of February and March. By gift of the King.
Northampton. 13 March.

[As these payments were always made to both Conrad and Henry at the same time, the clerk has noted that, with regard to money for firewood and litter, it was given '*ad opus eorundem per vices*'.

f. 69^{r} 1 mark for certain necessaries bought for him. By gift of the King.
Westminster. 16 July.
[Money for both, given to Conrad]

1302/3 Add. MSS. 35292. f. 29^{v}

1 mark to Henry and Cunrad, King's geige-players, for their wages.
Dunfermline.

1302/3 E101/364/13. f. 32^{v}

1 mark, prest, for *Henricus* and *Scundradus* to buy certain necessaries for themselves.
By order of the King. By the hand of Sconred.
Reading. 27 November.

1304/5 E101/368/6

f. 8^{r} 3s. prest to Cunrad *gigator*, for those things which were ordered for him in the Wardrobe.
Kempsford (Glos.). 6 December.

f. 21^{v} 20s. to Conrad *gigator Regis* to buy himself a gown/outfit (*roba*).
Kingston Lacy. 12 January.

1305/6 E101/369/11.

f. 98^v 20s. to Conrad, to buy himself a gown/outfit. By gift of the King.
Kingston Lacy. 2 January.

f. 102^v £12 18s. 8d. to Henry and Cunrad, King's geige-players; minstrels from Germany who have been staying at Court by order of the King; making their minstrelsy at his wish. The money given to them at various times, by order of the King, during the years 1301 to 1305/6.

1305/6 E101/368/27.

f. 46^v 3s. prest, for his wages. Given to him in cash by Peter de Brembe.
Charminster. 22 January.

1306 E101/369/6.
Present at the Whitsun Feast. Received 2 marks per Monsire Henri le Gigour.
See HENRY, GEIGE PLAYERS

D

DAA (HUGH)

1306 E101/369/6
Hugo Daa, probably a Welsh harper attached to the household of the L'estrange family.
Present at the Whitsun feast. Received 2s.

DANCERS (4) (13)

1332/3 E101/386/7. f. 7^v
20s. to 4 minstrels, for dancing and making their minstrelsy before the Lady Eleanor.
By gift of the lady, by the hand of the treasurer.
Malines. 15 May.
60s. to 13 minstrels, for dancing and making their minstrelsy before the Lady Alianora (Eleanor).
By gift of the lady, by the hand of John le Smale.
Bruges. 10 May.

DARE (JOHN)

1311/12 MS. Cott. Nero. C.viii

Minstrel of the King's (Ed. II) Household and later of the Household of Ed. III.

f. 194v £4 19s. 8d. to John Dare, minstrel of the King's Household, for money owed to him for his wages, and his outfit. By his own hand. By a bill.

9 July 1318/19

f. 226r 20s. to Janin Dare for his outfit.

DASSA (RICARD)

1311/12 E101/374/19

f. 8r minstrel of the Countess of Norfolk.

See FRAMLINGHAM (ROBERT)

DAVEROUNS (ROBERT)

1317/18 Archaeologia. xxvi 344

£3 to Robert Daverouns, vielle-player ('violist') of the Prince of Tauntum, making his minstrelsy in the presence of the King (Ed. II). By gift of the King.

Newburgh. 1 November.

DAVID (ap REES)

Welsh trumpeter of Ed. II

1307/8 Add. MSS. 35093.

f. 1r 10s. for his shoes.

10 July.

DAVID (LE CROUTHER)

1306 E101/369/6.

Present at the Whitsun Feast. Received 12d. Probably a Welsh crowder and one of the squires of the royal household.

DEPE (JOHN)

1294/5 King's Trumpeter. His fellow Trumpeter was John de London.

Fryde. 43. (Book of Prests)

£18 5s. to both, at 6d. per day, wages for the whole year, because they were never absent.

£12 18s. 4d. owing to them.

London (1297).

13s. 4d. for his wages (p. 174); 20s. for his wages (p. 176).

Wengham. 25 September.

20s. for his wages.

Canterbury. 26 October.

1296/7 Add. MSS. 7965.

f. 55r 60s. in compensation for his bay rouncy, killed in the King's service at Langestok in February.
Maghefeld. 30 March.

f. 56v 20s. for repair to his trumpet.

f. 79r 47s. 6d. for his wages, from 13 August, on which day his horse was valued, to 19 November, both days included; 99 days bar 4 in March. 12d per day; 6d. from the Marshalcy and 6d. from Court. By the hand of his fellow trumpeter, John de London.
Westminster. 19 March (1298).

f. 126v 20s. for his winter outfit.

1298 Gough. 198
His horse, a bay rouncy, valued at 6 marks.

1299/1300 Add. MSS. 35291. f. 155r
Prest for his wages: John de Depe.

1300/1 Add. MSS. 7966. ff. 175v, 178v
6s. 8d. prest, for the price of 20 ells of canvas.

1300/1 E101/359/6. f. 14r
To John de Depe, trumpeter, prests, for his wages:
1/2 mark. 30 September. Dunipace.
10s. 8 November. Linlithgow.

1302/3 Add. MSS. 35292. f. 4v
1/2 mark for his wages.

1302/3 E101/364/13.
Prests, for his wages:

f. 79v 1/2 mark. 17 March. London. By Nicholas, the King's Harper.
1/2 mark. 23 June. St. John de Perth.
10s. 27 April. York.
6s. 8d. 29 May. Roxburgh.

f. 81r 100s. to John de Depe, trumpeter, to buy his gear for the Scottish War.
York. 23 April.

DEVENISH (THOMAS)

Thomas le Deveneys; King's Tailor (subcissor)

1294/5 Fryde, 126
5s. to Thomas le Deueneys, prest, for his wages.
Plymouth. 7 May (1296).

1296/7 Add. MSS. 7965. f. 78^v
58s. 9d. to Thomelus Deueneys for his wages from 14 August on which day his horse was valued, to 19 November, both days included; 98 days bar 4, during which he received victuals: going with the King to Flanders. Paid $4^1/2$d. per day at the Marshalcy and $7^1/2$d. per day at Court.

1299 E101/357/15. f. 2^r
29s. $6^1/2$d. owing to Thomas Deuenays. (for 1299)

1300 E101/371/8. (Part I)
frag. 41 Thomas le Deueneys - 10s.
frag. 92 Prest for his wages - 30s.

1300/1 E101/359/5.
f. 3^r 4s. to Thomas le Deueneys, for the carriage of the King's clothes (robae).
Worcester. 20 April.
f. 4^r Prest, for his wages.

1302/3 E101/363/10.
f. 6^v 2s. prest, for the carriage of the King's clothes.
Coxton (Lincs.). 1 April.

1302/3 E101/364/13.
f. 34^v £17, prest, for carriage of the King's clothes, from St. Albans to London; 2s. St. Albans, 17 February; 2s Hertford (?) 21 February; 2s. in cash, given to him by John de Drokenesford at Newcastle-on-Tyne, 12 May. 6s. 8d. for carriage of the King's clothes from York to Newcastle.
York. 21 April.
f. 38^v 12d. for carriage of the King's clothes.
Roxburgh. 30 May.
f. 50^r 2s. in cash, for carriage of the King's clothes. Given him by Peter de Brembre, at Croxton, 1 April; 3s. for same, at Lenton. 10 April.
f. 77^v Prests, for his wages:

$^1/2$ mark.	6 April.	Brechin.
10s.	19 April.	York.
5s.	24 April.	York.
10s.	18 October.	Dundee.

1304/5 E101/368/6. f. 6^{v}

4s. prest; for carriage of the King's clothes; by the hand of Thomas Snel, sometarius (sumpter-man), at Wallingford, 23 November.

[and several other journeys. Total - 17s.]

f. 1 of 2 sheets sewn in at back of MS: 18s. prest, for carriage of men and of the King's clothing. Paid into his own hands. Chertsey. 10 November.

1305/6 E101/369/11. f. 36^{v}

3s. to Thomas le Deueneys for a gaming-board, with counters for the same; bought by him for the King's use, for playing with (coram) the King himself. Durham. 7 August.

1305/6 E101/368/27.

f. 21^{v} £6 16s. 10^{1}/2d. for his wages at 4^{1}/2d per day, for 365 days, because he was not absent from Court during the whole year.

f. 35^{v} 2s. prest, for carriage of the King's small Wardrobe. By the hand of D...fitz Ralph. Woburn. 24 June.

ff. 36^{v}, 38^{v} for carriage of King's clothes.

f. 36^{v} 3s. by the hand of Thomas Snel. Wallingford. 23 November.
3s. by the hand of Henry, groom of Gervase de Holeway.
Kempsford. 4 December.
5s. at Say 16 December.
2s. by the hand of Nicholas de Burton.
Christchurch. 21 December.

f. 38^{v} 2s. by the hand of Ricard Rolfe Middleton. 13 January; 18d. by same. Byere. 19 January. 12d. by same. Wareham. 21 January; 18d. by same. Dorchester. 31 January; 3s. by same Hamptoworth. 15 February. 18d. by same Winchester. 18 February. 2s. 8d. into his own hands. Farnham. 15 May.

f. 59^{r} 20s. prest, for his wages. Westminster. 17 June.

f. 61^{v} ^{1}/2 mark, for same, Lazenby. 30 July.
10s. for going to London on the King's business. Lanercost. 14 October.
10s. paid into his own hands, at Thrapston. 5 July.

f. 63^{r} 20s. prest, for his wages.
Newborough in Tyndale. 4 September.

f. 63v   5s. prest, for his wages.
Hexham. 16 August.
f. 65v   4s. prest, for his wages. Bastildone. 22 November.
3s. Derebury. 9 December.
f. 68v   5s. Werdeforde. 26 January.
5s. Itchenstoke. Last day of February.
1/2 mark. Winchester. 10 May.
f. 70r   20s. Wareham. 26 February.

1306/7   E101/369/16. f. 28r
1 mark prest, for his wages. Lanercost. 25 November.
20s. Lanercost. 1 February.
10s. Carlisle. 26 April.
10s. Carlisle. 12 June.

1306   E101/369/6.
Present at Whitsun Feast. Received 20s. by the hand of Bruant.

1306/7   E101/357/15. (Debts of the Wardrobe) and Add. MSS. 8835 f. 25r
f. 23r   £18 12s. 9d. owing to Thomas Devenish.

DRAKE (JOHN)
King's (Ed. I) Waferer.

1290   C47/4/5.
f. 37r   20s. to John Drake, *Waffrarius Regis*, who is in place of *Perottus*, the Waferer, deceased; for his winter outfit.
26 January.

1290   E101/352/24. (Household Account of King and Queen)
sub *Menestralli*:
John Drake, King's Waferer; issued summer and winter outfits.

1290   C47/4/4. f. 22v
£4 14s 4½d. paid to him, for his wages, at 7½d. per day, from 1 January to 31 May, both days included: 151 days.

1294/5 Fryde 14/27; 39; 181; 185, 207.
101s. 3d. for his wages, for 162 days, because he was never absent £41 8s. 1^{1}/2d. wages for the whole [Aberconway] year, because he was never absent.
26s. 8d. for his wages.
St. Albans. 2 January (1295).
16s. on account, for 2 quarters of wheat, given to him at Aberconway.
Price per quarter, 8s.
Memorandum: that there is owing to John Drake, King's Waferer, £4 4s. 2^{1}//2d.; minus the 2 quarters of wheat.

1297 Add. MSS. 7965.
f. 18^{r} 5^{1}/2 marks to Master John, the Waferer for a black horse, bought for a lady-in-waiting (domicella) of the Countess of Holland (Princess Elizabeth).
f. 52^{r} 20s. for making his minstrelsy at the wedding of Princess Elizabeth.
f. 77^{v} 35s. 3d. for his wages from 14 August, on which day his horse was valued, to 19 November, both days included; 98 days bar 4 at 4^{1}/2d. per day [? at the Marshalcy] Ghent. 21 November.
f. 123^{r} 20s. for his winter outfit.

1299 E101/356/13.
1st Roll/Daily issue of bread: Drake, 1 pennyworth. 16 April.

1299/1300 E101/357/5
Membrane 3: 20s. for his summer outfit. York. 9 September. On reverse of longest membrane: 5s. prest, for his wages, 21 October, Carlisle. 10s. 30 October, Carlisle. 16s. 13 November. Carlisle.

1306/7 E101/370/16.
f. 1^{v} (p. 42) 1 mark, for his wages. Lanercost. 26 November.
5s. 4d. for the payment of 10 tailors, furnishing the King's chamber at Lanercost and for thread bought by same over 2 days. Lanercost. 30 November.
f. 6^{r} (p. 51) 20s. for his wages. Lanercost. 1 February.
f. 17^{r} ^{1}/2 mark to Thomas Deueneys. Carlisle. 4 July.

DONCASTER (NICHOLAS)

1303/4 One of Earl Warenne's trumpeters.

Add. MSS. 8835. f. 42^v
13s. 4d. each to Nicholas of Doncaster and Robert Crackstrings, the Earl Warenne's trumpeters, who were staying in the King's Household, by order of the King, after the departure of the said earl from Dunfermline, to buy themselves 2 horses for their riding-out (equitatura).
By gift of the King.
Stirling. 14 May.

DORCHESTER (JOHN)

1311/12 Groom of the Household of the two young princes, Thomas and Edmund.

E101/374/19 f. 8^r
12d. to John of Dorchester, for making his minstrelsy in the presence of the princes.
28 October.

See MAPPARIUS (JOHN), WINDSOR (PHILIP)

DORUM (GERARD)

King's Yeoman/Squire.

c.1300 E101/371/8 (Part I). This MS. is a box of fragments containing miscellanea from the Marshalcy. The fragments are of various dates. The information is usually in the form of a name and a sum of money assigned to it.
fr. 16 Gerardus Dorum.

1306/7 E101/370/16
f. 10^r (p. 59)
49s. 10d. to Gerard Dorum, for money owing to him.
Carlisle. 13 April.

1314/15 (or later) E101/376/7. f. 122^v
£7 to Gerard Dorum, King's Squire, owing to him for his expenses out of Court.

1299/1300 Add. MSS. 35291. f. 155^v
Prest, for his wages.

1299/1300 LOG. 314
2 marks for his winter outfit. Westminster 23 March (1302).

1300/1 Add. MSS. 7966A. f. 136[r]
Received no money for his winter outfit, because he had been given a roll or length (pannus) of cloth by the Queen.

c. 1300 E101/371/8 (Part I)
fragment 16. Master John the Waferer. 10s.
" 41. John the Waferer. 1 mark.
" 48. 1 mark for his wages.
" 101. 10s. for his wages.

1302/3 Add. MSS. 35292
f. 4[v] 10s. for his wages.
f. 9[v] 10s. for his wages. Brechin. 11 August.
f. 12[r] 20s. to Master John Drake. Gask (Perthshire). 25 October.
f. 26[v] 20s. for his wages. Dunfermline. 8 February.

1302/3 E101/364/13. f. 75[v]
Prests, for his wages: 20s. 28 December. Odiham; 2s. 16 February Watford; 20s. 27 May Roxburgh; 10s. 28 June St. John de Perth; 20s. 12 August Brechin; 20s. 20 April York; 10s. by the hand of Master Peter de Collingbourne, for money which he owed him in 1301; in cash, given to him by Peter de Brembre. 5 April. Lenton (Notts.) 10s. in cash given to him by John de Flete. 8 May. Newcastle-on-Tyne.

1303 Add. MSS. 8835. f. 51[v]
40s. to Master John Drake the Waferer, in compensation for a dun-coloured sumpter-horse, returned to the Almonry at Dunfermline, in the current year. 4 October.

1304/5 E101/368/6. f. 12[r]
Prests, for his wages: 5s. 8 December. "Slecombe"; 5s. 19 December. Ringwood; 5s. 24 December. Kingston Lacy. (see E101/368/27 f. 66[v]).

1305/6 MS. Harley 152. f. 20[v]
Prest, for his wages. Lanercost.

1305/6 E101/369/11. f. 204[v]
Prests, for his wages.
1/2 mark 27 January. Charminster (Dorset).
10s. 26 February. Itchenstoke (Hants.).

1306 E101/369/6.
Present at Whitsun Feast. Received 2 marks.

1305/6 E101/368/27.

f. 20r £10 8s. 9d. for his wages, for 365 days bar 21, when he was absent from Court. 4 October. Westminster.

f. 60r Prests, for his wages:

13s. 4d.	7 June	Westminster.
10s.	30 July	Lazenby (Yorks).
40s.	16 September	Thirlwall.
5s.	13 July	Grantham.
1/2 mark.	5 July	Thrapston.
10s.	31 October	Lanercost.
10s.	1 November	Lanercost.

f. 62v 20s. prest, for his wages. 4 September Newborough in Tyndale.

f. 63v	5s.	16 August	Hexham.
f. 66v	5s.	8 December	Elcombe (Wilts) (1305)
	5s.	19 December	Ringwood (1305)
	1/2 mark	23 December	Kingston Lacy

f. 70r 2 marks, prest, for his wages. 6 February. Wareham.

1306/7 E101/369/16. f. 10r
24s. 6d. being the price of 7 ells of blue and green cloths (3 1/2 ells of each). Given to him by Ralph de Stokes, clerk of the Great Wardrobe.

1306/7 E101/370/16.

f. 1r 1 mark 25 November. Lanercost.

f. 4r 1 mark, for his wages. 28 December. Lanercost.

f. 6r 20s. for his wages. 1 February. Lanercost.

f. 9r 1 mark to Master John Drake, by order of the bishop (? of Carlisle). 26 March (Easter Day). Carlisle.

f. 17r 1 mark. 4 July. Carlisle.
[John had just 2 more days to make wafers for his master. Edward I died in the morning of 7 July].

1306 Walter de Wenlok. (ed. Ernest Harold Peace. Lond. 1920.) p. 85. [Gifts given by the abbot to various servants of the royal household]. Mandate from the abbot to the reeve of Denham (Bucks.) "We order you to deliver to the carrier of this letter a quarter of fine wheat, of our gift, to John, the Waferer of our Lord, the King."

1307 Fryde. E101/364/13.
f. 24^v^ £11 8s. $1^1/2$d. for his wages, at $7^1/2$d. per day, for the whole year (probably 1302/3), because he was never absent.
Westminster. 4 October (1307).

1307 Add. MSS. 8835. f. 112^r^
2 marks for his winter outfit.
Westminster. 4 October.

1306/7 E101/357/15. (Debts of the Wardrobe)
f. 16^r^ Owing to John Drake: £48 13s. $5^1/2$d.
f. 21^r^ Master John Drake, the Waferer: £30 2s. $1^1/2$d.
Foedera. II Pars I. 213.
Letters of protection for those who will set out with the King (Ed. II) for parts overseas: Johannes Drake. 3 May. Westminster.

1307/11 The Cartulary of Holy Trinity, Aldgate. (Lond. Record Soc. 1971).
No. 134. St. Olave, Hart Street.
1267/8. Grant by Gilbert, prior, and convent to John le Waffrere of lands with houses built upon it; abutments, the land and houses formerly of Richard Hakenay, on the east, on those of the prior and convent, formerly of Stacius de Gardino, clerk, on the west, and extending from the King's Highway to the former gardens of Richard Hakeney. Rent, 9s. per annum. The grantee is not to destroy the houses but to repair and maintain them. If John or his heirs wish to leave or sell, the prior and convent are to have the preference, by a bezant of 2s.
No. 135. In a list of those paying rent to the Convent:
1307/11 John Waffrer.

1316 CCR. 329.
On 20 March, 1316, Ed. II sent one Gaven le Corder, on account of his service to the King and Queen, to the Prior and convent of Christ Church, Canterbury, to receive the same allowance as 'John Drak', deceaed, had in that house. If this were John le Waferer then he died between 1313 and 1316.

DRUET

King Herald and vielle-player: minstrel of the Earl of Gloucester.

1296/7 *Add. MSS. 7965*. f. 52^r and *Add. MSS. 8934*. f. 124^v
40s. to Druett, for performing at the wedding of Princess Elizabeth.

1303/4 *Add. MSS. 8835*. f. 44^v
30s. paid to John de Claxton, for money which he distributed, by order of the Bishop of Chester, Treasurer of England, to King Druett, John de Maunte, Arnulett, the vielle-player, John de Swaneseye, James le Mazon and other minstrels, for making their minstrelsies in the presence of the Lady Maria, the King's daughter.
At Burstwick (Yorks.)

1311/12 *E101/374/19*.
f. 8^r 13s. 4d. to King Druett, vielle-player, minstrel of the Earl of Gloucester (*Rex Durettus, Violarius, menestrallus domini Comitis Gloucestrie*) and John Purley, trumpeter, minstrels of the lord Earl of Gloucester, for making their minstrelsy in the presence of the 2 (young princes, Thomas and Edmund).
By the hand of Master J. de. Weston.
Striguil. 31 December.

1306 *E101/369/6*.
Present at the Whitsun Feast. Received 40s.

DUFFELD (WILLIAM)

1306 *E101/369/6*.
Willelmus de Duffeld. Duffeld - $4^1/2$ miles N. of Derby. Present at the Whitsun Feast. Received 40d.

DUREME

1296/7 Probably a minstrel of Anthony Bek, bishop of Durham.

Add. MSS. 7965. f. 52^r
20s. for performing at the wedding of Princess Elizabeth.

DUZEDEYS (PETER)

1311/12 King's Minstrel.

MS. Cott. Nero. C viii. f. 87v
20s. each to Peter Duzedeys, Roger the Trumpeter and Janin the Nakerer, King's Minstrels.
York. 29 January.

1312/13 E101/375/8. f. 30r
10s. to Peter Duzedeys, King's Minstrel, by gift of the King, by the hand of Gilbert de Rishton, the money being given by order of the King, at Pontefract, on 1 July, as is stated in the particulars of Master John de Okham, in the Wardrobe.
Westminster. 26 October (1313/14)

DYNYS (THOMAS)

1312/13 King's Minstrel; probably a citole-player.

E101/375/8. f. 29v
socius of Jerome Vala le Cetoler.
both called 'menestralli Regis' in margin, by Clerk.

See VALA (JEROME)

E

EGIDIUS ("GILES")

1311/12 Giles, Court or King's Trumpeter.

MS. Cott. Nero. C.viii.
f. 193r £4 12s. 8d. for money owed to him.
21 February.
f. 226r Listed as a household minstrel.

1335/8 20s. to Egidius Trympour, minstrel in the household of Ed. III for his outfit.

1328 E101/383/4. (pp. 375/6)
Listed among the squire minstrels of Ed. III's household.

1330 E101/385/4. (p. 381)
as above: Egidius le Trumpour.

EILLIAME [or/SILLIAME]

1306 E101/369/6.
Present at the Whitsun Feast. Received 20s.

ELAND (JOHN)

1322 Cal. Chancery Warrants. I.529
Pardon granted to John de Eland, harper, for adhering to Thomas of Lancaster.
Rothwell. 22 April.

ELENA

1307 A female waferer and minstrel.

E101/373/15.
Wife of Ricard Pilke, King's Waferer.

See PILKE (RICARD)

ELIAS

1296 Rotuli Scotiae I. 28.
Master Elyas, le Harpeur. Harper of the Earl of Fife. Mandate from the King (Ed. I) to the Sheriff of Fife, ordering him to restore to Elias all his lands and goods, which were at that time being held in the King's hands, because the Earl of Fife was a minor.

ELIAS (the Piper)

1358/9 MS. Cott. Galba. E xiv. f. 52^r
20s. to Elias, the piper of the lord Prince, for making his minstrelsies in the presence of the Lady Queen, on Whitsunday. By gift of the same, on the same day (? 9 June 1359).

ERNOLET

Court vielle-player.

1306 E101/369/6.
Present at the Whitsun Feast. Received 40s.

See ARNULET.

ERNULPH

1290 Vielle-player of Count St. Pol.

C. 47/4/5. f. 45^v
40s. for performing at the wedding of Princess Joanna. By gift of the King.

LE ESTIUOUR (GEOFFREY)

Geffrai Le Estiuour.
An estive-player of one of the royal households.

1306 E101/369/6.
Present at the Whitsun Feast.
One of La Comune.

ESUILLIE

1306 E101/369/6.
"who is with Monsire Peter de Mauley"
Perhaps one of his minstrels.
Present at the Whitsun Feast. Received 1 mark.

EUSTACHE (DE REYNS)

1266 Eustache of Rheims. King's (Hen. III) minstrel.

CPR. 195.
Mandate to Ricard of Ewell and Hugo de Turri, buyers at the Wardrobe, to have an outfit made for Eustache de Reyns our 'minstrel'. By gift of the King.
Northampton. 26 May.

F

FAIRFAX

Perhaps John Fairfax. Squire/sergeant of the King's Household.

1298 Gough. 48, 49.
Letters of protection to Johannes Fairfax, to go with the army to Scotland.
5 July.

1306 E101/369/6.
Present at the Whitsun Feast. Received 20s.

FAIRFAX (William)

King's squire-at-arms.

1319/20 E101/378/4. f. 25^r
28s. to Willelmus Fairfax, who had his horse valued in the Scottish war, in the present year, from the last day of August, on which day his horse was valued, to 28 September, the first day included but not the last. 28 days at 12d. per day.
London. 11 November.

FLISKE (Henry)

Minstrel of Lord Cardinal Lucio de Fliske.

1317/18 MS. Soc. of Antiq. 121. f. 57^{r}
40s. to Master Henry de Fliske [MS. Fluske], minstrel of Lord Lucio de Fliske, Cardinal, playing (ludenti) in the presence of the Lord King, by the hand of John Pecocke the Elder, giving the money to him there on 4 December.

FOL (Robert Le)

post 1328 Queen Philippa's fool.

MS. Cott. Galba. E iii. f. 188^{v}
12 ells, 1 lamb's fur, 2 budge furs and 1 budge for a hood, to Master Robert le Fol, minstrel, to have an outfit made for himself, of striped cloth of Ypres.

FOLESTHANKE (Ralph)

King's Minstrel.

1285 E101/351/17.
£4 each to Ralph Folesthanke and Peter the Waferer.

See DRAKE (JOHN) for Peter, King's Waferer.

FOX (WILLIAM)

Singer.

1306 Warton. p. 85 n. 1. and MS. Bodley; Hearne's Diaries. 123.
MS. Bodley (Hearne, p. 8)
To William Fox and Craddoc, his socius, singers; 20s. for singing in the presence of the Prince and other nobles there in his entourage, at London, in the month of December.
By gift of the Prince, by the hand of the said William, who received the money from Ringwood.
5 December.
To William Fox and Craddoc, his socius, singers, 20s. (for singing) in the presence of the Prince and other nobles, at London. By gift of the Prince, by the hand of John de Ringwood, who gave them the money there on 8 January.
Warton.
20s. to William Fox and his companion, Cradock, singers, for singing in the presence of the Prince and other nobles of his entourage, at London.
8 January, by the hand of John de Ringwood.

FRAMLINGHAM (ROBERT)

1311/12 Minstrel (harper) of the Countess of Norfolk.

E101/374/19. f. 8^r
13s. 4d. to Robert de Framlingham, harper, and John, his companion, and Ricard Dassa, minstrels of the 'Countess Marshal', coming in the train of the Countess and making their minstrelsy in the presence of the 2 (young princes, Thomas and Edmund).
By gift of the princes.
Framlingham. 15 June.

FRANCISKIN (FRANCEKIN)

Prince's, later King's (Ed. II) Nakerer.

1306/7 Add. MSS. 22923. f. 7^r
10s. to Franciskin, the Nakerer (*tartarensis*), minstrel of the Prince's Household, to buy himself a pair of nakers.
By gift of the lord Prince.
22 April.

1310/11 E101/373/10.
f. 3^v 3s. to Franciskin, King's Nakerer (*nacarius Regis*) for his wages. 29 March.
f. 5^v 2s. for his wages. 28 April.

1310/11 E101/374/5.
f. 91^r Prests, for his wages.
2s. 24 October. Linlithgow.
3s. 8 November. Berwick-on-Tweed.

1311/12 MS. Bodley. Tanner. 197.
f. 50^r
3s. prest, for his wages. 29 March. Berwick-on-Tweed.
2s. for the same. 28 April. Berwick-on-Tweed.

1311/12 E101/373/26.
f. 76^v 2s. prest, for his wages.
20 June. Burstwick.

See KENNINGTON (JOHN); SCOT (JOHN)

FYNCHESLEY (ROBERT)

Robert Finchley, King's Watchman.

c. 1300 E101/371/8. (Pt. I).
fragment 16. Robertus de Fynchesle. 5s.
" 41. 10s.
" 101. 10s. for his wages.

1302/3 E101/364/13. f. 26^{r}
£6 16s. $10^{1}/2$d. for his wages, at $4^{1}/2$d. per day, for the whole of 1302/3, because he was never absent from Court.

1305/6 E101/368/27.
f. 21^{v} £6 16s. $10^{1}/2$d., prest, for his wages. at $4^{1}/2$d. per day, for 365 days, because he was never absent from Court. London. 1 March.
f. 63^{r} 1 mark, prest, for his wages. 4 September. Newborough in Tyndale.
f. 63^{v} 5s. prest, for his wages. 24 August. Newborough in Tyndale.
f. 64^{v} Prests for his wages:
4s. 5 July. Thrapston.
$^{1}/2$ mark. by the hand of Adam Skyrewith. 1 November. Lanercost.
f. 66^{r} 3s. prest, for his wages. 26 November (1305). Abingdon.
f. 69^{v} Prests for his wages:
5s. 23 February. Winchester.
5s. 22 March. Winchester.
5s. 10 May. Winchester.
f. 70^{v} 2 marks. prest for his wages. 23 February. Winchester.

1306/7 E101/369/16. f. 26^{v}
Prests for his wages: 10s. by the hand of Adam Skyrewith. 24 December. Lanercost. 10s. 4 February. Lanercost. 10s. 24 April. Carlisle. 10s. 30 May. Carlisle. 6s. 8d. 7 July. Tower of London.

1306/7 E101/370/16.
f. 1^{r} (p. 41) 10s. (for his wages) 25 November. Lanercost.
f. 3^{v} (p. 46) 10s. by the hand of Adam Skirewith. 24 December. Lanercost.
f. 11^{r} (p. 61) 10s. 24 April. Carlisle.

GARSIE (JOHN)

1302/3 Trumpeter of Prince Edward (later Ed. II)

E101/363/18.

f. 21^v 12s. for playing, with Thomasin, John de Catalonia and Janot the Nakerer, in the presence of the Prince, on Trinity Sunday, at Newbattle (Edinburgh).
By gift of the Prince, to buy himself a black silk cloak.
2 June. Newbattle.

f. 23^r A gift of the price of a habergeon and iron collaret, to Master John Garsie, trumpeter, Prince's minstrel, bought from Ricard the lorimer.
[A like gift made to John de Catalonia, trumpeter and Janot the nakerer. Cost, for the 3 sets - 33s.]
Dunfermline. (January)

1307 CLL. Letter-book C. 208
John, the 8 year-old son of John Garsie, 'tromppour', was placed in the custody of William Pontefract (Pountfreyt), together with 20 marks sterling and 1/2 mark quitrent, bequeathed to the said John by John Dunstable, by mainprise of William atte Ramme, brewer, and Robert Pontefract wardrobe/furniture dealer. The custody of the boy was legally handed over in the presence of the mayor and aldermen on 11 November 1307; who bound themselves jointly and severally to see that the said William would safeguard the boy, John, and answer for his property, etc.

GARSINGTON (ELIAS)

1312/13 King's (Ed. II) Harper.

E101/373/26. f. 24^v
Elias de Garsynton, Citharista Regis, first admitted on King's wages, on 27 January of the current year; receiving 4 1/2d. per day for his wages from that day up to 7 July, both days included; for 163 days, bar 19, when he was absent. £5 0s. 3d.
Windsor. 18 January.

GASCONY (MARTINET of)

1299/1300 A Fool from France.

LOG. p. 166 (f. 131)
2s. to Martinet, of Gascony, fool, for playing before the Prince Lord Edward, at Carlisle.
By gift of the Prince, by the hand of Lord/Sir (Dominus) John de Leek at Carlisle. 14 October.

GASKES (BERNARD)

1306/7 E101/370/16. f. 10^v (p. 60)
"To Bernard Gaskes, minstrel...
[a large water-patch on MS. throughout has rendered this particular entry illegible]

GATTE [GAYTE] (PETER)

c. 1300 (?)Watchman/Minstrel of the Master of the Order of St. John of Jerusalem.

E101/371/8. (Part I).
frag. 118.
40s. to Peter la Gatte, minstrel of the Master of the Order of the Hospice of St. John of Jerusalem and Acon.
By gift [of the King].
frag. 120
40s. to Peter la Gayte, for making his minstrelsy in the presence of the King.
By gift of the King 'per manus proprias'

GAUNSILLE (ROBERT)

1302/3 E101/363/18. f. 21^r
4s. to Robert Gaunsille, minstrel, for making his minstrelsy in the presence of the Prince.
By gift of the Prince, per Thomas de Burton, who gave him the money.
1 December.

1306 E101/369/6.
Present at the Whitsun Feast. Received 2 payments:
40d. Robertus Gaunsille (Latin list)
1 mark. Gaunsaillie (French list).

GAUTERON (LE GRANT)

1306/6 E101/369/6.
Present at the Whitsun Feast.
Probably a Court minstrel, since he was deputed, with others, to distribute the remainder of the 200 marks among 'les autres.'

GAUTERON (LE PETIT)

'Le Petit Gauteron'.

1306 E101/369/6.
Present at the Whitsun Feast. Received 40s.
Deputed with others, including Gauteron le Grant, to distribute the remainder of the 200 marks among 'les autres'.

See WOODSTOCK (WALTER of)

GEIGE-PLAYERS (GERMAN)

1299 E101/356/13 [Issues of daily bread and wine, at Court]
Roll I. 'Gygor'. One pennyworth of bread, Thursday and Friday, 1 and 2 April, only.
Roll 2. 'Gygors'. One pennyworth of wine per day.

1300/1 E101/359/5.
f. 3v 2 marks to the 2 German geige-players. By gift of the King. Kempsey. 30 April (Sunday)
f. 8r 2 marks to the 2 [German] geige-players. Berwick-on-Tweed. 16 July (Sunday).

1302/3 Add. MSS. 35292. f. 12r
1/2 mark each to the 2 geige-players.

1302/3 E101/364/13.
f. 32v To Scondrad and Henry, King's geige-players, 1 mark, prest, for them to buy certain necessaries for themselves, by order of the King. By the hand of Sconred, at Reading, 27 November.
10s. 26 April. York. by the hand of Cunrad.
20s. 29 July. St. John of Perth: into their own hands.
13s. 4d. 3 September. Banff: into their own hands.
13s. 4d. 17 October. Dundee: into their own hands.

See CUNRAD, HENRY

GEOFFREY (harper)

A harper (probably a retired Court harper)

1172 Pipe Roll. 18 Hen. 2.
Et in Corredio Galfridi Cytharedi. 5s. per breve Regis.
(Abbey of Hyde)

GEOFFREY (trumpeter)

Trumpeter of Lord Robert de Monhaut.

1306 E101/369/6.
Present at the Whitsun Feast. Received 12d.

GEOFFREY (harper)

1306 E101/369/6.
Harper of Earl Warenne.
Present at the Whitsun Feast. Received 20s.

GERARD

1299/1300 E101/358/20. f. 7r
6s. 8d. to Gerard. [No indication here that he was a minstrel; but compare next].

GERARD

1306 E101/369/6.
Gerard: Present at the Whitsun feast. Received 12d.

GERARD (vielle-player)

1302/3 Lord of (?) Sutting's minstrel. A Fleming.

E101/363/18.
f. 21v 13s. 4d. to Gerard the vielle-player, minstrel of the lord (dominus) of ?Sutting, who came to the Prince on behalf of his master, to Straddle (Herefs.) and made his minstrelsy in his presence. The money was given to him on his departure the same day. 7 April (Sunday). Straddle.
[The Clerk has written in the margin: Menestrallus Flandrie].

GEYTE (JOHN LA)

Watchman/minstrel.

1300/1 Add. MSS. 7966A. f. 67r
15s. to John La Geyte, for an outfit and other necessaries bought for him. By gift of the King.
Northampton. 7 January.

GIFFARD (John)
MINSTREL OF

1285/6 E101/352/4. (Counter roll of Jewels)
Membrane 1.
(No. 1980). From William de Faringdon 1 silver gilt cup with foot and cover, of 2 marks 4d. weight, value 54s. given by the King to the minstrel of John Giffard 28 March.

GIGOUR (LE TIERZ)

'The third geige-player'.

1306 E101/369/6.
Present at the Whitsun Feast. Received 2 marks.

See PEFER (CONRAD LE)

GILBERT (harper)

1251/2 Book of Fees. 1276. (Warwick and Leicester).
Hugh de Loges sold a virgate of land to Gilbert le Harpur, for the yearly rent of 12d. and its value is 20s. per annum.

GILBERT (trumpeter)

1311/12 Trumpeter of the 2 young Princes, Thomas and Edmund.

E101/374/19. f. 11r
Issue of outfit and shoes to him.
Gilbertus Trumparius.

GILBERT (Waferer)

1301/5 E101/362/20. [A long parchment roll of prests, relative to the expenses of the Queen's Household, when she was not with the King.]
Gilbert was probably Queen's Waferer, or one of the Court Waferers. The roll lists payments 'by the hand of': therefore, it is impossible to be certain whether the 'John, the Waferer' was John Drake or another Waferer in the Queen's Household. Since I have not come across any other Queen's Waferer, it is at least likely that Gilbert was hers.
4s. by the hand of Gilbert the Waferer. 12 January. Kingston.
4s. by the hand of Gilbert the Waferer. 14 January.
3s. 6d. by the hand of Gilbert the Waferer. 30 January.
2s. by the hand of Gilbert the Waferer. 9 January.
4s. 2d. by the hand of Gilbert the Waferer. 12 March. Windsor.

GILLOT

Harper of Lord Peter de Mauley.

1306 E101/369/6.
Present at the Whitsun Feast. Received 10s.

GILLOT (LE HARPOUR)

King's (Ed. I) Harper. William de Morley.

See MORLEY (WILLIAM)

GILLOT (LE TABORER)

The Earl of Warwick's taborer.

1306 E101/369/6.
Present at the Whitsun feast. Received 3s.

GILLOT (trumpeter)

King's, later Prince's Trumpeter: styled 'Monsire Gillot le Trumpour'.

1300/1 Add. MSS. 7966. f. 178r
To Gillotus Trumpator, prest, for his wages for those days on which he was out of Court in the entourage of the Lord Edward, the King's son, during the month of January: 18d. by the hand of Master R. de Chishulle; 4s, by the hand of Master Roger, at Lincoln, on 19 February; 13s. 4d. into his own hands at Lincoln, on 19 February.

1306 E101/369/6.
Present at the Whitsun Feast. Received 1 mark.

See JANUCHE (his fellow-trumpeter) and WILLIAM (the Trumpeter)

GILOT

Harper of Lord Hugh de Cressingham.

1296/7 Add. MSS. 7967. f. 52r
20s. to Gilot citharista, returning to his master, in Scotland.
By gift of the King.
Bury St. Edmunds. 20 November.

GLAMORGAN (Ricard de)

1310/11 E101/373/26.
f. 87v. Ricardus de Glamorgan: on court wages.

GODESCALK (the Piper)
King's Piper/Minstrel.

1314/17 MS. Cott. Nero. C.viii
f. 192v 54s. 3d. to Godescalc, the Piper, King's Minstrel. By a bill. 23 January.
f. 226r Minstrel of Ed. III's Household.
20s. to Godescalk, piper, for his outfit.

GODFREY (trumpeter)
(thirteenth-century stone coffin, found under the Guildhall, London and now in the Guildhall Museum.

"Godefrey Le Trompour cist ci."

GOUGH (DAVID)
King's Welsh squire/archer.

1296/7 Add. MSS. 7965. f. 108r
Carrying letters to Aberconway and Caernarvon.

1299/1300 LOG. 101
Present at the seige of Caerlaverock, with 8 other Welsh archer/squires.
5s. for his winter shoes.

1306/7 E101/357/15. f. 12r
20s. owing to him, at end of the reign for shoes (1306/7)

1317/18 MS. Soc. of Antiq. 121. f. 25r
12d. each to David and Adinettus Gogh, Welsh archers, for their outfits for the whole of the present year.

1322 Cal. Chancery Warrants.
Pardon granted to David Gogh (Gouth), for adhering to Thomas of Lancaster. Rothwell. 22 April.

GOGH (ADINETT) [?EDNYFED]
1317 MS. Soc. of Antiq. 121. f. 25r

See GOGH (DAVID) above.

GOGH (OWEN)
1307 E101/357/15. f. 25r
18d. owing to Audoenus Gogh, at end of reign.

GRACIOS

King's Minstrel (Taborer)

1311/12 MS. Cott. Nero. C.viii. f. 86^v
20s. to Gracios, King's Minstrel, for making his minstrelsy in the presence of the King.
By gift of the King. 'Honeden' [?Honeydon/or/Hoveden]. 30 June.

1311/12 E101/373/26. f. 53^r
Appears in a list of those who, in the train of John of Brittany, were holding the castle of Scarborough.

1319/20 MS. Soc. of Antiq. 121. f. 130^r
1 mark to Graciouse le tabourer, for his summer outfit. London. 14 April.

GRENDON (JOHN)

1303/4 Minstrel of Anthony Bek, Bishop of Durham.

Add. MSS. 8835. f. 44^r
40s. to John de Greyndone, minstrel of Lord Anthony, Bishop of Durham, for making his minstrelsy in the presence of the King on the day of the Translation of St. John (of Beverly) at Burstwick on 25 October. By gift of the King.

f. 121^v (sub Jocalia)
A silver-gilt cup, valued at 76s. 8d., given, by order of the King to John de Greyndon, minstrel of the Bishop of Durham, for bringing...on the part of the King. Burstwick. 25 October.

1306 E101/369/6.
Present at the Whitsun Feast. Received 1 mark.

GRESSYL

1299 Minstrel of the Earl of Gloucester.

Add. MSS. 24509. f. 61^r
20s. (or 10s.each) to Gerard le Boone and Gressyl, minstrels of the Earl of Gloucester, for making their minstresly in the presence of the King.
By gift of the King, into their own hands.

See BOONE (GERARD)

GREY

1290 King Herald.

C47/4/5. f. 45v
50s. to King Grey 'de henaldis', who came to the wedding of the Earl of Gloucester and Joanna, daughter of the King.
By gift of the King.

GRILLO

1311/12 MS. Cott. Nero. C.viii. f. 4r
31s. to Grillo menestrallus, for his wages from 22 September, on which day his horse was valued, to 22 October, both days included; for 31 days, according to the contract drawn up with him at Berwick-on-Tweed, on 19 November. Paid, per Okham, at Berwick, by the hand of Cusin the minstrel.

13 March 1312.

See COSYN (JOHN)

GRIMMESHAWE (ADAM)

1305 Cal. Chancery Warrants. 251
Order to cause inquisition to be made whether it will be all right for the King to grant certain tenements in Hampton, Salop. to Adam of Grimmeshawe, which he has acquired on the death of Roger le Strange, at an annual rent of 5s.

Leeds (Castle). 24 July.

1306 E101/369/6.
Present at the Whitsun Feast. Received 2 marks, by the hand of Monsire Robert de Clou (Clough), harper.

1312 CPR. 494
Pardon, at the instance of James Daudele, King's yeoman and kinsman (of John), to John le Harpour of Trentham, for the death of Adam de Grymmeshargh.

Westminster. 15 September.

[Grimmeshargh. Lancs.]

GRISCOTE

1296/7 Add. MSS. 7965. f. 52r
20s. for making his minstrelsy, with Visage and Magote, in the presence of the Lady Elizabeth, on her wedding day. By gift of the King.

Ipswich. 8 January.

GRYMESAR' (WILLIAM)

1306 E101/369/6.
A harper: probably 'Grymesargh'.
Present at the Whitsn Feast. Received 40d.

GUILLEME (harper)

William, *alias* Guilleme, Gillot: harper of Anthony Bek.

1304 Add. MSS. 8835. f. 44[r]
5s. to Gillot, harper of the lord Bishop of Durham, for bringing to the King, on behalf of his master, a sparrow-hawk; and for looking after it during the time he was journeying with the King betyween Alverton and Beverly; and he was given licence by the King, to return to his own parts.
By gift of the King.
[No date; possibly mid-October, when Ed. I was at Beverly]

GUILLOT (taborer)

1306 E101/369/6.
Present at the Whitsun Feast. One of 'La Comune'.

1310/11 CLL. Letter-book B. 22.
Recognizance by Godewyn le Pheliper, who bound himself to William de Gaytone, taborer, in the sum of 50 marks.
[The debt was repaid on 25 July 1313].
[This may not be the same person as Guillot, above; but the sum he lent was the kind of money royal minstrels were able to lend. Perhaps William de Gaytone was taborer of Thomas of Lancaster. There is a Gayton 5 miles NE of Stafford.]

1325 CPR. 161.
Grant for life to John le Scot, trumpeter, for his good service to the King (Ed. II), of a messuage, 8 acres of land, and an acre of meadow in the town of Pontefract and Friston, late of William le Taborer, a rebel, which have come into the King's hands by forfeiture; to hold without rendering anything to the King.
Langdon Abbey (Kent). 26 August.

GUILLOT (vielle-player)

King's or Court vielle-player.

1285/6 E101/352/2. (Roll of divers payments)
No. 2328. And 100s. to Guillot, the King's vielle-player, to whom the King has allowed £10 annually, receiving it from his Wardrobe at the two periods of the year - that is to say, at the Feast of St. Michael (29 September) and at Easter, for his fee from the end of Easter, in the 14th year.

[Probably Guillot de Roos].

1294/5 Fryde. 187
100s. prest, to Guillot, vielle-player, for the fee which he receives annually from the King's Wardrobe. (quia allocatur in feodo suo).

THE GUITARIST

1314-16 Queen's Guitarist.
Henricus/or/?Drincus (the MS. is difficult to read)

E101/376/7.

f. 93r 2 marks to ?Drincus the Guitarist, Queen's minstrel, for his outfits for the current year; according to contract.

f. 124r 53s. 4d. owing to ?Drincus le Guttarer, for his outfits for 8 and 9 Ed. II.

26 December 1316/117.

1319/20 MS. Soc. of Antiq. 120.

f. 165r No issue of winter outfit to ?Drincus de Hispania, because he was out of Court.

1320/21 MS. Soc. of Antiq. 121.

f. 117r 2 marks to Drinco de Ispannia, for his livery for the whole year.
12 December. London.

[If he be the same person as the preceding, then he was a Spanish guitarist and his name was Drinco?]

HALEFORD (RICARD)

1306 E101/369/6.
Present at Whitsun Feast. Received 40s.
Styled 'Monsire Ricard de Haleford.'

HAMOND (estive-player)

1306 E101/369/6.
Present at Whitsun Feast. Received 2 marks.

See LESTIUOUR.

HARDING (JOHN)
HARDING (WILLIAM)

1311/12 MS. Cott. Nero. C.viii. f. 194[v]
King's Watchmen.
Payments for wages and outfits.

HARPER (anon.)

1299/1300 LOG. 166.
3s. to a certain harper, who made his minstrelsy before the Prince at Penrith on 17 September.
By gift of the Prince.

HARPER (Queen's)

WALTER DE WENLOK (ed. E.H. Pearce. Lond. 1920) p. 120.
1306 3s. to a harper of the Queen (cuidam citharede regine)
(Queen Margaret, second wife of Ed. I.)

HARPER (Comyn's)

1296/7 Harper of Lord John Comyn of Badenoch.
Add. MSS. 7965. f. 52[r]
1 mark, for performing at the wedding of Princess Elizabeth.

HARPER (Countess of Lancaster)

1306 A harper of the Countess of Lancaster (Alice, daughter of earl of Lincoln)

Present at the Whitsun Feast. Received 40d.

HARPERS (2. Bishop of Durham)

1296/7 Add. MSS. 7965. f. 52[r]
20s. each to 2 harpers of the Bishop of Durham, for performing at the wedding of Princess Elizabeth.

HARPERS (2. Oxford and Multon)

1296/7 Add. MSS. 7965. f. 52[r]
10s. each to 2 harpers of the earl of Oxford and Thomas de Multon, for performing at the wedding of Princess Elizabeth.

HARPERS (King's)

1296/7 Add. MSS. 7965. f. 52^r
Two King's Harpers (names not given).
20s. each for performing at the wedding of Princess Elizabeth.

1299 E101/356/13.
2nd Roll. Issue of wine to
'4 harpers' (who were, by this time, Adam Clitheroe. William Morley, John Newenton and Hugh de la Rose).

HARPERS (5, Scottish)

1303/4 Add. MSS. 8835. f. 42^r
5s. to 5 harpers who met the King on the sands between Durie and Sandford on 6 March.
By gift of the King, by the hand of Basculus (one of his bodyguard of arbalesters).
St. Andrews. 12 March.

HARPER (Bishop of Durham)

Another harper of Anthony Bek.

1306 E101/369/6
Present at the Whitsun Feast. Received 10s.
[The entry in the Payroll has been inserted in the list and immediately procedes that of Guilleme.]

HATHEWAY (WILLIAM)

Vielle-player

1300/1 Add. MSS. 7966A. f. 66^r and E101/359/15. f. 1^v
6s. 8d. to William de Hatheway, vielle-player, for making his minstrelsy with Gilbert of York in the presence of the King. By gift of the King.
Evesham. 2 April (Easter Sunday).

See YORK (GILBERT)

HENDELEKE (RICHARD)

1306 E101/369/6
Present at Whitsun Feast. Received 2 marks.

HENRY (German)

One of the 2 German geige-players at Court of Ed. I.

1299 E101/356/13. (Issues of Bread and Wine)
Gygor' - 1d. per day, Thursdays and Fridays only.
Gygors - 1d. per day [each, presumably].

1300/1 Add. MSS. 7966.

f. 66^v 13s. 4d. to Henry, the German geige-player, King's minstrel. By gift of the King. Kempsey. 29 April.

f. 67^r 20s. for certain necessaries bought for him. By gift of the King. Burton. 14 January.

6s. 8d. for a sumpter-saddle and girth, bought for his use. By gift of the King. Eston. 19 January.

8s. 2d. paid in cash to him for firewood and litter during the months of February and March.

f. 69^r 1 mark for certain necesaries bought for him. By gift of the King. Westminster. 16 July.

1302/3 Add. MSS. 35292. f. 29^v

1 mark to Henry and Cunrad, King's geige-players, for their wages.

Dunfermline.

1304/5 E101/368/6. f. 21^v

20s. to Henry, geige-player of the King, to buy himself an outfit.

By gift of the King. Kingston Lacy. 12 January.

1305/6 E101/369/11.

f. 98^v 20s. to buy himself an outfit.

By gift of the King. Kingston Lacy. 2 January.

f. 102^v £12 18s. 8d. to Henry and Cunrad, King's geige-players, minstrels from Germany, who have been staying in court by order of the King, making their minstrelsy at his wish. The money given to them at various times by order of the King during 1301, 1302, 1303, 1304/5.

1306 E101/369/6.

Present at Whitsun Feast. Received 2 marks.

See CUNRAD, GEIGE-PLAYERS.

HENRY (Harper)

Book of Fees. I. 117. (Details of the holding of lands in the Honor of Wallingford, in the Testa de Nevill).

1198 After the first coronation of King Henry, the lord King's (Richard I) father, Peter Boterel held the manor of Chaugrave, with its appurtenances; and, after his death the lord King Henry took the aforesaid manor into his own hand and gave Emma, in this manor, who had been the daughter of William de Grandune, together with her inheritance, to Henry the Harper [Henrico Citharedo]; and she was wont to render to the lord King for her tenancy, 60s. per annum; and the lord King Henry, by his charter, exempted the aforesaid Henry and his heirs by the aforesaid wife of the aforesaid 60s. for serjeanty of 1d. per annum.

[A very interesting example of the King giving a woman (heiress) to ?his harper, in marriage.]

HENRY (messenger)

Rotuli de liberate. (ed. Duffus Hardy. Lond. 1844) 149.

1210 King John's mounted messenger (Nuncius). 12d to Henry, the Messenger, going with letters to the Sheriff of Lincs.

Reading. February.

HENRY (harper)

Harper of Edmund Mortimer. 'Master Henry'

1289/90 Swinfield. 149

To Master Henry, the harper of lord Edmund Mortimer - 12d.

HENRY (harper)

1296/7 Add. MSS. 7965. f. 52r

10s. to Henry the harper for performing at the wedding of Princess Elizabeth.

HENRY (harper)

1322 Cal. Chancery Warrants.

Pardon granted to Henry le Harper, for being an adherent of Thomas of Lancaster.

York. 10 May.

HENRY (fool)

1299 E101/355/17. (Sub Dona; one membrane only)
Henricus Stultus. The Fool of the Count of Savoy.
12d. to Henry the Fool by gift of the Lord Edward (Prince of Wales) son of the King; and 10d. from the same Lord Edward by William de Hertfeld, for gaming (ad ludendum ad talos).

HENRY (trumpeter)

1299/1300 LOG. 137
Trumpeter/squire of Lord Robert de Clifford.
Henry the Trumpeter, his/Clifford's) vallettus, had a white dapple horse, valued at 10 marks, at Caerlaverock.

HENUER/HENVER

1306 E101/369/6.
Present at the Whitsun Feast. Received 30s.

HEREFORD (WILLIAM)

1311/12 E101/374/19. f. 8r
5s. to William de Hereford, at one time harper of Sir John ap Adam, for making his minstrelsy in the presence of the 2 young princes, Thomas and Edmund.
Striguil. 31 December.

HERT (WALTER)

1358/9 MS. Cott. Galba. E. xiv. f. 51v
13s. 4d. to Walter Hert, returning to Court from London, from the School of Minstrelsy (de scola Menestralcie) [This is the only reference I have come across to a royal minstrel attending a school of minstrelsy - and at London].
By gift of the Queen (Isabella), by Peter de S. Paul (? Pol) into his own hands.
31 March.

HESEL (JOHN)

1298 Earl of Norfolk's harper?

Gough. 33
Letters of protection for John, the Harper of Hesel, who was with Roger Bigod, while he was staying in Scotland.

HORSHAM (WILLIAM)

Archaeologia. xxvi. 344.

1317/18 20s. to "William de Horsham and 3 others, his companions, singing before the King in his chamber at Westminster, of the King's gift, being the price of 20s. of striped cloth, bought of John Mahoun and given to them to make garments of."

HUGH (harper)

c. 1300 E101/371/8. (Part I)
fragment 16. Hue le Harpor.
Probably Hugo de la Rose, King's Harper.

1306 E101/369/6.
Present at the Whitsun Feast. Received 2 marks. Called the 'campaignon' of Gillot de Morley, John de Newenton and Adam of Clitheroe: styled 'Hughethun Le Harpour.'

1306/7 E101/369/16.
f. 9v 27s. 6d. prest, to Hugo le Harpour, being the price of 3 1/2 ells of bluet cloth, 3 1/2 ells of striped and 1 lamb's fur, given to him by Ralph de Stokes, clerk of the Great Wardrobe.
f. 10v 24s. 6d. prest, being the price of 7 ells of blue and green cloths (3 1/2 ells of each), given to him by Ralph de Stokes, clerk of the Great Wardrobe.

1322 Foedera. III 375.
Pardon to Hugo le Harper, re Thomas of Lancaster.

See ROSE (HUGH DE LA)

HUGHETHUN (LE HARPOUR)

see HUGH (harper)

HUGO

1289 Harper of the lord Abbot of Reading.
Swinfield. 147.
HUGO citharista.

HURELL

1312/13 Minstrel of the King of France.

E101/375/8. f. 30r
40s. to Hurell, minstrel of the King of France, on his departure from the same King of France.*
7 July "Maubusshar".
[Not clear. Should it be *'King of England'?]

IANIN

1303/4 Mounted messenger (nuncius) of the Count of Savoy.
Add. MSS. 8835. ff. 43v and 45v
...to Ianin, nuncius of the Count of Savoy, who came to England with news to the King, from the Lady Mary, Queen of France.

IPRE (HANEKIN)

post 1328 MS. Cott. Galba. E. iii. (Wardrobe Account of [probably] Queen Philippa).
f. 175r
18 ells of cloth of Ypres, for 2 striped 'beguines' of Ypres, of green colour, for the minstrel, Hanekin de Ipre.

ISAMBERD (FRANCEKYN)

1330 E101/385/4.
One of Ed. III's sergeants-at-arms.

ISPANIA (ROCHERICO)

1290 Roderigo of Spain vallettus/or/sergeant-at-arms, in the service of Prince Edward.
C.47/4/4. f. 20r
7½d. per day for his wages from the 1st of January to the 30 April; 120 days, bar 47, when he was off duty/or/not in Court. - 45s. 7½d.

1290/2 Botfield, 96
Rotherico de Yspannia [? legatus Regine].

1299/1300 LOG 227.
£2 7s. 3d. to Rotherico de Hispannia, for his wages on active service from 1st July to 3 November. 126 Days.

IVGLETT

See JUGLETT

JACOMIN

1260 King's (Hen. III) Fool.

CPR. 321.
Order to Richard de Ewell and Hugh de Treni, buyers of the King's Wardrobe, that they shall have an outfit suitable made for Jacomin, the King's Fool and Minstrel (istrio). By gift of the King.
Windsor. 25 December.

JAKE (trumpeter)

1325/6 MS. Soc. of Antiq. 122.
f. 27^v 10s. to Jake, the Trumpeter, of Dover, who brought to the King from Dover, 47 goldfinches in a cage; and a terrine.
By gift of the King for his expenses and lodging.
Westminster. 9 October (Wednesday)
[N.B. the use of English: "en vne cage xlvij Goldfynches et vne terryne."
The goldfinches were to be a present to Hugh le Despenser's wife (who was Ed. II's niece), because the clerk goes on to say that William of Dunstable was to look after them until Madame le Despenser arrived at Westminster.]

JAKELINUS (vielle-player)

1198/9 Book of Fees. Appendix 1387/8. (Dorset).
The lord King (?Rich. I) gave Jakelin the vielle-player (vilator) a burgage in Bridport to hold for as long as it pleased him; and after the death of the aforesaid Jakelin Walter de Bur[gh], who was the lord King's steward of escheats came and gave the aforesaid burgage to William de Hollewell and his wife, Agnes.

JAKEMIN

1299/1300 Messenger of Lord John de Bar.

LOG. 157
6s. 8d. to Jakemin, nuncius of Lord John de Bar, to help toward his expenses in coming to the King with letters from his master, and returning to his own country. By gift of the King.
Newington (Kent). 26 February.

JAKET

1290 Minstrel of the Marshal of Champagne.

E101/352/21.
[This MS. is a Roll, of monies given to various people; and should be read in conjunction with the relevant Wardrobe entries.]
40s. to Jaket, minstrel of the Marshal of Champagne, for remaining in Court (at Havering-atte-Bower) while other minstrels went to the Earl Marshal's wedding in London. This Jaket, appears to have been the Juglett, Iuglett of the Wardrobe books.

See C47/4/5/ f. 47v. JUGLETT, JANIN (Albemarle)

JANIN

1285 Prince Edward's minstrel.

E101/351/17. (A counter-roll of domestic payments to the King's Household.)
£4 each to Janin the minstrel of the Lord Edward and John the lutenist.

JANIN (Albemarle)

1290 C.47/4/5. f. 47v and E101/352/21.
40s. for remaining in court while other minstrels went to London to the Earl Marshal's wedding.
E101/352/18. f. 17r
60s. prest, paid to the Lady Queen, the King's Consort, for paying Janyn, the Earl of Albemarle's minstrel, Ricard, the Earl of Gloucester's harper and Juglett, the Marshal of Champagne's minstrel; 20s. each because they remained with the King and did not go to the wedding-feast of the Earl Marshal on St. John the Baptist's Day (24 June).

JANIN (Savoy)

1299/1300 The nuncius of the Count of Savoy.

LOG.
p. 157 10s. to Janin, the nuncius of the Count of Savoy, to help with his expenses in returning to his Lord with letters of the King, by gift of the King; by the hand of Thomas de Buterwick; at Ospringe, 21 or 25 February (the only 2 days when the King was at Ospringe.)

p. 159 5s. to Janin, <u>nuncius</u> of the Count of Savoy, returning to his Lord with letters of the Lord Edward, the King's son; by gift of the same, to help with his expenses; into his own hands.
30 March. Westminster.

JANIN (Bagpiper)

1311/12 MS. Cott. Nero C.viii. f. 82v
40s. to Janin le Cheueretter, for making his minstrelsy in the presence of the King, in the House of the Preaching Friars of London.
By gift of the King; by the hand of Oliver de Burgedala, giving the money for cash which was paid to him (Janin).
Berwick. 3 October.
[Chevrete: the bag of a bagpipe; made of goatskin]

JANIN (trumpeter)

Prince Edward's Trumpeter.

1285 E101/351/17. (Counter Roll)
Janin, minstrel of the Lord Edward.
[at that time Edward was 1 year old]

1300/1 E101/359/5. f. 2r
6s. 8d. to John the Trumpeter of Edward, the King's son, prest, for his wages.

1300/1 E101/360/10.
Membrane 1. (a list of the names of servants accompanying the Queen and Prince Edward, when they set out from Langley in January, to join the King at Lincoln)
'Johann le Trumpeur.'

1303/4 Add. MSS. 8835. f. 130v
Two silver trumpets, bought by the Prince, and given to Janin and Januche, his trumpeters, by his order, for their good service to the Prince in the Scottish War.
Dunfermline.

1307 E101/373/15.

f. 5v To Janin the Trumpeter, for his wages:
10s. 29 July. Carlin.
10s. 2 September. Carlin.
13s. 4d. 20 October. Leighton Buzzard.
All paid into his own hands.

f. 19r £4 to the King's minstrels - William of Queenhithe, Janin the Trumpeter, Januche the Nakerer and Janin the Organist, for making their minstrelsy in the presence of the King at Dumfries on 10 August.
20s. to each by gift of the King, by the hand of the said William.

1319/20 MS. Soc. of Antiq. 121. f. 117r
1 mark to Janin the Trumpeter for his winter and summer outfits.
York. 26 October.

JANIN (DE LA TOURE)

One of Henry de Beaumont's trumpeters.

1306 E101/369/6.
Present at the Whitsun Feast. Received 1 mark.

1310 E101/373/10. f. 7v
20s. to John de la Tour, trumpeter of Lord Henry de Beaumont. By gift of the King; into his own hands.
14 July.

JANIN (juggler)

1311/12 MS. Cott. Nero. C. viii. f. 86v
20s. to Janin le Tregettur, for making his minstrelsy in the presence of the King.
By gift of the King; by the hand of Janin le Nakerer.
Swineshead. 7 July.

JANYN (psaltery-player)

1330 E101/385/4.
p. 381 In a list of minstrels of the Household of Ed. III.

JANYN (psaltery-player. Percy's)

1306 E101/369/6.
Minstrel of Lord Henry de Percy.
Janyn le Sautreour: Present at the Whitsun Feast.
Received 1 mark.

JANOCHE (JANUCHE)

Prince Edward's Trumpeter.

1302/3 E101/363/18. f. 22r

8s. each to Janoche the Trumpeter and Janin the Nakerer, for making their minstrelsy in the presence of the Prince. By gift of the Prince, to buy themselves aketons; by the hand of Robert of Durham, armourer.

Newcastle-on-Tyne. 6 May.

1303/4 Add. MSS. 8835. f. 130v

A silver trumpet, bought by the Prince, and given to him for his good service in the Scottish War.

See JANIN (trumpeter) and JOHN (nakerer).

JANOT (messenger)

1317/18 MS. Soc. of Antiq. 121. f. 56r

(?40s.) to Janot, the nuncius of Lord Lucio de Fliske, Cardinal, coming to the King with letters of the said Lord (Cardinal) and returning to him with letters of the King.

By gift of the King; into his own hands.

York. 5 September.

JANOT (psaltery-player)

Queen's Psaltery-player.

[1316/17] E101/376/7. f. 93r

2 marks to Janot the Psaltery-player, Queen's minstrel, for his outfits for the whole of the current year.

26 December.

1314/16 Ibid. f. 124r

53s. 4d. owing to Janot le Sautreour, for his outfits for 8 and 9 Ed. II.

JOHN (nakerer)

also - Janin, Janyn, Januche, Janot.

Prince Edward's (and later King's) Nakerer.

1302/3 E101/363/18

f. 17r

20s. paid to Hugh de Naunton, for a sorrel hack of his, which was bought by the Prince for John the Nakerer's riding-out (equitancia).

f. 21v

3s. to Janin le Nakerer, Prince's minstrel, to buy skin for covering and repairing his nakers.
By gift of the Prince.

Straddle. 11 April.

f. 22r

8s. for making his minstrelsy with Janoche the trumpeter, in the presence of the Prince; by gift of the Prince to buy himself an aketon.
See JANOCHE (trumpeter)

f. 23r

A gift of the price of a habergeon and an iron collaret, from the Prince, to Janot le Nakerer, Prince's minstrel.
See GARSIE (JOHN)

1306 E101/369/6.

Present at the Whitsun Feast (under title of Le Nakarier). Received 1 mark.

1307 E101/373/15.

f. 5v to Janin le Nakerer; for his wages:

10s.	29 July.	Carlin.
10s.	2 September.	Carlin.
13s. 4d.	2 October.	Nottingham.

f. 19r 20s. to Januche le Nakerer, for making his minstrelsy in the presence of the King (Ed. II).
By gift of the King, by the hand of William de la Queenhithe.
Dumfries. 10 August.

1307 E101/357/15. f. 25r

Owing to Johannes le Nakerer, at the end of the reign of Ed. I, £4 19s. 4d.

1311/12 MS. Cott. Nero. C.viii. f. 86v

Appointed to give the King's gratuity of 20s. to Janin le Tregettour.

1314/17 MS. Cott. Nero. C.viii. f. 192^{v}
20s. to Janin Nakerer, menestrallus hospicij Regis, in part payment of £6 8s. 2d. owing to him for his wages and outfits.
3 February.
f. 226^{r} (see below)

1319/20 MS. Soc. of Antiq. 120. f. 106^{v}
40s. to Johannes le Nakerer, in compensation for his bay horse, returned to the Almonry at Nottingham, in the month of December of the present year, (?1318/19).
York. 29 October (?1320)

1319/20 MS. Soc. of Antiq. 121.
f. 117^{r} 20s. to John le Nakerer, for his outfits for the whole year. York. 26 October.
f. 129^{r} 20s. for his summer outfit. York. 26 October.

1325/6 or later MS. Cott. Nero. C.viii. f. 226^{r} and E101/381/11.
Listed as a minstrel of the Household of Ed. III.
20s. for his outfit.

1323 CCR. 694.
Letter to abbot and convent of Burton-on-Trent, requesting that they grant maintenance for life to John le Nakerer ('Janyn nostre Nakerer') who has long served the King.
[They excused themselves on the ground of poverty].

JOHN (crowder)

1304 CPR. 254
Pardon to John de le (sic) Crouther for the death of Richard del Croft and for homicides.
Jedburgh. 23 August.
[Ed. I was at Jedburgh on that day (a Sunday)].

1306 E101/369/6.
Present at the Whitsun Feast; one of La Comune, and therefore a royal or Court minstrel: Johan le Croudere.

J(OHN) (harper)

1290 Wenlok. (Accounts) 177.
6^{d} given to John the harper, on Wednesday, 'in septimana Pasche'.

JOHN (HENGFOSSHE)

1313 <u>Foedera</u> II Part I. 230
John le Harpour de Hengfosshe, pardoned for supporting Thomas of Lancaster, re the death of Gaveston.

JOHN (organist)

King's Organist.

1306 <u>E101/369/6</u>.
Janin Lorganistre. Present at the Whitsun Feast. Received 2 marks.

1307 <u>E101/373/15</u>
f. 5v prests, for his wages:
10s. 31 July. Carlin.
13s. 4d. 2 October. Nottingham
f. 19r 20s. to Janin le Organiste, <u>menestrallus Regis</u>, for making his minstrelsy in the presence of the King (Ed. II). By gift of the King; by the hand of William de Queenhithe.
Dumfries. 10 August.

1307 <u>E101/357/15</u>. f. 25r
£4 6s. 3d. owing to John the Organist, at end of reign of Ed. I.

1310/11 <u>E101/374/5</u>. f. 29r
To John the Organist, receiving 4½d. per day for his wages, from 8 July of the current year now beginning, to 23 January, of the same year, both days included; 200 days, during which time he was present in Court for 81 days - 30s. 4½d.
Berwick-on-Tweed. 23 January.

1311/12 <u>MS. Cott. Nero. C.viii</u>
f. 4r (or 5v new foliation)
To John the Organist, receiving 4½d. per day for his wages, from 8 July 1309 to 7 July of the same [regnal] year; both days included; for 365 days, during which time he was in Court for 87 days - 32s. 7½d.
To the same, for his outfits for the whole of the aforesaid year - 26s. 8d.
According to the contract drawn up with him at Berwick-on-Tweed. Total - 59s. 3½d. paid by a bill (on the Exchequer).
Berwick. 11 December (1310).

f. 7^v
There is owing to John the Organist, for his wages and outfit, up to 23 January 1310; according to the contract drawn up with him at Newcastle-on-Tyne on the said 23 January - 57s. $0^1/2$d.
He has a bill.

JOHN (psaltery-player)

1331 Cartularium Monasterii de Rameseia. (Rolls Ser. III) 102
Complaint to the King (Ed. III) of the burden being placed on the monastery, for the upkeep of retired royal servants.
3 March: "And it is not long since, Most Serene Lord, that you burdened our house with Johannes [l]e Sauterion, who received his sustenance at your command in this house, even as one of our free brothers".

See JANOT, the Queen's psaltery-player. Probably the same person.

JOHN (Trumpeter)

Janyn, King's Trumpeter.

1329 CCR. 538/9
To the abbot and convent of St. Albans. Whereas the King lately granted to John le Trumpour, his minstrel, the maintenance in that abbey that Vivian de Luk had for his lifetime therein by the late King's order, and John afterwards delivered to the King the letters patent of the abbot and convent concerning the maintenance; and the King, at the request of Queen Isabella has granted to Isabella de la Helde, damsel of her chamber, the aforesaid maintenance for her life; the King therefore requests the abbot and convent to make letters patent to her granting to her the said maintenance for life, to be received both in her absence and in her presence, notwithstanding the aforesaid grant to John." ['Janyn nostre trumpour' in Privy Seal].
Wallingford. 25 April.

1330 CCR. 142
John le Trumpour, who has long served the King, is sent to the prior and convent of Durham, to receive such maintenance from their house as William de Leschekier, deceased, had therein by the late King's request.

JOHN (Cantilupe)

1298 Gough. 178

Johannes le Harpour, vallettus of Sir William de Cantilupe, has a pommely grey rouncy, valued at 5 marks.

f. 140r

The little orphan, Tom Scot, whom Queen Isabella befriended, was sent to London to stay with Agnes, the wife of John Gallicus, the organist.

40s. for his keep from the Feast of St. Michael (29 September) of the current year (1311/12) to the same feast in the year now completed (revoluto).

12s. 8d. for other necessaries bought by Agnes for him; for putting on the scab (or scurf) on his head.

Total - 52s. 8d. received by Agnes in cash, at the Queen's Wardrobe.

17 August. (1312/13)

[See Menestrellorum Multitudo p. 116).

JOHN (WARENNE)

JANIN, (the organist of Earl Warenne)

1300/1 Add. MSS. 7966A.

f. 66v 2 marks to Janin, organist of Earl Warenne, for playing in the presence of the King and Queen, in turn, or, on various occasions, with John de Cressy and Martinet.

By gift of the Queen. Lincoln. February.

[An example of money being distributed to minstrels according to their status: Janin, the most highly paid, received 26s. 8d.: John de Cressy, 20s. and Martinet, 13s. 4d.]

f.67v 40s. for playing before the King and Queen. Lincoln. 22 February.

1302/3 E101/363/18.

f. 5v To Master John, the organist of the Earl Warenne, for 15lbs of tin, bought by him for repairing the Prince's organ in his Manor at Langley, against the coming of the King and Queen there in the month of February of this present year; together with various other small things bought by him - 7s. 6d.

To the same, for his expenses re horse and boy for 9 days, during which time he was at Langley, in the same month, repairing the said organ; at 9d. per day - 6s. 9d.

Total 14s. 3d.

1303/4 Add. MSS. 8835. f. 42^r
20s. to John, organist of the Earl Warenne, for making his minstrelsy in the presence of the King.
By gift of the King. Dunfermline. 21 February.

JOHN (Lancaster)

1296/7 Harper of Lord Thomas de Lancaster, son of Edmund, the King's brother.

Add. MSS. 7965. f. 57^v
£14 6s. 8d. paid to Lord Thomas of Lancaster, 'having been made knight', at Ghent, on the Feast of All Saints, for bringing minstrels to perform before the King. By gift of the King, by the hand of John, the Harper of the said Lord Thomas.
Ghent. 4 November.

1297 C47/4/6. (MS. is one of Issues and Receipts)
2s. to the harper of the Earl of Lancaster.
8 February - 29 March.

1298 Gough. 181
John le Harpeur, *vallettus* of Thomas, earl of Lancaster, has a dappled iron-grey rouncy, valued at 12 marks.
[It was killed at the battle of Falkirk, which seems to confirm that minstrels were on the field].

JOHN (harper)

King's (Ed. III) minstrel.

1328 E101/383/4. (pp. 375/6)
Johannes le Harper listed among the squire minstrels of the Household of Ed. III.

1330 E101/385/4.
As above: *Johannes* le Harpour.

1335/8 MS. Cott. Nero. C.viii. f. 226^r
Johannes Harpour, minstrel of the Household of Ed. III.
20s. for his outfit.

JOHN (harper)

CCR. 533

1335 Hugh le Joigner is sent to the prior and convent of Bath, to receive such maintenance for life from that house as John le Harpour, deceased, had there at the late King's request.
By Privy Seal.

JOHN (vielle-player)

1306 E101/369/6.
The vielle-player of Lord John fitz Reginald.
Johannes le Vilour *domini J. Renaud*.
Present at the Whitsun Feast. Received 12d.

JOHN (Clynton)

1306 E101/369/6.
Harper of John de Clynton.
Present at the Whitsun Feast. Received 2s.

JOHN (fitz Payn)

Trumpeter of Lord Robert fitz Payn.

1304/5 E101/368/6. f. 21^v; and E101/369/11/. f. 99^v
20s. to John, the Trumpeter of Lord fitz Payn, for playing his trumpet before the King on the day of Epiphany.
By gift of the King.
Wimborne. 12 January.

1306 E101/369/6.
Present at the Whitsun Feast. Received 12d.

JOHN (Leyburn)

1300/1 E101/359/5. f. 2^r
John le harpour, *vallettus* of Lord William de Leyburn.
40s. to Lord William de Leyburn, concerning his fief and affairs. By the hand of John le harpour, his *vallettus*.

JOHN (Norfolk)

1311/12 E101/374/19.
Minstrel (probably a harper) of the Countess of Norfolk.
socius of Robert the harper.

See FRAMLINGHAM (Robert)

JOHN (Henry Lancaster)

1307 CPR. 495
Pardon granted to Henry of Lancaster, the King's nephew, for aiding the evasion of John le Harpour from the goal of St. Briavels (Glos.) and for receiving him; whereof he was indicted before John Boutetourte and his fellow justices.

[Perhaps the same as John, the harper of Thomas? Or one of Henry's own minstrels?].

JOHN

1307 E101/357/15. f. 13r
21s. 5½d. owing to Master John the minstrel (Magister Johannes menestrallus), at the end of the reign of Ed. I. Evidently a Court Minstrel.

JOHN (trumpeter)

King's Trumpeter.

1285 E101/351/17. (Counter roll of domestic payments)
Johann, listed with Bertin, as trumpatores, menestralli Regis.

1290 E101/352/24.
Issues of summer and winter outfits to Royal Household Minstrels. '2 King's Trumpeters' - of whom John was probably one.

1290 C47/4/4. f. 26r
John and Ranulph. two trumpeters.

1300/1 Add. MSS. 7966. f. 178r
2s. 6d. to John the Trumpeter, prest, for ?linen/canvas/hessian/(canabus) and for other different things at different times and in various places.

1305 E101/371/8. Pt. I.
fragment 37. John the Trumpeter, half a mark.
fragment 48. (part of an account of monies paid to various officers of the Royal Household, on 12 August, apparently at Newport Pagnell.)
To the Clerk of the Kitchen, concerning duties in Hall.
To Master John le Trumpour, half a mark for his wages.

1306/7 E101/357/15. f. 13r
9s. 2d. owing to John the Trumpeter (at end of the reign of Ed. I).

1318 MS. Cott. Nero. C.viii. f. 195r
115s. 3d. by the hand of John the Trumpeter, minstrel of the Lord King, for money owed to him for his war-wages and his outfits. By a bill.
21 July.

1319/20 MS. Soc. of Antiq. 121.

f. 130r 1 mark to Janin le Trumpour for his summer outfit.
York. 26 October.

JOHN (trumpeter)

1305/6 E101/368/12.

f. 4v One of the trumpeters of the 2 young princes, Thomas and Edmund.
20s. to Martinet the Taborer, William and John, trumpeters, minstrels of the 2 (young princes) for making their minstrelsy in their presence on the Eve and Feastday of Epiphany. By gift and grace of the aforesaid two.
Windsor. 5/6 January.

f. 8 Issue of winter and summer outfits to Richard the Trumpeter and John his companion (7 ells and 1 lamb's fur).

JOHN (trumpeter)

1323/4 Abbrevatio Rotulorum Originalium in Curia Scaccarii I. (Lond. 1805)
p. 272 (Roll 8) 'The King gives to John the Trumpeter, for his good service, those houses, lands and tenements with their appurtenances, which belonged to William the Taborer in the town of Pontefract and Friston.

[Perhaps John Scot, King's Trumpeter, who had been a boy minstrel in Ed. II's household when he was Prince of Wales. His 'good service' no doubt included his loyalty and support at Boroughbridge in 1322. William the Taborer was probably one of Thomas of Lancaster's minstrels].

JOHN (trumpeter and his son)

King's Trumpeters.

1305/6 MS. Harley 152. f. 17
Prest of 100s. to John the Trumpeter and his son for their wages 'present and future'; and for remaining at Court.
London. 18 August.

1305/6 E101/369/11. f. 202^v and E101/368/27. f. 62^r
100s. prest, for their wages, 'future and present', by the hand of Master John de Drokenesford; given to them in cash at London on 18 August; as well for their expenses in coming to the King by command of the King, as for their wages while remaining at Court.

1306/7 E101/370/16.

f. 1^r 20s. to Johannes Trumpator et Johannes filius suus.
Lanercost. 22 November.

f. 3^v 10s. each.
Lanercost. 24 December.

f. 6^r 20s.
Lanercost. 1 February.

f. 9^r 1 mark each.
Carlisle. 21 March.

f. 10^v 10s. to Janin the Trumpeter Junior.
10s. to John the Trumpeter.
by the hand of Janin.
Carlisle. 22 April.

f. 11^r 13s. 4d. for their wages; by the hand of John, the son.
Carlisle. 30 April.

f. 12^r 40s. for their outfits.
Carlisle. 4 May.

f. 12^v 1 mark. for John de London, sick, at Carlisle. Saturday, 13 May.

f. 16^r $^1/2$ mark each to John the Trumpeter and his son.
Carlisle. 13 June.

f. 17^r $^1/2$ mark each.
This was the day before Ed. I set out for Burgh-on-Sands. The following Thursday, 7 July, the King died. So that, John and his son were with him to the last.
Carlisle. 4 July.

JOHN (VIELLE-PLAYER)

1266 CPR. 617
Pardon, at the instance of Edmund, the King's (Hen. III) son, to John le Vilur of Midhurst, for the death of Llewelin Voyl of Bedhampton and of any consequent outlawry.
Kenilworth. 18 July.

JOHN (vielle-player)

Court minstrel (?)

1296/7 Add. MSS. 7965.

f. 52r 50s. to Johannes Vidulator, for making his minstrelsy on the wedding day of Princess Elizabeth [bracketed with King Page and a minstrel of Earl fitz Simon].
Ipswich. 8 January.

JOHN THE TRUMPETER

Prince's Trumpeter. (Probably, JANIN)

1302/3 E101/364/13.

Magister Johannes Trumpator.

f. 96r Prests, for his wages.

6s. 8d.	29 July.	'Barry' (?) [? Bury St. Edmunds]
10s.	27 August.	Aberdeen.
1/2 mark.	26 June.	St. John de Perth.
4s.	24 September.	'Tailglanny'.
13s. 4d.	17 October.	Dundee.
2 marks.	9 November.	Dunfermline.

JOHN THE WAFERER

1301/5 E101/362/10. (Parchment roll)

Payments from Peter de Chichester, Clerk of the King's Pantry and Butlery. Prests relative to the Queen's household expenses, when she was not with the King.

2s.	7 February.	
12d.	24 January.	(Windsor)
9d.	27 June.	(St. Albans)
5s.	19 May.	(Wolvesley. Hants)
3s.	8 July.	(Pitchley. Northants.)

all by the hand of Johannes Waffrarius.

See GILBERT

[The dates and places do not tally with those in the King's itinerary].

JOHN THE WAFERER

1306 Waferer of the Countess of Lancaster.

E101/369/6.

Present at the Whitsun Feast. Paid 40d.

[The Countess was Alice, daughter of Henry de Lacy. Married Thomas of Lancaster when she was 13 (and he, 16) in 1294. Died 1342].

JOLIET

1289/90 Swinfield. 155.
'A certain minstrel, Joliet.'

JUGLETT

Minstrel of the Marshal of Champagne.

1290 C47/4/5.
f. 47v 20s. by gift of the King, for staying in Court at Havering-atte-Bower, while other minstrels went to London, to the Earl Marshal's wedding.

See JAKET

[The name of the excellent minstrel in Guillaume de Dole (c. 1210/14) was Jouglet.]

K

KENNINGTON (JOHN DE)

King's Trumpeter.

1310/11 E101/373/10.
f. 3v 3s. to Johannes de Kenynton, for his wages. By the hand of Franceskin the Nakerer. 29 March. Berwick.
f. 5v 2s. for his wages. 28 April. Berwick.

E101/374/5.
f. 91r 3s. prest for his wages, to John de Kennington, Trumpator. 8 November. Berwick.

1311/12 MS. Bodley. Tanner. 197.
f. 50r Prests for his wages:
3s. by the hand of Franceskin the Nakerer. 29 March. Berwick-on-Tweed.
2s. 28 April. Berwick-on-Tweed [see above].

1311/12 E101/373/26. (Account of the Clerk of the Marshalcy)

f. 20r £26 handed to John de Kennington, receiving the money for the wages of carters, sumpters and other grooms.

20s. handed to the same at the same place, on the same day.

19 May. Newcastle-on-Tyne.

£17 8s 6 1/2d. by the hand of John de Kennington, receiving the money for wages of carters, sumpters and other grooms, for 5 days.

31 May Newcastle.

3s. 4d. by the hand of John de Kennington, for hay and oats.

7 July. Swineshead.

f. 76v 2s. prest for his wages.

20 June. Burstwick.

KESTRE (BAUDET DE)

Squire of the Household of Ed. III.

1330 E101/385/4.

Baudettus de Kestre.

KING'S BOYS (choristers)

1272/3 Issue Rolls 79.

£60 to Thomas de Pampleworth, clerk of Geoffrey de Picheford, Constable of Windsor Castle and Keeper of the King's boys in the same castle for the expenses of the boys aforesaid.

KINGORN (JOHN DE)

King's PIPER.

1303/4 Add. MSS. 8835.

f. 42r 13s. 4d. to *Johannes* de Kingorn, *fistulator Regis*, being the cost of 6 ells of striped cloth, bought from Simon of Westminster, for a *roba* given to the said John and then made, by order of the King. The money paid to the said Simon at St. Andrews.

14 March.

Price per ell 2s. and for making the *roba*; (so that the cloth cost 12s. and the making 1s. 4d.)

LAUNDE (PETER DE LA)

1311/12 MS. Cott. Nero. C.viii.
f. 82r 20s. to Perrotus de la Launde, minstrel of Sir/Lord Hugo de Nevill, for making his minstrelsy in the presence of the King. By gift of the King. 19 July. Berwick.

LAURENCE (harper)

1296/7 Add. MSS. 7965.
f. 52r 10s. to Laurentius le Harpour, for performing at the wedding of Princess Elizabeth.

1306 E101/369/6.
Laurentius Citharista.
Present at the Whitsun Feast. Paid 1/2 mark.
[He seems to have been one of the Court minstrels].

LAURENCE (herald)

1312 Bain. III. 423.
Laurencius Harald has a black bay horse, valued at 10 marks.

LAURENCE (horn-blower)

1325/6 King's Household minstrel.
E101/381/11.
In a list of minstrels in the King's Household:
Laurence le Cornour.

LENBURY (WILLIAM DE)

1358/59 MS. Cott. Galba. E xiv.
f. 52r 13s. 4d. to William de Lenbury, acrobat (saltator) for making his minstrelsies in the presence of the lady Queen, during Whitsun. By gift of the same. 24 May.

LESTIUOUR (HAMOND)

Hamo or Hamond, Court estive-player

'Hamond' may have been a surname (and therefore might be entered under H).
He was valet/groom of Master John de Drokenesford, Treasurer/Keeper of the King's Wardrobe.

1296/7 Add. MSS. 7965.

f. 15^r 10s. to Hamon Lestiuour, vallettus domini J. de Drokenesford, Treasurer of the Wardrobe, for carrying letters of the Treasurer to the lord bishop of Coventry and Lichfield, in great haste, on the King's business; for the money paid by him for his passage between London and Gravesend, by water; for divers hackneys, used by him for his riding-out on the aforesaid journey and for his expenses in going to Dover and returning, in the month of February.
Paid into his own hands at Westminster.

f. 17^r £10 to Hamon Lestivour, for a bay horse bought from him, through Ralph de Manton, at Westminster, in the month of April, and given to William le Fissher, for draught work in a certain long cart, which was assigned at the Wardrobe to the Duchess of Brebant, for transporting the King's treasures (jocalia) and other accountrements (harnesia) of the Wardrobe.
By the hand of James de Molendinis, at Portsmouth.

f. 52^r 20s. to Hamon Lestiuour, for performing at the wedding of Princess Elizabeth, Countess of Holland.

1304/5 E101/354/10.
or 1305/6 f. 14^v 18s. 4d. prest, to Hamon Lestiuour by the hand of William de Thorntoft; in a charter concerning a gift with a fee (or fief) 'Comellar' given to him by master W. on the same day 'there'.
23 August. Westminster.
(I do not understand the references here)

1306 E101/369/6.
Present at the Whitsun Feast. Received 2 marks.

LEUTOR (JOHN LE)

King's Lutenist.
(could be entered under J.)

1285 E101/351/17. (Counter-roll of Domestic Payments to members of the King's Household).
Johannes Le Leutour. Occurs in the list of the King's minstrels.

1290 E101/352/24.

20s. for his summer outfit [cited by Denholm-Young, in History and Heraldry, 56.]

1290 C.47/4/4.

f. 33^v paid $7^1/2$d. per day as wages while he was in Court.
[Top of folio torn].

1294/5 Fryde.

[N.B. Fryde has misread the MS. throughout. He calls him Lentour – a very understandable error]

p. 31 Janin le Leutour; paid 60s. $7^1/2$d. wages, for 162 days, during which time he was in Court for 97 days.

p. 32 47s. 6d. wages, from 1 May to 18 October, both days included, during which time he was in Court for 76 days.

p. 164 13s. 4d. prest, for his wages, 'on the march in Bar, 1293'. By the hand of lord Roger de L'Isle.

1295 CPR. 144.

Exemption, for life, at the instance of Edmund, the King's brother, and of Henry de Lacy, earl of Lincoln, and with the assent of the commonalty of the city of London, to John le Leutur, citizen of London, from all tallages, aids, watches and contributions whatsoever, which might be expected from him by the King or his ministers, by reason of the said John's lands, tenements, rents or other things, or merchandize within the said city or without; and from being put on assizes, juries or recognizances, or from being made mayor, sheriff, escheator, coroner, reeve, alderman or any other minister there against his will.

21 August. Westminster.

1296/7 *Add. MSS. 7965*.

f. 52^{r} 50s. for playing before Princess Elizabeth and her husband, the Count of Holland, at their wedding.

f. 77^{r} 34s. 11d. to John le Leutor, for his wages, from 7 September, on which day his horse was valued, to 19 November, both days included; for 78 days at 12d per day, of which 7^{1}/2d. was allowed him in the Marshalcy and 4^{1}/2d. in the Wardrobe, except 4 days, when he was absent.

f. 126^{v} 20s. for his winter outfit, at Harwich. January 1297.

f. 131^{v} 20s. for his summer outfit.

1298 *Gough*. 173.

Johannes le Leuteur has a pommely grey rouncy, valued at 8 marks.

1300 *CPR*. 542.

Protection, with clause *volumus*, until Whit Sunday, for John le Leutur, going beyond seas with Henry de Lacy, earl of Lincoln. By letter of the earl.
He nominated John de Triple, to act as his attorney during his absence.

15 November. Carlisle.

1302/3 *E101/363/18*.

f. 23^{r} £10 to John le Leutour, minstrel, as a gift from the prince; a donation to help him in the building of his house in London.
He received the money from Master J. de Drokenesford, Keeper of the Wardrobe.

1302 *CLL. Letter-book B*. 122.

On Thursday, the eve of St. Thomas, 21 December, came John de Triple and Andrew de Staunford and acknowledged themselves jointly and severally bound to John le Leuter in the sum of £50; to be paid within a fortnight of Easter. On Monday, before the feast of St. Barnabas, 11 June, the said John le Leuter came and acknowledged satisfaction. Therefore, the debt cancelled.

1304 <u>CLL. Letter-book B</u>. 135.

Saturday, the eve of Pentecost (16 May). Pledges of Adam the Tailor placed in the hands of Sir John de Sandale, for £4, which Stephen le Moreschal owes to Nicholas Pycot by statute, which pledges the said Sir John delivered to John le Leuter for safe custody until Midsummer next. And the aforesaid Adam came before the Chamberlain on Saturday, the eve of Holy Trinity (23 May) and agreed that unless he paid the said £4 at the said time, the said pledges should be sold. The said pledges are sealed with the seal of Thomas Sely in the name of the said Adam.

1304 <u>CCR. 135</u>.

To Roger de Higham, Walter de Gloucestre and John de Sandale, appointed to assess and levy the King's tallage in the city of London and its suburbs.
Order to cause John le Leutur, citizen of that city to be acquitted of the tallage and to release any distress that they may have levied for it, as the King, at the instance of Edmund, his brother and of Henry de Lacy, earl of Lincoln, and by the assent of the citizens of that city, has granted, by his letters patent, to John that he should be quit during his life of all manner of tallages that might be exacted by the King or his heirs from him by reason of his lands or rents or other goods and wares within the city.

13 April. Inverkeithing (Co. Fife).

1304 <u>CLL. Letter-book C</u>.

p. 137 Roger Higham, Walter de Gloucestre and John de Sandale to the Mayor, Sheriffs and Aldermen, notifying the receipt of the King's Writ, dated at Inverkeithing, 13 April 1304, to the effect that John le Leutor should be exempted from tallage, such exemption having been granted at the instance of Edmund, the King's brother and of Henry de Lacy, earl of Lincoln, with the assent of the citizens of London, and bidding them see that the King's orders were executed.
Dated at York 27 April the year aforesaid.

p. 138 On Friday (7 August) before the Feast of St. Laurence (10 August) (1304) came John le Leutour before Sirs John le Blound, Mayor, John de Wengrave, Walter de Finchingfeld, Simon de Paris, Salalmon le Cotiller [and] Nicholas Pycot, aldermen, and complained that the Serjeant of the Chamber of the Guildhall and other bailiffs of the City had unlawfully distrained him for the 1/15th. granted to the King in Parliament at Lincoln, in the 29th year of his reign (1300), contrary to the terms of the charter of exemption from such burdens granted him by King Edward I and now produced. It was thereupon ordered that his name should be removed from the Roll and that he should not in future be assessed.
Charter of exemption from assessments, mentioned _supra_, granted to the above John le Leutour at the instance of Edmund, the King's brother and of Henry de Lacy, earl of Lincoln. Dated. Westminster. 26 August 1294/5.

[This entry seems to be post 1306, because John le Blound was not knighted until 22 May 1306].

1305 CPR. 380.
Protection until Easter for the following going beyond seas on the King's service with Henry de Lacy, earl of Lincoln: [16 of them, including John le Leutur. 2 October. Sheen.

1306 E101/369/6.
Present at the Whitsun Feast. Received 40s.

1306/7 E101/364/13.
f. 22v 26s. 3d. to Johannes Le Leutor, for his wages, at 7 1/2d. per day, for the whole of the current year, i.e. for 365 days, during which time he was in Court for 50 days.
24 February. Lanercost.

1307 Add. MSS. 8835.
f. 114r Nothing for his winter outfit, because he was out of Court on Christmas Day.
23 February. Lanercost.

?1306/7 E101/368/27.

f. 19r 10s. to John le Leutor, for his wages, at 7 1/2d. per day, for the whole of the current year, i.e. for 365 days, during which time he was in Court for 16 days.
24 February. Lanercost.

1307 E101/357/15. (Debts of the Wardrobe at the end of the reign of Ed. I).

f. 13r 21s. 5 1/2d. owing to 'Master John, the minstrel.'

[May be another minstrel].

LEWELIN

Llewelyn, Welsh Trumpeter of Ed. II.

1307/8 Add. MSS. 35093.

f. 1r 10s. for his shoes. 10 July.

LEYLOND (RICARD DE)

Harper of either Countess Warenne or Lady Despenser.

See QUITACRE (RICARD DE)

1306 E101/369/6.

Present at the Whitsun Feast. Received 1/2 mark.
[As there were other men with this name, it is difficult to ascertain the identity of the harper; yet, it is worth noting that a squire of Fulk fitz Warin, in 1298, was a Ricard de Leyland and that, in 1313 and 1318 a Ricardus de Leylaund was pardoned for rebellious behaviour re Gaveston and the Despensers.]

See Gough, 205; Foedera I pars. 2, 231 and P.W. II div. ii. 127].

LINCOLN (HUGH DE)

King's Watchman.

c.1300 E101/371/8. Pt. I.

frag. 16. Hugo de Lincoln 5s.
frag. 41. 10s.
frag. 48. 1/2 mark, for his wages.

(See JOHN the Trumpeter)

1305 MS. Harley 152.

f. 17v named as Vigil Regis.

1305/6 E101/369/11.

f. 203^{v} 3s. prest for his wages to Hugo de Lincoln, Vigil.
18 August. Newborough in Tyndale (Northumberland)

See STAUNTON (JOHN DE)

5s. prest for his wages.
24 August. Newborough in Tyndale.

1305/6 E101/368/27.

Prests for his wages:

f. 60^{r}	10s.	7 June.	Westminster.
	4s.	5 July.	Thrapston.
	1/2 mark.	1 November.	Lanercost per Adam Skirewith.
f. 63^{r}	13s. 4d.	4 September.	Newborough in Tyndale.
f.63^{v}	3s.	18 August.	Newborough in Tyndale.
	5s.	24 August.	Newborough in Tyndale.
f. 68^{r}	5s.	25 January.	'Werdford'. [Gough says Bindon (Dorset)]
	5s.	26 February.	Itchenstoke. (Hants.)
	4s.	29 April.	Winchester.
	5s.	10 May.	Winchester.
f. 70^{r}	2 marks.	6 February.	Wareham.

1306/7 E101/369/16.

Prests for his wages:

f. 26^{v} 10s. by the hand of J. de Stanton. 25 February. Lanercost.
10s. 24 December. Lanercost.
10s. 4 February. Lanercost.
10s. by the hand of Robert de Fynchesle. 24 April. Carlisle.
20s. 8 May. Carlisle.
6s. 8d. 30 May. Carlisle.

1306/7 E101/370/16.

Prests for his wages:

f. 1^{r} (p. 41) 10s. 25 November. Lanercost.
f. 3^{v} (p. 46) 10s. 24 December. Lanercost.
f. 11^{r} (p. 61) 10s. by the hand of R. de Finchesle. 24 April. Carlisle.

1310/11 <u>E101/374/5</u>.

Prests for his wages:

f. 88v	3s. 4d.	10 July.	Westminster.
	3s.	4 September.	Durham.
	3s. 4d.	15 October.	Renfrew.
	3s.	9 November.	Berwick-on-Tweed.

<u>LION</u> (DE NORMANVILLE)

1306 <u>E101/369/6</u>.

An unidentified minstrel on the Pay roll:
(Latin) Received 2s.
Perhaps a squire in the Prince's Household.

1312 <u>BAIN Cal. Docs. rel. Scot. III</u>. 428.

Roll of horses:
Leo de Normanville has a black dapple (<u>nigrum liardum</u>) or dark iron-grey horse. Perhaps a son or kinsman of Thomas de Normanville, King's Escheator ultra Trent (before 1295).

<u>LONDON</u> (JOHN DE)

King's Trumpeter.

1294/5 <u>Fryde</u>.

p. 43.	£18 5s. wages for the whole year (6d. per day; for himself and John Depe.) during which time he was not absent. London 26 Ed. I (1297).
p. 174	13s. 4d. wages.
p. 176	20s. wages. 25 September. Wengham.
p. 180	20s. wages. 26 October. Canterbury.

1296/7 <u>Add. MSS. 7965</u>.

f. 123v	2 marks for his winter outfit.
f. 56v	20s. for repairing his trumpet. 25 July. Westminster.

1297 <u>C.47/4/6</u>.

f. 7r 6s. 8d. prest, for his wages. 17 February. St. Albans.

1300/1 <u>Add. MSS. 7966</u>.

ff. 175v, 178v 6s. 8d. prest, for the price of 20 ells of canvas.

c. 1300 <u>E101/371/8</u>. (Part I)

fragment 16.
John de London 10s.
fragment 41.
John de London 1 mark.

1304/5 E101/368/6.

f. 21r To Master Johannes de London, Trumpator, 20s. d.d. Regis.
By gift of the King.
10 January. Brianston.

1305/6 MS. Harley 152.

f. 18v 13s. 4d. prest, for 'their' wages. 3 November. Lanercost. [Since the clerk has written against this entry, 'ad huc Joh. de London et filius, trumpatores, it seems certain that 'their' refers to John and his son (also John) and not to John Depe and his son. 1/2 mark each to 'Master John de London and John, his son, trumpeters', prest, for their wages.
3 November. Lanercost.

1305/6 E101/369/11.

f. 99v

Magister Johannes ['de London' in margin] trumpator et Johannes filius suus, 40s. [20s. each] for remaining in Court on Christmas Day and returning from Court to London.
By gift of the King.
10 January. Brianston.
[Gough: Kingston Lacy]

f. 203v Master John de London and John, his son, 1/2 mark each, prest, for their wages.
3 November. [Lanercost].

1305/6 E101/368/27.

f. 65r To Master John de London and John, his son, trumpeters, to each of them 1/2 mark, prest, for their wages. 3 November. Lanercost.

f. 21v 116s. 3d. prest, for his wages, at 71/2d. per day, for the whole of the current year (1305/6); for 365 days, bar 179, during which he was absent from Court.

f. 60r Prests, for his wages:
13s. 4d. 7 June. Westminster.
7 marks. 27 August. Carlisle.
10s. 'at the beginning of June'. Westminster.
10s. 2 October. Lanercost.
13s. 4d. 2 November. Lanercost.
20s. 'by the hand of G. de Monte Reuelle' 4 November. Lanercost.
20s. 5 November. Lanercost.

f. 62v 20s. prest, for his wages, by the hand of John [MS. has G.] his son.
4 September. Newborough in Tyndale.

1306/7 E101/369/16.
f. 26r John de London and John, his son, King's Trumpeters: prests, for their wages:
20s. 22 November. Lanercost.
20s. 24 December. Lanercost.
20s. 1 February. Lanercost.
2 marks (1 mark each) 22 March. Carlisle.
10s. each, by the hand of John, the son, 22 April. Carlisle.
13s. 4d. (each) by the hand of John, the son, 25 April. Carlisle.
13s. 4d. into their own hands.
15 May. Carlisle.
40s. (20s. each) by the hand of John, the son, 4 May. Carlisle.
1/2 mark each. 21 June. Carlisle.
1/2 mark each, by the hand of John de Staunton. 4 June. Kirkandrews [Co. Cumberland].

1306/7 E101/370/16.
f. 12v (p. 64)
1 mark to John de London, ill, at Carlisle.
13 May. Carlisle.

LOWYS (Simon)
King's/Queen's mounted messenger.

1294/5 Fryde. 83
40s. in advance. for the expenses of Master Nicholas Merien, dean of Gurnsey, Robert de Vivario, of their clerks and valets, coming from Montgomery to London and there awaiting the coming of the King.
[It was Simon who came from Montgomery, to meet and escort the strangers to the King.]

1296/7 Add. MSS. 7965.
ff. 107 to 131v
Among minstrels, receiving their winter outfits.
Simon Lowys, Nuncius, [20s.] for his winter outfit.

1304/5 E101/368/16.
f. 22r Simon Lowys, Nuncius, 4s. for carrying letters of the King, to the earl and countess of Gloucester. For his expenses.

LOWYS (Thomas)

1290/2 Botfield, 125.
11s. given to Thomas Lowys, '*quondam nuncio Regine*', by the Queen's executors.

LUCAT

1306 E101/369/6.
?King's Sergeant-at-arms.
Received 30s. paid to him by Le Roy Capenny.
Perhaps the same person as John de Luke.

LUKE (John de)

1294/5 Fryde. 160 (E36/202)
1296/7 King's Sergeant-at-arms.
Johannes de Luk', prest of 100s. into his own hands, on his going into Gascony.
24 August.
To John de Luke, 100s. by the hand of William de Melton, on 24 August, for his going to Gascony.'

1296/7 Add. MSS. 7965.
f. 124r In a list of the King's Sergeants-at-arms – John de Luca.

1299/1300 Add. MSS. 35291.
f. 92r
Was transferred to duty on the fortifications around Dumfries 20 November to 12 July.
£6 10s. for his wages, from 13 July, on which day he returned from Dumfries and went with the King's army into Galloway (after the siege of Caerlaverock), until 19 November. 130 days at 12d. per day.

1299/1300 LOG.
p. 215 same as entry in Add. MSS. 35291, f. 92r
p. 317 *Johannes* de Luk'
2 marks for his winter outfit.
13 January. Newcastle.

1300/1 E101/359/5.
f. 3v 1/2 mark (with 15 other sergeants) to John de Luke, sergeant-at-arms, for his wages.
5 May. Kempsey (Worcs.).

1300/1 E101/359/6.
f. 10v 10s. prest, for his wages.
9 November. Linlithgow.

1302/3 E101/364/13.

f. 70v 10s. prest, for his wages.
27 April. York.

1303/4 Add. MSS. 8835.

f. 61r £10 6s. 0d. for his wages and for those of one of his fellows, from 29 April, on which day he came from the fortifying of the peel of Linlithgow, with horses and arms, to stay in the King's army at Stirling, until 9 August, both days included. 103 days, receiving for himself and his fellow, 2s. per day, because his horses were valued for the same period on 29 August at Berwick-on-Tweed.

1306/7 E101/357/15. (Debts of the Wardrobe)

f. 18v [Owing] to John de Luke - £10 5s. 8d.

1309 Cal. Chancery Warrants, 211.

13 July. Langley. The King sends his sergeants, John de Luke and John de Coreby and Henry de Hetch and John de Borch, two of his mariners, against whom some people of Flanders have made divers trespasses. Mandates to make letters to the Count of Flanders and to the mayor and commonalty of Bruges, asking them to send to the King the bodies of the trespassers, whom the mariners will name.

1310/11 E101/374/5.

f. 42v Johannes de Luca serviens Regis, aquarius
4d. prest, for his expenses relating to ?Sir [Br]ankulun de Puerpeffry of Scotland, ? serving [for] the same from London to Scotland to the King 'in duabus picheris'.
18 and 19 May.

1310/11 E101/374/7.

p. 9 Johannes de Luke.

p. 24 15s. 4d. for money owing to him for his expenses in going to the parts of Flanders on the King's business in the 3rd year (1309).

p. 25 Magister Johannes de Lucy, 21s. for his expenses in coming to the King from London to Berwick and remaining there 13 days at 6d. per day.

1311/12 E101/373/26.

f. 56r £10 to Johannes de Luca, King's Sergeant-at-arms, prest, for his wages and for those of certain others remaining with him in the aforesaid castle (Odiham); by Henry Nasend.
9 May.

f. 48r 60s. to John de Luke, sent by the King to Odiham castle, to take in charge and repair the same castle; prest, for [cost of] repairs.
10 March. York.

f. 68v prests, for his wages:
1/2 mark. 12 September. London.
26s. 8d. 24 November. Westminster.

1311/12 MS. Cott. Nero C.viii.

f. 9v (10v) £10 8s. for his wages from 8 July of the current year to 31 January of the same year, both days included 208 days.
2 marks to the same, for his winter outfit for the aforesaid year (? 1310)
£6 14s. to the same, for his wages and those of others, for the fortifying of the town of Berwick, from 20 September to 31 January, 134 days.
Total allocated to him - £18 18s. 8d.
He received 3 prests in 1310 - 26s. 8d.
And so there is owing to him £17 2s.
He has a bill.

f. 100r To John de Luke, King's Sergeant-at-arms, £9 3s. for his wages from 8 July to 7 January, on which day he was admitted custodian of Odiham castle, by order of the King; the first day included but not the second; for 183 days, receiving 12d. per day, because his horse was valued at the same time. According to contract drawn up with him.
21 October of the 6th year (1312/13) Windsor.

1314/15 E101/376/7. (Controller's Roll. Robin Wodehouse; sub Vadia Balistariorum).

f. 66v £10 8s. 0d. to John de Luke, King's Sergeant-at-arms, for his wages from 8 July of the present year to 31 January of the same year, both days included, for 208 days, because his horse was valued at the same time; by contract, at Cawood.
16 December of 13th year (1319/20).

?1315/16 (or later) f. 114v £167 18s. 4d. to John de Luke, King's Sergeant-at-arms, prest, owing to him for haketons and arbalesters' collarets, bought for 120 arbalesters, sent from London by the same to Berwick-on-Tweed; and for staying there; for their wages, in cash, given to him by the treasury.
6 February. London.

f. 122v 16d. to John de Luke, for his wages and outfit.

1314 CLL. Letter-book D. 308.
Indenture made between John de Gisors, mayor, Stephen de Abyndone and Hamo de Chigwelle, Sheriffs of London, on the one part, and John de Luka, the King's Esquire, on the other part, touching 'aketons, colerettes, arbalests', and quarels, quivres and money provided for the arbalesters, by the King's writ to carry them as far as the vill of Berwick-on-Tweed, for the defense of the same: viz:

Imprimis, there are delivered to the said John de Luke.
120 aketons, each worth 6s. 9½d. preter 2s. 4d.
Total: £40 17s. 4d.

Item. 120 bacinets with colerettes of iron, each worth 5s. 1d. preter 2s.
Total: £30 12s.

Item. 120 arbalests, each worth 3s. 5d.
Total: £20 10s.

Item. 120 baldrics, each worth 12d.
Total: £6.

Item. 120 quivers each [3d.]
Total: 30s.

Item. 4,000 quarels at 20s. the thousand
Total: £4
Total £103 9s. 4d.

Item. delivered to the same for the pay of the under-written [here follow the names] 120 arbalesters for 28 days at 4d. a head per day and 6d. for the vintenars - £57 8s.

Item. for sarplers and casks for packing the arms - 24s.

Item for the carriage of 3 carts and and pay of 6 carters carrying the said arms from London to Berwick, for 18 days' travelling, each cart with 2 carters, receiving for pay and for provender and shoeing of 4 horses, 2s. 2d.
Total: 117s.
Sum Total £167 18s. 4d.

1325/26 E101/381/11. (Fragments)
In a list of household officers being issued clothing, to go with the King (Ed. II) to France: among the esquires.
Jaket de Luke.

1328 E101/383/4.
pp. 375/6 From a list of squire minstrels in the household of Ed. III. Recipients of the King's livery.
Jakinet de Luke.

1330 E101/385/4.
p. 379 Squires receiving the King's livery,
Jakinet de Luke, scutifer.
[Identity not certain. Probably same as John de Luke, who was now an old man, having served a minimum of 35 years in the King's household. If not, may have been his son?]

LUND (Walter)

1296/7 Add. MSS. 7965.
f. 55r A harper of Chichester, whom the King (Ed. I) found playing his harp in the cathedral, in front of the tomb of the Blessed Richard.
6s. 8d. by gift of the King.
26 May. Chichester.

M

MACHEYS (Roger)

1305/6 E101/369/11.
Herald (prob. (MARCHEYS)
f. 100v 20s. for his expenses on his journey from Winchester to London.
6 April. Winchester.

See NORFOLK (Thomas de)

MADDOK ARGLOUTH
(Madoc Arglwydd)

1307/8 Add. MSS. 35093.
Trumpeter of Ed. II.
f. 1r 10s. for his shoes.
10 July.

MAGOTE

1296/7 Add. MSS. 7965.
f. 52r 20s. for making his minstrelsy before the Lady Elizabeth on her wedding-day.
8 January. Ipswich.

See GRISCOTE and VISAGE.

MAHU
'qui est oue La Dammoisele de Baar'

1306 E101/369/6.
Unidentified minstrel accompanying Joan de Bar, grand-daughter of Ed. I to the Whitsun Feast.
Received 40s.
[She was the daughter of Princess Eleanor and Henry, Comte de Bar. Was about 11 years old and came to England on the death of her father; March 1305. [Henry died, 1303. Princess Eleanor, 1298] In May 1305 the King offered her in marriage to John de Warenne. See CCR. 321 (1305). The marriage took place on 20 May 1306. She died s.p. 1361. John did his best to divorce her, but she outwitted and outlived him.]

MAHU DU NORTH

1306 E101/369/6.
At the Whitsun Feast. Received 1 mark.
Unidentified; perhaps the minstrel of Sir Maheu de Redman.

MAHUET
'qui est oue Mons. de Tounny'

1306 E101/369/6.
At the Whitsun Feast. Received 2 marks. Unidentified minstrel of Robert de Tony, 'the Knight of the Swan', who was 28 at the time and who died s.p. 28 November 1309.

MAKEJOY (Matilda)

1297 Add. MSS. 7965.
f. 52r Matilda Makeioie Saltatrix.
2s, for making her vaults in the presence of Edward, the King's son, in the King's Hall, Ipswich.
By gift of the Lord Edward.
27 December. Ipswich.

1306 E101/369/6.
Present at the Whitsun Feast.
Received 12d.

1311/12 E101/374/19.

f. 8v 2s. to Matilda Makejoy, acrobat/dancer, for making her minstrelsy in the presence of the two young princes [i.e. Ed. I's sons by his second queen Margaret].
by gift and order of Lord Thomas.
24 June. Framlingham.

MALINES (John de)

1290 C47/4/5.
Vielle-player of John de Brabant.

f. 49r 40s. to Johannes de Malyns, vidulator Johanni de Brabant, for a German bay rouncy bought from him and given to the said John last winter...50s. to the same Janyn, vidulator of John de Brabant, on going from the Court at Langley to his own country.
By gift of the King.

1290 E101/352/21. (Roll of money paid to various people)
40s. to John de Malyns for a German bay rouncy etc. (as above).
50s. to Janin the vielle-player etc. (as above).

MANTOZT ('Alienus' de)

1296/7 Add. MSS. 7965.

f. 54r 17s. 6d. to a foreign minstrel from Mantozt coming from Gascony, with news, to the King; for certain small necessaries for his use.
By gift of the King.
5 April. Exeter.

MARCHIS (Walter le)

1298/9 Gough.
Letters of protection, 26/7 Ed. I. Scotch Roll. Chancery No. 3.

p. 17 Walterus le Rey et Rogerus de Cheyni, who will be setting out with Henry de Percy [Warden of the Marches, at Falkirk, 1298].

p. 31 Walterus le Rey Marchys, who has set out with Henry de Percy...
Walter was one of the Kings of Heralds and a King Minstrel.

1300/1 Add. MSS. 7966.

Walterus le Marchi Rex Haraldorum.

f. 66r 40s. for making a certain proclamation by order of the King, in the presence of the King, in his hall below Northampton Castle on Christmas Day, concerning prohibition of holding tournaments in England.
By gift of the King.
25 December. Northampton.

f. 102v Walterus le Marchis Rex menestrallus.
£4 8s. for his wages from 8 July, on which day his horse was valued, to 9 October, on which day he departed. 93 days at 12d. per day.

E101/369/6.
Present at the Whitsun Feast. Le Roy Marchis.
Received 5 marks.

MARCHIS (Ralph)

1312 Bain. III
p. 419 Radulphus Marchys has a white spotted (? pied - piolatum) horse valued at £10.

MARCHIS (ROBERT)

1312 Bain III.
p. 419 Robertus Marchys has a bay horse, with a star, valued at 8 marks.

MARCHIS (William)

1335/8 MS. Cott. Nero. C.viii.
f. 226r Willelmus Marchis, minstrel in the household of Ed. III.
20s. for his outfit.

MARKIN

1306 E101/369/6.
Monsire Markin, apparently a Court minstrel, who handed their gratuities at the Whitsun Feast, to the 3 anonymous minstrels of Sir John de Hastings. [Unless he was one of the 3]

MARTIN

1290 E101/352/24.
King's Sergeant-at-arms.

Martinus dictus parvus, serviens-ad-arma being issued his summer and winter outfits.
Probably the same as Martinet, whom see.

1284 C47/3/21. (Fragments).
'To Martin Parvus, King's Sergeant-at-arms...'

MARTINET

1300/1 Add. MSS. 7966A.
f. 66v Martinettus menestrallus.
1 mark for entertaining, in turn or on various occasions with John de Cressy and Janin, Earl Warenne's organist, the King and Queen, at Lincoln, in the month of February. By gift of the Queen.

See JOHN DE CRESSY and JANIN.

MARTINET (drummer)

1296/7 Add. MSS. 7965.
Taborer in the Royal Household.
f. 52r 10s. to Martinet le taburer, for performing at the wedding feast of Princess Elizabeth.

1305/6 Add. MSS. 37656. (Wardrobe Book of Thomas of Brotherton)
f. 1r Martinettus menestrallus.
2s. to Martinet, the minstrel, for making his minstrelsy in the presence of the two young princes and for repairing his tabor, broken by them.
By gift of the two princes.
12 July. Ludgershall.

1305/6 E101/368/12. (Household Account of the 2 young princes)
f. 3r Martinettus Taburarius.
11d. to Martinet the Taborer, for the repair of the little drums ['tymbrium' - tambours? tambourines?] of the King's sons and for money paid by him for parchment for covering same.
18 November.
f. 4v 20s. to Martinet the Taborer and William and John the trumpeters, minstrels [of the 2 [young princes] for making their minstrelsy in their presence on the Eve and the Feast (day) of Epiphany.
By gift of the princes.
5/6 January. Windsor Castle.

sub Robe, Martinet appears as 'Minstrel of Hall and Stable' menestrallus Aule et Stabuli; also as plain menestrallus; and allowed prest, for 7 ells of cloth and 1 lamb's fur for his outfit.
Ward. (Frag. 31 Ed. I. Queen's Remem.)
Green. (History of Royal Ladies) vol. III. 40. mention what appears to be a different version of another incident of the same kind: 'An odd illustration of the tumultuous mirth of the royal nursery occurs in the following wardrobe entry: 'For the Lords Thomas and Edmund, the King's sons, and the Lady Margaret, the daughter of Elizabeth, Countess of Hereford, paid to Martinet the tabourer, making minstrelsy for them; and also for the reparation of his tabor, broken by them - 7s.
[The baby, Margaret, was born at Tynemouth, at the end of September, 1303; and sent to Windsor, to be brought up with the 2 young princes].

1306 E101/369/6.
Present at the Whitsun Feast.
Received 1 mark.

MARTINET (Warwick)

1306 E101/369/6.
'qui est oue le Conte de Warwike'
Minstrel of Guy de Beauchamp, earl of Warwick.
[Perhaps a Taborer. See Gillot le Taborer. Present at the Whitsun Feast.
Received 40s. (handed to him by Baudet the Taborer).

MATTHEW (Crowder)

1305/6 E101/368/12.
Crowder of Edward, Prince of Wales.
f. 4v Matheus Crudarius menestrallus domini Principis. 5s. to Michael the Prince's trumpeter and Matthew, his crowder, for making their minstrelsy before the two young princes.
By gift of them (the same).
18 November. Northampton.

See MICHAEL.

MATTHEW (harper)

1306 E101/369/6.
Present at the Whitsun Feast.
Matheus le harpour. Unidentified.
Received 5s.

MATTHEW (Waferer)

1306 E101/369/6.
Waferer of Lord Robert de Monhaut.
Matheus Waffrarius domini R. de Monte Alto.
Present at the Whitsun Feast. Received 2s.

MAUNTE (John de)

Court minstrel.

1302 CCR. 66.
John de Maunte acknowledges that he owes William le Menestral £10; to be levied, in default, of his lands and chattels in London.

1303/4 Add. MSS. 8835.
f. 44^v made his minstrelsy with other minstrels in the presence of the King's daughter, the Lady Maria, at Burstwick (Yorks) and shared a gift of 30s.

See DRUET

MAUPRIVE

1328 E101/383/4. pp. 375/6.

1330 E101/385/4. p. 381.
Listed among the squire minstrels of the household of Ed. III.

MASCUN (Jaques de)

1306 E101/369/6.
Present at the Whitsun Feast.
Received 1 mark.

MAZON (James le)

1303/4 Add. MSS. 8835.
Court minstrel. Jacobus le Mazon.
f. 44^v One of the company of minstrels performing before Princess Mary, the nun, at Burstwick.

See DRUET

MELF (John de)

1325 CPR. 158.
(?) Nakerer of Ed. II.
Grant for life to John de Melf, nakerer, of the King's houses in the parish of St. Nicholas in the Shambles (de Marcellis), which Henry Scot, deceased, held for life by grant of Thomas, late earl of Lancaster.
By the King.

MELIOR

1296/7 Add. MSS. 7965.
harper of Lord John Mautravers.
f. 54v Melior Citharista qui fuit quondam cum domino Johanne Moutravers.
20s. for making his minstrelsy in the presence of the King during the time of his blood-letting in April, at Plympton.
By gift of the King, by the hand of W. Sturton.
23 April. Plympton.

1304/5 E101/368/6.
f. 21v Melior Citharista Johannis Mautravers.
40s. for playing his harp in the presence of the King on the day of Epiphany (6 January).
By gift of the King.
12 January. Wimborne.

E101/369/11.
f. 99v same as above.

MELLERS

1306 E101/369/6.
Present at the Whitsun Feast.
Unidentified.
Received 1/2 mark, handed to him by Roy Baisescu.

MELLET

1306 E101/369/6.
Present at the Whitsun Feast.
Unidentified. Received 1 mark.

MERLIN

1306 E101/369/6.
Present at the Whitsun Feast.
Received 1 mark.

MERLYN (JOHN)

1307/8 Add. MSS. 35093. Johannes Merlyn Scutifer.
f. 3r £33 6s. 8d. to Lord Aymer de Valence, prest, for certain bow(s) which were ordered from the King's Wardrobe, for 60 men-at-arms, who were being retained in parts of Scotland.
Received by the hand of his squire, John Merlyn, at Dumfries.
By order of the King and his Council. 7 August.

1311/12 Foedera. Vol. II. pars. I

p. 212 Johannes Merlyn listed among those who were to set out with the King for parts overseas. He was in the group of people who were in Aymer de Valence's train.

p. 231 John Merlyn. pardoned re the death of Gaveston.

1312/13 E101/375/8.

f. 30r

Johannes Merlyn, vallettus domini Adomari de Valens Comitis Penbrochi.

Paying a minstrel for his performance.

See JAKEMIN DE MOKENOR.

MERLIN (vielle-player)

1320/1 Add. MSS. 9951.

Minstrel of the Earl of Richmond.

f. 21r 20s. to Merlin, vielle-player, minstrel of the lord Earl of Richmond, for making his minstrelsy in the presence of the lord King. By gift of the lord King into his own hands. 12 May. Westminster.

MERLYN (le Vieler)

1330 E101/385/4.

p. 381 Merlynus le Vieler occurs in a list of minstrels of the household of Ed. III.

1330 MS. Cott. Galba E iii. (Issues of summer livery in the Queen's Household).

f. 187r To Merlin, the minstrel, vielle-player [Merlin vidulator menestrallus] 6 1/2 ells of yellow and striped Cloth of Samite and 1 lamb's fur to make an outfit for himself.

MERLYN (John, le Skirmishour)

CCR. 411.

1295 To the sheriff of Devon and the coroners of that county. Order to restore to John Merlyn le Skirmishour his goods and chattels which were taken into the King's hands, because he fled [for sanctuary] to Church for a trespass committed by him in so striking a man that he thought he had killed him, as the King has granted to John his goods and chattels for his good service to the King in his expedition to Wales.

22 April. Llanfaes (Anglesey),

MERTON (Geoffrey de)

1311/12 E101/373/26.
King's Watchman.
f. 76v Galfridus de Merton, Vigil, prests for his wages:
5s. 20 June. Burstwick.
5s. 21 April. Newcastle-on-Tyne.
f. 77v Galfridus de Merton, Vigil Regis, 6s. 8d. prest, for his wages. per Wengesfeld.
5 February. York.

MICHAEL (trumpeter)

1305/6 E101/368/12.
Prince of Wales' trumpeter.
f. 4v Michaelis Trumparius...menestrallus domini Principis 5s. to Michael the Trumpeter and Matthew the Crowder, minstrels of the lord Prince, for making their minstrelsy in the presence of the two young princes.
By gift of the two princes.
18 November. Northampton.

MILLY (William de)

1313/14 E101/375/9.
Magister Willelmus de Milly. Cantor Milly. (in margin)
f. 14v 74s. to Master William de Milly, Singer, paid 2s. per day for his wages, from 8 July of the 7th year (1313) to 7 July of the same year, both days included, for 365 days, during which time he was present in court 37 days, according to the contract drawn up with him by Master John de Forest.
At York. 20 July of the 8th year (1314/15).
[This is an unusually high wage for a minstrel; it is the equivalent of the daily wage of a knight.]

ANONYMOUS MINSTRELS

[in chronological order]

1283/90 WENLOK 243
Household Ordinances: "...e qe ce checun home dastat soit assis a son droit a la table e menestrals e messagers par els bas e servi solom lur estat...

1296/7 <u>Add. MSS. 7965</u>.

f. 55v £4 8s. 4d., by gift of the King (Ed. I) to 14 minstrels, making their minstrelsy before the statue of the Blessed Mary, the Virgin, in the crypt (<u>vouta</u>) of Christchurch, Canterbury.

<u>NORFOLK</u>

1296/7 <u>ADD. MSS. 7965</u>.

f. 52r 20s. each to two minstrels of the Earl Marshal (Hugh Bigod, Earl of Norfolk), for performing at the wedding of Princess Elizabeth.

<u>FITZ SIMON</u>

1296/7 <u>Add. MSS. 7965</u>.

f. 52r 30s. to the minstrel of Earl fitz Simon, for making his minstrelsy at the wedding of Princess Elizabeth.

See: <u>PAGE</u> (John) (<u>vidulator</u>)

1299 <u>Add. MSS. 24509</u>.

f. 61r 20s. to a certain minstrel, who was with the Lady Alienor, sometime queen of England, mother of the King, coming to the King's son and bringing to him a certain book of Romance [<u>librum de Roman</u>] which the aforesaid queen had bequeathed to the King.
By gift of the King's son, by the hand of Master John...

[As Q. Eleanor died in 1291, eight years elapsed before the book arrived].

1299/1300 <u>LQG</u>. 163.

12d to a certain boy, playing [<u>ludens</u>] in the presence of the prince, at Rosington.

1299/1300 <u>LQG</u>. 163

3s. given to various people, minstrels and others, by Prince Edward, between 12 May and 9 June/
<u>Videlicet</u> 'to 2 minstrels, making their minstrelsies in the presence of the said Lord Edward, at Bury St. Edmunds, 12 May.

1300/1 Add. MSS. 7966A.

f. 67v 3s. to 'a certain minstrel', for making his minstrelsy in the presence of the Queen.
By gift of the Queen.
7 January. Northampton.

PERTH

1303/4 Add. MSS. 8835.

f. 42v Menestralli de Perth.
4s. to divers vielle-players, timpanists and other minstrels, going into the presence of the King, on his departure from St. John (de Perth) and making their minstrelsies.
By gift of the King.

1303/4 Add. MSS. 8835.

f. 132r [Humphrey de Bohun, earl of Hereford, married Princess Elizabeth on 14 November 1302]
On the day of her churching/purification, two monks from Westminster Abbey travelled to Knaresborough, where she and her baby son were, with the girdle of the Blessed Virgin: and Gilbert de Dromle, a clerk detailed to see to the expenses of her household, made a gift to minstrels who performed before her and other members of the nobility. Later on, the baby was sent to Windsor Castle, to be nursed with the King's 2 sons (by Margaret), Thomas and Edmund, but the little fellow died on the way, at Stony Stratford, 24 October. the minstrels referred to were probably King Robert and a company of 15 of his fellow-minstrels.

See King Robert.

COUNTESS OF NORFOLK

1306 Ward and Hearne

p. 85, 4s. to the minstrel of the Countess Marshal, for making his minstrelsy in the presence of the Prince.
Penrith.

MONTMORENCY

1306 E101/369/6.

Minstrel of Sir John de Montmorency, kinsman of the King (Ed. I), through Simon de Montfort, earl of Leicester, who married Eleanor, sister of Henry III. Simon's mother was Alix de Montmorenci.
Present at the Whitsun Feast. Received 2 marks.

BELLS

1306 E101/369/6.
'The minstrel with the bells'.
Present at the Whitsun Feast. Unidentified.
Received 1 mark.

MINSTRELS OF VARIOUS NOBLES

1305/6 E101/369/11.

f. 185^{v} The account of Master Reynolds, of the expenditure of the Lord Prince of Wales: for gifts given by the Lord Prince, in money, to various minstrels who came to him on the parts of various nobles; making their minstrelsies in his presence; to palefreteers leading palfreys to him from various nobles; money given to divers soldiers, squires and servants of the Prince's household, together with compensation for horses, as well as those valued for his soldiers and squires in the Scottish war of this current year as those found killed (but not valued) in the Prince's service; and for other things (*facta*) during the same aforesaid time; as is revealed by this (account) book.

£1,268 18s. 1d.

[An entry which seems to me to be typical of Walter Reynolds, skating over huge expenses and seemingly giving no proper details. It also indicates the Prince's extravagance; and the nobles were obviously taking full advantage of it. In our terms the sum is equivalent to about 1/4 million pounds.]

GAVESTON'S WEDDING

1307 E101/373/15.

f. 21^{r} £20 given, in cash, by the King (Ed. II) and his council to divers minstrels, for making their minstrelsies in the presence of the King, on the Feast of All Saints (1 November), that is to say, on the wedding-day of the Earl of Cornwall.
By the hand of William de Baillol; by gift of the King.
3 November. Berkhamsted.

HASTINGS

1306 E101/369/6.

1 mark each to 'the three minstrels of Monsire de Hasting(s). Present at the Whitsun Feast. Sir John Hastings of Abergavenny. Steward of Queen Margaret. ob. 1313. [his widow m. Ralph de Monthermer].

1306 E101/369/6.

Present at the Whitsun Feast.
3s. each to 'three different minstrels'. Unidentified.

BERWICK

1306 E101/369/6.

Present at the Whitsun Feast;
40d. to 2 minstrels (possibly trumpeters) of Sir John de Ber(wick), King's Clerk and Keeper of the Queen's gold.

UNKNOWN

1312/13 E101/375/8.

f. 32[r] 20s. to Thomas de Derby, groom of the King's Chamber, for cash paid by him, by order of the King, to a certain minstrel who made his minstrelsy in the King's presence.
11 June.

SAVOY

1316/17 MS. Soc. of Antiq. 120.

f. 100[v] 40s. to a certain minstrel of the Count of Savoy, who came, with his master's permission, to the lord King and returned to his master with the lord King's letters. By gift of the lord King, by the hand of Roger le Trumpour.
30 May. Westminster.

VARIOUS

1332/3 101/386/7.

f. 7^{r} 12d. to a certain minstrel for making his minstrelsy in the presence of the Lady Alianora, on her journey between Osprynges (Ospringe, Kent) and Canterbury.
By the hand of the Lord Steward, who gave him the cash.
3 May.
2s. to divers minstrels, for making their minstrelsies before the statue of the Blessed Virgin, in the volta in Christchurch, Canterbury.
By gift of the Lady [Eleanor] by the hand of the Treasurer.
4 May.

f. 7^{r} 10s. to 4 minstrels, for making their minstrelsies in the presence of the Lady Alianora, coming from Mare to Lesclues.
By gift of the said lady, by the hand of the Treasurer.
6 May.

f. 7^{r} 13s. 4d. to 4 minstrels of Arragon, who came to the Lady Alianora and made their minstrelsies in her presence. By gift of the same, by the hand of Henri de Newenton.
7 May.

f. 7^{v} 6s. 8d. to 2 minstrels from the parts of Hoyland, coming from England to Novum Magnum (?) in the train of the Lady Alianore.
8 May. Bruges.

ULSTER

1358/9 MS. Cott. Galba. E xiv.

f. 5^{v} 10s. to 2 minstrels of the Countess of Ulster, for making their minstrelsies in the presence of the Lady Queen, on the Tuesday of Easter Week (25 April).
By gift of the same by the hand of Robert Louth, on the same day.

[Lionel of Clarence, earl of Ulster, 1347-68, son of Edward III, married Elizabeth de Burgh].

MOCHELNEYE (John de)

1306 E101/369/6.

Present at the Whitsun Feast. Received 2 marks.

MOKENON (Jakemin de)

1312/13 E101/375/8.
King's minstrel.
f. 30r £7 3s. 1d. to Jakemin de Mokenon, King's minstrel, for making his minstrelsy in the presence of the King.
By gift of the King, by the hand of John Merlyn, valet of Lord Aymer de Valence, earl of Pembroke; paid to him in cash by order of the king.
28 May. St. Richer.

MONET (John)

1304/5 E101/368/6.
Minstrel of Lord Robert fitz Payn.
f. 21r 60s. to John Monet, vallettus domini Rob. filii Pagani, for making his minstrelsy in the presence of the King.
6 January. Wimborne (Dorset).

1305/6 E101/369/11.
f. 99v Johannes Monet menestrallus domini Roberti filii Pagani.
60s. for making his minstrelsy before the King on the day of Epiphany.
By gift of the King.
6 January. Wimbourne.

1306 E101/369/6.
Present at the Whitsun Feast.
Received 20s.

MONHAUT (John de)

1290 E101/352/12.
Court minstrel; later, Herald and King of Heralds.
f. 11v Johannes de Mohaut, menestrallus.
40s. in sterlings paid to him on pawn of 8 belts remaining in the custody of John de Drokenesford, in the Wardrobe.
8 August. Carlisle.

1294/5 Fryde, 156.
13s. 4d. prest, for his wages when he was in Court.
17 July. Biriton (Salop.).

1296/7 Add. MSS. 7965.
f. 52r Monhaut [Rex haraldorun]. 40s. for performing at the wedding of Princess Elizabeth.

MONTESORI (John)

1358/9 MS. Cott. Galba E xiv.

f. 52v 6s. 8d. to John Montesori, harper, for making his minstrelsies in the presence of the Lady Queen (Isabella) at Hereford.
By gift of the same. 9 July.

MORAND (Taborer)

1303/4 Add. MSS. 8835.

f. 122v [Sub Jocalia]. A gold clasp, worth 70s., given to Morand le Taborier, by the King, for making his minstrelsy in the presence of the King.
3 February. Dunfermline.

MORAVIA (John de)

1312 Bain II 420.
Johannes de Moravia has a bay horse, valued at £10.

MOREL (Nicholas)

King of Arms. King Herald of Edward I.

1282 CCR.

p. 169 Gift by the King to Nicholas Morel of 4 oak stumps for fuel, from Clarendon Forest.
7 October. Rhuddlan.

1290 C.47/4/5.

f. 38r To Nicholas Morel, King of Heralds, 20s. for his winter outfit.

f. 40v 20s. for his summer outfit.
Chichester.

1290 E101/352/24. [Household Account of King and Queen].
Summer and winter outfits issued to Nicholas Morel, 'the other King of Heralds', alter Rex Haraldorum.

1290 C47/4/4.

f. 17v 20s. prest, for his wages.
22 April, Chichester.

f. 20v paid 7 1/2d. per day for his wages from 1 August to last day of April; 273 days, bar 171, when he was not at Court - 63s. 9d.

1291 CCR. 131.
Order to the Keeper of the Forest of Clarendon, to cause Nicholas Morell to have in that forest 2 leafless oak stumps for fuel, of the King's gift.
24 October. Abergavenny.

1293 *Fryde*.

p. 160 To *Colin Morel Rex*, 13s. 4d. for his wages.
On the march, in Bar.

p. 169 20s. for his wages.
14 May. Talybont. (Caernarvonshire)

p. 177 13s. 4d. prest, for his wages.
6 October. Canterbury.

p. 181 13s. 4d. prest for his wages.
21 November. Winchelsea.

1294 *CCR*. 367.

Gift, by the King, to Nicholas Morel, of 4 does from Clarendon Forest.
30 August. Down Amprey.

1294/5 *Fryde*.

p. 27 £4 11s. 10^{1}/2d. to Nicholaus Morel, King of Heralds, as prest for his wages (at 7^{1}/2d. per day) for 162 days, bar 15, when he was absent.
14 May. Talybont.

p. 43 78s. 9d. for his wages from 1 May to 19 November, during which time he was in Court 126 days.
[*Inde debentur ei* – 52s. 1d. London 1298].

1296/7 *Add. MSS. 7965*.

f. 52^{r} To *Morell, Rex*, 50s. for making his minstrelsy before Princess Elizabeth and her husband, at their wedding.

f. 126^{v} *Morellus Rex*.
20s. for his Winter outfit.

1297 *CCR*. 81.

To the prior and convent of Merton. The King is sending to them Nicholas Morel, who is incapacitated from work by infirmity of the body, and requests them to admit him into their house with a groom and a horse, and that they will find him his necessaries according to requirements of his estate. The King wills that he shall not long stay there, but that he shall stay for a time only, provided he behave himself courteously and honestly. If he behave otherwise, the prior and convent are to certify the King full of his behaviour.
24 January. Bury St. Edmunds.

1299 CCR. 244.
Order to the Treasurer and Barons of the Exchequer to cause N. Morel to be acquitted of a 10 marks fine, which had been imposed upon him before John de Vescy, Justice of the Forest beyond Trent, for taking a hind in Sherwood Forest without the King's permission, because the King had pardoned the fine in 1293.
20 April (1299) Westminster.

MORLEY (William de)

King's Harper.

1299/1300 E101/357/5. (4 membranes)

mem. 1. 27s. 11d. received (by the Wardrobe) out of the wages of Guillot, King's Minstrel, which were allocated to him in the Marshalcy in May and July, for the period in which he received hay and oats from the Marshalcy.

mem. 3/4 39s. 4 1/2d. paid to Guillot Menestrallus, for his wages for 63 days.
Knaresborough.

[This might be Guillot Le Sautreour or some other Guillot]

c. 1300 E101/371/8. (Pt. I. fragments)
frag. 101 Gillot de Morle.

1300/1 E101/359/6.

f. 11v 13s. 4d. prest, for his wages.
28 July. Peebles.

f. 12r Guillot Citharista collected Robert Parvus' wages.
19 October. Dunipace.
prests, for his wages:
10s. 19 August. Cambusnethan.
2s. 7 September. Bothwell.
1/2 mark. 18 September. Dunipace.
13s. 4d. 19 October. Dunipace.
1/2 mark. 9 November. Linlithgow.

1302/3 Add. MSS. 35292.

f. 26v 20s. for his wages, to Guillot de Morle harper; into his own hands.
[8 February] Dunfermline.

1302/3 E101/364/13.

f. 26r 71s. 3d. to Guillot de Morley, for his wages at 7 1/2d. per day, for the whole of 1302/3, during which time he was in Court for 114 days.

f. 75v 1 mark prest for his wages.
29 December. Odiham.
1/2 mark, by the hand of Nicholas the Harper.
17 March. London.
10s. 9 November. Dunfermline.

1304/5 E101/368/6.

f. 13r 20s. prest, for his wages.
8 January. Kingston Lacy.

1304/5 E101/368/6.

f. 13r £4 to Gillot de Morle, Johannes de Newenton, Hugo de la Rose and Adam Clyderhowe, on account. 20s. each by the hand of Master Gillot.
8 January. Kingston Lacy.

See CLITHEROE (Adam)

1304 CPR. 283

Commission of oyer and terminer to Ralph de Sandwich and John le Blund, mayor of London, on complaint by William de Morlegh, that while he was in Scotland on the King's service and under his protection, John de Hoy, merchant of Dinan (Dynaund) carried off (rapuit) Agnes, his wife, at London, and led her away, with his goods, which he still detains.

1305/6 E101/369/11.

f. 103v 46s. 4 1/2d. to Guillot de Morleye, King's Harper, who had his horse valued in the Scottish War 1299/1300, for his wages from 14 July 1300, on which day his horse was valued, to 4 September, on which day he departed from the King's army; the first day included, but not the last. 52 days at 12d. per day (7 1/2d. from the Marshalcy and 4 1/2d. from the Wardrobe).

[This entry proves that Gillot entered upon his 'army' duty on the day Caerlaverock Castle was taken and so proves that he was present at the rejoicings (if not at the siege itself). He did not leave until Sunday, 4 September, when the King was at Holmes-Cultram, in Cumberland.]

f. 114r 43s. 6d. for his wages, from 27 July (1301), on which day his horse was valued, to 19 November (1301), both days included; 116 days at 12d. per day. To the same, (Guillot de Morleye, <u>citharista Regis</u>), for his wages from 20 November (1302) to 10 February (1302), both days included; for 87 days at 12d. per day - 31s. 1½d.

f. 204v Guilot de Morle, taking John de Newenton his wages.

See <u>JOHN</u> (Newentone de)

1306 <u>E101/369/6</u>.
Present at the Whitsun Feast. Received 2 marks.
Styled: Monsire Gillot Le Harpour Le Rois.

1305/6 <u>E101/368/27</u>.

f. 22r 23s. 9½d. prest, for his wages, for the year, during which time he was in Court 38 days.
[1 March. London?]

f. 61v 20s. prest, for his wages.
31 January. London.

f. 67r 13s. 4d. prest for his wages. (<u>Willelmus</u> de Morle).
23 October. London.
20s. prest for his wages (<u>Guillotus</u> de Morle)
2 January. Kingston Lacy.

[He also collected 20s. each for his 3 fellow harpers: John de Newenton, Hugh de la Rose and Adam de Clitheroe].

1306/7 <u>E101/370/16</u>.

f. 3v (p. 46) <u>Gillotus</u> de Morle; 1 mark, by the hand of John de Newenton.
24 December. Lanercost.

f. 6r (p. 51) 1 mark.
1 February. Lanercost.

f. 8r (p. 55) Guillot de Morley, <u>Citharista</u>; 1 mark.
23 February. Lanercost.

f. 9r (p. 57) ½ mark.
26 March (Easter Day) [Carlisle].

f. 10v (p. 60) 1 mark.
21 April. [Carlisle]

f. 11r (p. 61) 1 mark.
24 April. [Carlisle]

f. 13r (p. 65) 1 mark.
21 May (Sunday) [Carlisle]

1310/11 E101/374/5.

f. 90v 1 mark, prest, for his wages.
'Edulnestone'. 26 September.
1 mark.
10 November. Berwick-on-Tweed.
100s. by the hand of Ricard Wolewych.
24 December. Berwick-on-Tweed.
40s. 6 January. Berwick-on-Tweed.
1/2 mark. 3 February. Newcastle-on-Tyne.

1311/12 E101/373/26.

f. 73v 1/2 mark, prest, for his wages.
22 December. Westminster.

1322 Foedera II, pars. I. 498 and CPR 210.

Grant for life to Willelmus de Morle, called 'Roi du North', ministrallus Regis, of the houses with their appurtenances, in Pontefract, which had belonged to Roi Bruant.

28 October. York.

See BRUANT.

1326 MS. Soc. of Antiq. 122.

f. 64v Will[elme] Roi des Heraux.
30s. paid, at Caversham, to William, King of Heralds, for a blue samite Haketon with a 'rue' on it and a helm with a visor ornamented at the sides. The haketon and helm were delivered to Monsire Thomas Wycher, knight, [by] the valet, master Hugh, of the said Thomas, at the Cascoigne, in the seventeenth year of our lord the King, and it was not then paid [for] and it is paid today.
Thursday, 22 May. 'Bristlesham'.

MORLEYNS (John)

1335/8 MS. Cott. Nero. C.viii.

f. 226r Johannes Morleyns (minstrel in the household of Edward III).
20s. for his outfit.

MOXHAM (John de)

1300/1 Add. MSS. 7966A.

f. 68v John de Moxham was the boy chosen to be Boy Bishop on the Feast of St. Nicholas (6 December) at Southwell.
40s. when he came to the King at Newstead in Sherwood.
By gift of the King; by the hand of Ralph de Stanford. Chaplain.
6 December. Newstead.

N

NAGARY

1306 Prince's Crowder.

E101/369/6.
Nagary le Crowder *Principis*. Present at the Whitsun Feast. Received 5s.

NAUNTON (Hugh de)

1300/1 Court Harper; later, King's Harper.
Add. MSS. 7966A.

f. 100v [£6 10s.] to Hugo de Naunton, for his wages from 13 July, on which day his horse was valued, to 20 November, both days included. 130 days at 12d. per day. (7½d. from the Marshalcy and 4½d. from the Wardrobe).
29 July [1301/2]. London.

?1298 C47/22/9. also, Bain, II 256.
fragment 123.
A letter, in French, from Hugh de Naunton to Walter Bedwynd, King's Cofferer 1303/7.
[Bain's translation not altogether reliable. The MS is not good; cut away in 4 places.]

1302/3 E101/363/18.

f. 17r 20s. to Hugo de Nauntone for a sorrel hackney bought from him for the riding-out (*equitancia*) of John the Nakerer, Prince's minstrel.
24 December.

1302/3 Add. MSS. 35292.
f. 13^{v} 33s. 4d. for the Lord Prince, by the hand of Hugo de Naunton.
[? Gask. Perthshire].

1303/4 Add. MSS. 8835.
f. 63^{v} [Sub: Vadia Scutiferorum; thus proving that Hugh was a Squire of the Royal Household].
£13 4s. for his wages for 264 days at 12d. per day, because one of his horses was valued at Berwick-on-Tweed.
18 August.

[On my way home from Oxford, 2 August 1975, I called at Naunton, which is a small, charming, quiet village. In the Church was a list of known rectors; among them "Henry de Nawnetone 1301", I am not in the habit of indulging in speculation, but it seems to me that this Henry could have been a relative of Hugh; perhaps his father. Such a social background would have been fitting for one who became a court musician/singer.]

1304/5 E101/371/8. (Pt. I)
fragment 31. On it are given details of Hugh's appointment as Court Harper. He arrived at Court on wages, for the first time, 20 May, with two horses and a groom. There follows a list of the periods during which he was at Court, on duty, until the following August twelvemonth.

See Menestrellorum Multitudo, pp. 21/2.
fragment 41. Hugo de Naunton, harpator - 1 mark.

1305/6 E101/368/27.
f. 59^{r} prests, for his wages:
1 mark. 17 June. Westminster.
10s. 1 November. Lanercost.

1306/7 E101/370/16.
f. 1^{v} (p. 42) 10s. for his wages. 26 November. Lanercost.
f. 3^{v} (p. 46) 1 Mark. 24 December. Lanercost.
f. 6^{r} (p. 51) 1 mark. 1 February. Lanercost.
f. 9^{r} (p. 57) 1/2 mark. 26 March [Easter Day] [Carlisle]
f. 10^{r} (p. 59) 20s. to Hugo de Nauntone vallettus for money owing to him in the Scottish war in 1303/4.
13 April. [Carlisle].

1310/11 E101/374/5.

f. 51r 34s. to Hugh de Naunton; prest, for his expenses in going, for the King, from Windsor to Wallingford; in cash; given him by Wengefeld. 22 July. Windsor.

f. 87v prests, for his wages:
40s. by the hand of Laurence de Elmham. 9 July. Westminster.
40s. by the hand of Walter, his groom 27 July. St. Albans.
100s. receiving the money himself from Lymburgh.
9 October. London.

1311/12 E101/373/26.

f. 73r 60s. for his wages/
14 November. Westminster.

1315/16 E101/376/7.

f. 91r His name heads a list of 19 who were out of Court at Christmas, 9 Ed. II, and so received 'nihil' for their winter outfit.

f. 123v £4 18s. 1 1/2d. owing to Hugh de Naunton for his outfits for 8 and 9 Ed. II.

1319/20 MS. Soc. of Antiq. 120.

f. 165r No issue of winter outfit to him, because he was out of Court.

1320/21 MS. Soc. of Antiq. 121.

f. 116v 20s. to Hugo de Naunton for his winter outfit. 14 December. London. (?1319/20)

f. 129r 20s. for his summer outfit.
11 December 1320/21. London.

NEWENTON[E] (John de)

King's Harper.

c.1300 E101/371/8. [Miscellanea from the Marshalcy. A box of fragments.]

frag. 16 Johannes de Newentone, harpator.

frag. 41 Johannes de Newentone, harpator – 1 mark.

frag. 48 1/2 mark, for his wages.
12 August. apparently at Newport (Pagnell) but the year is not specified.

frag. 101 [a page from a Wardrobe Account, which has been entered and therefore crossed out. Among the names: Johannes de Newentone].

1302/3 Add. MSS. 35292.

f. 7v 10s. for his wages.
11 August. Brechin (Forfarshire)

f. 9v 10s. for his wages.
Brechin.

f. 12r Johannes de Neutone, citharista.
1/2 mark (for his wages).
17 October. Dundee.

1302/3 E101/364/13.

f. 74r Johannes de Neutone, Citharista: prests, for his wages:
2s. 4 December. Hungerford.
1 mark. 29 December. Odiham.
1/2 mark, by the hand of Nicholas, Citharista.
17 March. London.
10s. 11 August. Brechin.
1/2 mark. 29 May. Roxburgh.
10s. 28 June. St. John de Perth.
1/2 mark. 17 October. Dundee.
10s. 9 November. Dunfermline.

f. 81v Johannes de Newentone, Citharista Regis.
10s. prest, for his wages.
1 September.

f. 82r collecting the wages of Nicholas.

See BLUND, (Nicholas le)

1303/4 Add. MSS. 8835. (sub Jocalia).

f. 122v A gold clasp, worth 8 marks, given by the King to John de Newentone, Harper, at Dunfermline. 4 February.

1304 CPR. 283.

Commission of oyer and terminer to Ralph de Sandwich and Robert de Burghersh, touching persons who by night broke the houses of John le Harper of Newenton, at Newenton, co. Kent.
9 August. Stirling.

1304/5 E101/368/6.

f. 13r 20s. prest, for his wages, by the hand of Master Gillot (de Morley).
8 January. Kingston Lacy.

See CLITHEROE, (Adam de)

1305/6 <u>E101/369/11</u>. and <u>MS. Harley</u>. 152.
f. 203^{v} 20s. prest for his wages, by the hand of Guillot de Morley.
2 January. Lanercost.

1305/6 <u>E101/368/27</u>.
f. 67^{r} 20s. prest for his wages: collected for him by William de Morley.
2 January (1305). Kingston Lacy.

N.B. f. 62^{v}
20s. prest for his wages to
<u>Hugoni de Newenton, Cithariste</u>.
This entry could refer to either John de Newenton or Hugh de Naunton, because the clerk has entered, in the margin, <u>De Newentone, Citharista</u>, but has put the prest down to Hugo de Newenton, as above. I am inclined to think that the Clerk meant John, but got mixed in his mind with the Christian names. [A not uncommon fault].
4 September. Newborough in Tyndale.

1306/7 <u>E101/369/16</u>.
f. 19^{v} <u>Johannes</u> le Harpour, [who can be no other than John de Newenton, because he receives the following prest with Adam de Clitheroe and Hugh].
27s. 6d. prest, the price/value of $3^{1}/2$ ells of bluet cloth, $3^{1}/2$ ells of striped and 1 lamb's fur: given to him by Ralph de Stokes, Clerk of the Great Wardrobe.
f. 10^{v} <u>Johannes</u> de Newe(n)ton.
24s. 6d. prest, the price of 7 ells of blue and green cloths ($3^{1}/2$ ells of each), given to him by Ralph de Stokes, Clerk of the Great Wardrobe.
f. 27^{v} prests for his wages:
10s. 28 November, per Adam de Cliderhou. Lanercost.

13s. 4d.	24 December.	Lanercost.
13s. 4d.	1 February.	Lanercost.
6s. 8d.	9 February.	Lanercost.
6s. 8d.	11 March.	Carlisle.
6s. 8d.	26 March.	Carlisle.
10s.	30 March.	Carlisle.
13s. 4d.	21 April.	Carlisle.
1 mark.	24 April.	Carlisle.
5s.	10 May.	Carlisle.
10s.	15 May.	Carlisle.
13s. 4d.	21 May.	Carlisle.
10s.	6 July.	Burgh-upon-Sands.

1306/7 E101/370/16.

f. 1v (p. 42) 10s. [for his wages, by the hand of *dominus Adam* (i.e. Adam de Clitheroe)]. 26 November. Lanercost.

f. 3v (p. 46) 1 mark. 24 December. Lanercost.

f. 6r (p. 51) 1 mark. 1 February. Lanercost.

f. 9r (p. 57) 1/2 mark. 26 March (Easter Day). [Carlisle.]

f. 10v (p. 60) 1 mark. 21 April. [Carlisle].

f. 11r (p. 61) 1 mark. 24 April. [Carlisle].

f. 12v (p. 64) 10s. 15 May (Whit Monday) [Carlisle].

f. 13r (p. 65) 1 mark. 21 May (Trinity Sunday) [Carlisle].

1306 E101/369/16.

Present at the Whitsun Feast. Received 2 marks.

1342 *Cal. Fine Rolls. V. 288*.

Order to the Escheator, John de Vielston, to take into the King's hands the lands late of John of Newenton.

NEWENTON (Robert)

King's/Prince's *Nuncius*

1302/3 E101/363/18.

f. 5r 8s. to Robert de Newentone, *nuncius*, for making journeys at one time from London and at another from Odiham to the Constable of Windsor Castle, fetching the 5 boys [the choristers. See *Menestrellorum Multitudo*, s.v. *Pueri Principis*] to Court at Warnebourne (?) for the Prince's chapel, to serve there on Christmas Day: for the price of 5 hackneys, for carrying the boys, together with other expenses between the places. Into his own hands. 24 December. Warneborne.

{NEWSOM (Henry)
{NUSHAM

Prince's/later, King's (Ed. II) harper.

1306 E101/369/6.

Present at the Whitsun Feast. Received 1 mark.

1325/6 E101/381/11. (Two collections of fragments, chiefly mandates for knights' liveries, with receipts; and a list of household officers being issued clothing, to go with the King (Ed. II) to France). Among the minstrels: Henri Neusom.

1326 Soc. of Antiq. MS. 122 (Account of the King's Chamber. In French).

f. 50r King's Harper. 40s. paid to Henri Newsom, harpour le Roi and Richardyn, Cytoler le Roi, for making their minstrelsy before the King and the Countess Marshal [Countess of Norfolk, King's sister-in-law], who was dining with the King ce jour. 20s. to each of them.
Thursday, 30 January.

NICHOLAS (harper)

Harper of Robert de Vere, earl of Oxford.

1298 GOUGH 39.
Letters of protectiom for Nicholaus le Harpour qui cum Robert de Ver, Comite Oxonie, while he is staying in Scotland.

1299 CPR. 444, 447.
Nicholas le Harpour, nominated by 'Robert de Veer, earl of Oxford', for one year, as one of his attorneys, while the earl, accompanied by John de Drokenesford, went overseas.

1300 Cal. Chancery Warrants.
Mandate to make letters of attorney for Nicholas le Harpour, general attorney of Robert de Vere, earl of Oxford. Robert had gone overseas and had nominated Nicholas to be his attorney in a suit the abbot of St. Albans was prosecuting against himself, Stephen the Bailiff of Dylewyk and Richard le Fevre, also of Dylewyk, for trespass.

NICHOLAS (trumpeter)

King's or Court Trumpeter.

1314/17 MS. Cott. Nero. C.viii.

f. 192v 46s. into the hands (per manus) of Nicholaus Trumpour, in part payment of 106s. owed to him for his war-wages and livery and compensation for his horses.
23 January. By a bill.

?1318/19 f. 196r 60s. into the hands of Nicholas the Trumpeter, for money owed to him.
19 December. By a bill.

NOBLET (Bastin)

1290 C47/4/5.
f. 48r 10s. to Bastin Noblet of Liege, acrobat, (saltator) by gift of the King.
[He had evidently come to perform at the wedding festivities of Princess Margaret].
18 July. Westminster.

NORFOLK (John de)

King's mounted messenger.

1319/20 Add. MSS. 17632.
f. 39r 12d. to John de Norfolk, nuncius, for his expenses, when carrying letters of the King (Ed. II) under Privy Seal, to Sir Andrew de Harclay (Andreas de Hercla).
16 July.

NORFOLK (Thomas de)

King's Herald.

1302/3 E101/364/13.
f. 97v Prests, for his wages:
10s. 26 June. St. John de Perth.
20s. 31 August. Fyvie (Aberdeen).
13s. 4d. 20 October. Dundee.
1 mark. 11 November. Dunfermline.

1305/6 E101/369/11.
f. 100v Thomas de Norffok, harald.
20s. for his expenses on his journey [with 2 other heralds, Roger Macheys and John Butler] between Winchester and London.
6 April. [Winchester).

1306 E101/369/6.
Present at the Whitsun Feast. Received 40s.

NORRIS (Andrew)

1311/12 MS. Cott. Nero C.viii.
King of Heralds for Ed. II and Ed. III.
[Perhaps the 'Master Andrew' of the 5 boys of the Prince]
f. 195r Andreas Noreys, Rex h[a]raldorum [MS. 'hor']
53s. 4d. into the hands of Andrew Norris, King of Heralds, for money owed to him for his war-wages and his livery.
21 July [?1318]. By a bill.

1335/8 f. 226r 20s. for his outfit. (He was now King of Heralds in the household of Ed. III).

NORTHLEY (Roger de)

Court Minstrel.
1325/6 E101/381/11. (fragments)
From a list of the King's household minstrels (Ed. II)

Roger de Northle.
1328 E101/383/4. (pp. 375/6)
Listed among the squire minstrels of Ed. III's household.

Rogerus [d]e Northley.
1330 E101/385/4. (p. 381)
Again, as above: Rogerus de Northley.

O

OWYNFLET (John de)

1311/12 Harper of the King's household.

MS. Cott. Nero. C.viii.
f. 194r 24s. 3½d. into the hand of John de Owynflet Citharista hospicii regis, for money owing to him for his outfit.
24 February. By a bill.

O[YSE]L

1300/1 E101/359/5.

f. 2r 10s. paid to Master Ralph de Manton, by the hand of O...l, minstrel of Lord John of Bretagne.

[This is a purely speculative reading on my part; Oysel was an ordinary surname. cf. CPR (1301/7): Richard Oysel; Tout, State Trials of the Reign of Ed. I. (Camden Ser. 3rd. Ser. Vol. ix. ii. Henricus Oysel].

OYSELE (Janyn de)

1285/6 Vielle-player of the Duke of Burgundy.

E101/352/4.
Membrane 3.

no. 2015 And for 1 cup, silver gilt, worked with enamel, with foot and cover, of 2 1/2 marks' 16d. weight; value 60s; given by the King to Janyn de Oysele, vielle-player of the Duke of Burgundy.

OYSILLET

1290 Minstrel of the King of Scotland.

C47/4/5.

f. 45v 40s. to Oysillet, the minstrel of the King of Scotland, by gift of the King (Ed. I), when he attended (and performed at) the wedding of Princess Joanna.
8 May.

P

PAGE

1296/7 King of Heralds [?of the Count of Holland]
Add. MSS. 7965.

f. 52r 50s. to King Page, for making his minstrelsy on the wedding-day of Princess Elizabeth [she married the Count of Holland].
By gift of the King.
8 January. Ipswich.
25s. by gift of the King, being the price of a habergeon bought from a certain sailor and given to Page, by the Seneschal, at Harwich.
18 January.

PARVUS (Brother Andrew)

1302/3 E101/363/18. Prince's Minstrel.

f. 13v 24s....for silk and satin and cloth [*felum*, *velum*] together with the making of 18 'garnishings' of various cloth, given to the Prince and bought...at different times in the Scottish war...which garnishings (*garniamenta*) he afterwards gave to his minstrels and squires; for cash given to brother Andrew *parvus* [*fratri Andree paruo*], his minstrel, by order of the Prince, to buy a tunic for himself.

[Payment to Michael Cissor, valet and tailor of the Wardrobe. The cloths and garnishings were for the clothes the Prince wore at Christmas, Easter and Whitsun. It is not clear from the MS. whether Andrew was 'little brother Andrew' or Brother Andrew Little].

PARVUS (Robert)

King's Herald/King of Heralds.

1277 MS. Cott. Vesp. C.xvi.

f. 3 "to King Robert, Minstrel squire-at-arms [*Rex Robertus Ministrallis scutifer-ad-arma*] staying, on King's wages, in the fortification of Berwick-on-Tweed, receiving 12d. per day..."
(Quoted by Ward: *Cat. Rom*. I. 610-15).

1285 E101/361/17. (Counter Roll of domestic payments to members of the King's Household).

Listed among the minstrels:
'Master Robert'.
(in all probability, Robert Parvus).

1285/6 E101/352/4. (Counter-roll of Jewels).

Membrane 1.

No. 1983 By Lady de Gorges for 1 cup of the same type (i.e. silver gilt with foot and cover) of 3 marks 2 ounces weight, value 60s., given to the lady Queen consort by order of the King, to be carried (given) to Master Robert Parvus, King.

[From a later entry (no. 1986) we learn that she was Lady Elena de Gorges].

No. 1987 By Roger de Insula, 1 cup of the same type, of 3 marks' weight, value 70s. given by the King to the wife of Master Robert Parvus, King of heralds. 24 May.

1286/7 MS. Addit. Roll. 6710. (Issue of outfits to those remaining in Court)
To Robert Parvus, King of Heralds, for his winter outfit for the 15th and 16th years - 40s.

1290 C.47/4/5.
f. 38r 20s. to Robert Parvus, King of Heralds, for his winter outfit for the present year. Paid into his own hands.

1290 E101/352/24. (King's and Queen's Household Account)
sub Menestralli being issued winter and summer outfits:
Robert Parvus, King of Heralds.

1294/5 Fryde.
p. 46 Memorandum, that Robert Parvus, King of Heralds, is not on the Marshalcy Roll for the whole of the year.
p. 164 13s. 4d. prest, for his wages.
p. 185 Magister Robertus Parvus, Rex Haraldorum. 20s. 2 1/2d., on account, for money owing to him in payment of his wages for the year 1293/4, for prests made to him the same year beyond his wages, which he had, on account, in 1293 and 1294 in 3 parcels [particulis], 113s. 4d.; and his wages came to £4 13 1 1/2d. and so in payment of the aforesaid account the same as above (i.e. 20s. 2 1/2d.) is owing.

1301 Add. MSS. 7966.
f. 178r 1 mark to King Robert, King's Trumpeter. (Trumpator Regis), prest, for his wages.
18 July. Peebles.
To the same, into his own hands, 20s.
19 August. Cambusnethan (Lanarks.)
To the same, 13s. 4d.
7 September. Bothwell.
To the same, by the hand of William, the harper. (i.e. William Morley) 20s.
20 October. Dunipace
Total: 65s. 8d.
f. 178v 20s. to Robert, Rex Haraldorum, into his own hands.
9 November. Linlithgow.

1301 E101/359/6. [cf. with Add. MSS. 7966, above]

f. 11v To King Robert, Trumpator Regis, prest for his wages - 13s. 4d. into his own hands.
28 July. Peebles.

f. 12r To Robert, Rex haraldorum, prest for his wages, 20s. into his own hands.
19 August. Cambusnethan.
13s. 4d. prest for his wages, into his own hands.
7 September. Bothwell.
20s. by the hand of Guillaume Citharista (Wm. Morley).
19 October. Dunipace.
20s. into his own hands.
9 November. Linlithgow.
Total: 65s. 8d.

1302/3 E101/364/13.

f. 81v Robertus Rex Haraldorum.
10s. prest for his wages:
22 April. York.

1303/4 E101/365/20. (A roll of divers expenses of the household of the Countess of Hereford).
6 marks to King Robert, the minstrel and 15 of his minstrel companions, for making their minstrelsies in the presence of the Countess and other of the nobility on the day on which the countess was purified ("churched").
by gift of the Countess there*
11 October [?Knaresborough].
*[The account begins in July, in Linlithgow and she and her household gradually journeyed southward. As she made an oblation at the tomb of Robert of Knaresborough, on 13 October, the household may have been there (or near it) on 11 October. The last place noted on the roll is 17 October, Pocklington].

1303/4 Add. MSS. 8835.

f. 42r Rex Robertus. 40s. to Robert, king of heralds, for making his minstrelsy in the presence of the King.
By gift of the King, into his own hands.
1 January [Feast of Circumcision] Dunfermline.

1306 E101/369/11 and MS. Harley. 152 f. 18^v

f. 96^r 200 marks to King Robert and certain (other) Kings of Heralds, and also to other divers minstrels, for making their minstrelsies before the King and other nobles, at Westminster on the day of Pentecost, when the Prince was Knighted.
The gift of the Prince, by order of the King, by the hand of Walter Reynolds, Keeper of the Prince's Wardrobe.
The money [to be] distributed in the name of the Prince.
23 May (Whitmonday). London.

f. 203^v 1 mark to King Robert, King of heralds, prest for his wages.
4 November. Lanercost.

1306 E101/369/6.
Le Roy Robert. Present at the Whitsun Feast.
Received 5 marks.

1306 E101/368/27.

f. 65^r 1 mark to King Robert, King of Heralds, prest for his wages.
4 November. Lanercost.

1306/7 E101/369/16.

f. 9^v 27s. 6d. prest, to King Robert, being the cost of 3 1/2 ells of bluet cloth, 3 1/2 ells of striped and 1 lamb's fur; given to him by Ralph de Stokes, Clerk of the Great Wardrobe.

f. 26^r prests, for his wages:

1 mark.	25 November.	Lanercost.
10s.	29 December.	Lanercost.
13s. 4d.	1 February.	Lanercost.
30s.	15 April.	Carlisle.

1306/7 E101/370/16.

f. 6^r (p. 51) 1 mark to King Robert (together with 1 mark each to King Copinii, Adam de Clitheroe and Hugh de Naunton)
1 February. Lanercost.

1311/12 <u>E101/374/16</u>.

<u>Robertus Rex menestrallorum</u>.

p. 3. 13s. 4d. to Robert, King of the minstrels, for his wages.

15 November. Berwick-on-Tweed.

p. 4. <u>Rex Robertus Taborarius</u>.

26s. 8d. to King Robert, the Taborer, for his wages, concerning the fortification of the town of Berwick.

19 November. [Berwick].

1311/12 <u>MS. Cott. Nero. C.viii</u>.

f. 84v To King Robert and other divers minstrels, for making their minstrelies in the presence of the King and other nobles, in the Houses of the Friars Minor, at York, on the day of the purification of the Lady Margaret, Countess of Cornwall [niece of Ed. II, sister of Earl Gilbert of Gloucester and wife of Piers Gaveston].

By gift of the King; by the hand of the said King Robert, given the money for distributing among them - 40 marks.

20 February. York.

f. 86r 40s. to King Robert, for carrying to the King, large, white pearls, of his own accord [<u>ex parte sua propria</u>]. By gift of the King.

25 April. Newcastle-on-Tyne.

1312 <u>Bain</u> III.

p. 399 <u>Rex Robertus, menestrallus scutifer-ad-arma</u>.

To King Robert, minstrel squire-at-arms, remaining on King's wages in the aforesaid [Berwick] fortification, receiving 12d. per day for his wages from 1 August of the 5th year [i.e. 1311/12] to the last day of December, both days included; for 153 days, £7 13s.

p. 417 (Roll of Horses).

King Robert the Minstrel has a dappled sorrel horse, valued at £20.

1312/13 <u>E101/375/8</u>.

f. 14v [...] to King Robert for a dappled sumpter-horse bought from him and given to Robert Gascoigne, sumpter of the King's butlery, for carrying the vessels of his office.

17 May. London.

1316/17 *MS. Soc. of Antiq. 120*.

f. 104^{v} 70s. to King Robert, staying at York and coming to the lord King there, to get help, in the month of October of the present year. By gift of the King, as for [*nomine*] his wages and 2 of his horses which were taken there; by the hand of Sir Simon Warde, Sheriff, who gave him the money, by order of the King under Privy Seal.
28 May 11 Ed. II (1317/18). York.

1317/18 *MS. Soc. of Antiq. 121*.

f. 59^{r} 40s. 10d. to King Robert, ill, at York. By gift of the lord King, as for his expenses for 2 grooms and their horses.
By the hand of the (said) Sheriff, paid to him in cash, by order of the King.
26 May. Westminster.

1319/20 *Add. MSS. 17632*.

f. 33^{v} *Rex Robertus menestrallus*.
33s. $2^{1}/2$d. to King Robert the minstrel, by gift of the lord King for a livery (*roba*) with three garnishings, to be made for him; being the cost of $4^{1}/2$ ells of coloured cloth and $4^{1}/2$ ells of striped given to him by Master Robert de Riston, against the feast of Pentecost of the present year (as is to be seen in the details [of the account] of the same Master Robert); and the cost of 2 budge furs for his over-tunic; given to him by the same for the aforesaid livery.

1320/21 *Add. MSS. 9951*. (Baldock's *Journal*)

f. 19^{n} *Robertus Rex Heraldorum...et Regalium functionum*.
£20 to Robert, King of Heralds and of Royal functions, and to other minstrels of the King, for making their minstrelsies at a banquet of the lord King, held at Amiens. By gift of the same lord King [or, of the lord King himself] into [or, by] his own hands.
8 July, the beginning of the present [regnal] year. [i.e. 1320]. Amiens.

PARVUS (Walter)

1297 One of the King's 'runners' or foot-messengers.

C. 47/4/6.
f. 12v and f. 14r to Walter parvus, for carrying letters of the King to the bailiff of Monmouth and letters of Lord J. de Hustwayt to South[ampton], on the King's business, 8d. for his expenses.

1304/5 E101/368/6.
f. 22r 22d. to parvus Walterus, for carrying letters of the King to the Sheriff of Berkshire.

1306 Add. MSS. 3766.
f. 5v 6s. to Walter parvus, for carrying letters of the King to the bishop of Chester; for his expenses.
1 August. Lazenby (Yorks.)

1306 E101/369/6.
if the same person; see GAUTERON (Le Petit).

1311/12 MS. Cott. Nero. C.viii.
parvus Walterus; Queen's messenger.
f. 148r expenses for carrying the Queen's letters:
to the Abbot of Newborough 6d.
3 August.
for going into Kent 17d.
29 October.
to John de Thweyt, bailiff of Cotyngham 2s.
22 November.
to Hugh de Wake, with a letter from the Exchequer 15d.
28 November.
to William Ingre 6d.
29 January. etc.

PARVUS (William)

1306 E101/369/6.
Organist of the Countess of Hereford.
Present at the Whitsun Feast. Received 5s.

1300/1 **N.B.** Add. MSS. 7966 (A).
f. 187r In a list of officers in the household of Elizabeth, Countess of Holland, under the heading: Camerarii, Sometarii et Palefridarii, there occurs: 'parvus Willelmus cum garc[i]one, comedit in aula'. Elizabeth married Humphrey de Bohun, earl of Hereford in 1302.

PATRICK

1296/7 Earl's Falconer/Trumpeter.
Add. MSS. 7965.
f. 54r 40s. to Patrick, Trumpeter, Falconer, for coming to the King with a certain falcon, on behalf of Earl Patrick [to receive licence to hunt?].
21 February. Denham.

PAVELY (Walter)

1300/1 E101/359/5.
f. 8r 20s. to Master Ralph de Manton, by the hand of Walter Pavely, trumpeter.
[16] July. Berwick-on-Tweed.

PEFER (Conrad Le)

1305/6 A geige-player from Germany.

E101/369/11.
f. 100v 60s. to Conrad le Pefer [or Fefer], geige-player, coming to the King, at the command of the King of Germany and staying in England during the months of March and April; for his expenses while so staying and returning to his own country, by licence of the King. By gift of the King.
10 April. Winchester.
[N.B. He stayed on for the knighting of the Prince in May. See GIGOUR (Le TIERZ)].

PERCY (Nicholas de)

Trumpeter of Ed. II.

1310/11 E101/373/26.

f. 26r First taken on Court wages on 21 November, at squire's pay of 7 1/2d. per day.

f. 74v 5s. for going to Scarborough and staying there; prest, for his wages. Paid to him at York, 18 March.

f. 76r 13s. 4d. prest, for his wages.
20 June. Burstwick.

1314/15 E101/376/7.

f. 40v 100s. to Nicholas de Percy, minstrel, for bringing to the King a certain book of customs (moribus) and the life of Lord Edward, the King's father. By gift of the King.
8 November. Clipstone.

1318/19 MS. Cott. Nero. C. viii.

f. 192v 46s. to Nicholas the trumpeter, in part payment of wages and outfits.

f. 196r 60s. in money owing to him.
19 December. [date uncertain].

PERINUS (TEUTONICUS)

Minstrel of Henry III.

1250 CCR. 308

For Peremis, the German. The King has given to Perin, the German, his player/minstrel [istrioni suo] the house, with all its appurtenances, in the parish of St. Laurence, London, which was the house of the Jew, Abraham de Berchamsted; and the justices responsible for the custody of the Jews are ordered to see to it that the aforesaid house, with its appurtenances, be handed over, in full seisin, to William [Chubb, King's Sergeant].
28 July. Clarendon.

PERICUS (ALEMANNUS)

1251

CPR. 104.

?the same person as Perinus?

Protection, until Christmas, for Pericius [in margin of MS. 'Pelerimus';] Alemanni, the bearer, the King's player/minstrel [istrioni].
4 August. Windsor.

See ALEMANNUS.

PERLE IN THE EGHE

1306 E101/369/6.
Present, with his companion, at the Whitsun Feast. Received 12d. and 1 mark; and 1 mark for his companion. Probably a blind or purblind minstrel. 'Pearl in the Eye' is the name for cataract or white spot in the eye. His socius or compaignon was, no doubt, his guide.

PERROT

1290 E101/352/21. (Roll, of money given to various people)
20s. to Perottus, a minstrel of Laner..., coming from the Earl Marshal to the King.
By gift of the King.

PEROU, PYREWE (Adinet de)

Minstrel of the Count of Flanders.

1289 Add. MSS. 35294. (Wardrobe Account of Queen Eleanor)
f. 10v 100s. to Adinettus de Perou (or, Perow?), minstrel of the Count of Flanders. By gift of the queen; by the hand of Master G. Feuer.
17 July. Havering-atte-Bower.

1290 C47/4/5.
f. 47v 66s. 8d. to Adinet de Pyrewe, minstrel of the Count of Flanders, by gift of the Countess of Gloucester, the King's daughter; by special order of the King.
26 June. Havering-atte-Bower.

E101/352/21. [Roll of money given to various people]
66s. 8d. to Adinet de Pyrewe, minstrel of the Count of Flanders, by gift of the King's daughter, the Countess of Gloucester: by special order of the King.

PETER (The Guitarist)

1306 Add. MSS. 22923. and MS. Harley 5001. f. 44v.
f. 10r 24s. to Peter le Guytarer, for coming to Lambeth, to the Prince's Court and making his minstrelsy in the presence of the lord Prince and other nobles in his entourage there.
By gift of the Prince, to buy himself an outfit.
By the hand of J. de Ringwood, who gave him the money there on the same day.
12 June.

MS. Harley 5001.

f. 48r Prince's Minstrels. 39s. to Peter le Gutterer and Henry de Blida, minstrels, for remaining in Court by order of the Prince and making their minstrelsies in his presence, in turns, or, on various occasions, for 52 days during the present year. As wages to both, at 4 1/2d. per day. On account, in cash, given to them at Ringwood.

E101/369/6.
Le Gitarier. Present at the Whitsun Feast. Received 1 mark.

PETER (the Taborer)

1306 E101/369/6.
Perotus le Taborer. Present at the Whitsun Feast. Received 40d.

See DUZEDEYS (PETER). May be the same person.

PETER (the Taborer)

Perhaps a minstrel of John de Vescy.

1278 CCR. 282.
Licence for John de Vescy to demise for life (by a writing which the King has inspected) to Peter le Taberur, land to the value of 100 marks yearly, in his manor of Chatton, held on chief.

13 November. Westminster.

[p. 420. Respite for life to John de Vescy of his debts to the king, on condition that his heirs answer for them after his death.]

1278/9 CCR. 512, 562.
Enrolment of a grant by John de Vescy to Peter le Taberer for life of 100 marks yearly of land in his manor of Chatton; rendering therefor a dove yearly. He also grants to Peter, for life, common of turbary and of heath (bruere) in the said manor and 20 cartloads of brushwood yearly in John's woods in the manor, except from John's park.

7 November. Westminster.

1279 Peter le Taberur acknowledges that he owes to John de Vescy 578 marks, to be levied, in default of payment, of his lands and chattels in Co. Northumberland.

26 April. Westminster.

PIRYE (PETER DE)

1318/19 MS. Soc. of Antiq. 121.

f. 126v 20s. for his summer outfit.
(He was a sergeant of the Pantry and Butlery, with R. Pilke and may, therefore, have been another King's Waferer.)

PETER (the Waferer)

1285 E101/351/17. Perotus le Vaufrur. King's Waferer.
Listed among the King's Minstrels and given £4.

PETER (the Waferer)

1335/8 MS. Cott. Nero. C.viii.

f. 226r Petrus Gaffrer. Waferer in the household of Ed. III.
20s. for his outfit.

PHILIP

1289 Add. MSS. 35294. (Wardrobe Account of Q. Eleanor)

f. 9v 40s. to Robert de Berneville, a minstrel of the King of France, by gift of the Queen, by the hand of Philip, the minstrel/player [istrio] of Lord Edmund, the King's brother.
11 May. Westminster.

PILKE (RICARD) (RICHARD)

First, Prince's then King's (Ed. II's) Waferer.

1295 CPR. 158.
Pardon, on account of his services in Gascony, to Richard Pilke for the death of Stephen de Fraunketon; and of his outlawry, if any, for the same, on condition that he stand trial on his return.
16 November. Udimore (Sussex).

1306 E101/369/6.
Present at the Whitsun Feast.
Received 1 mark.

1307 E101/373/15.

f. 5v Prests, for his wages:
1 mark, by the hand of Elena, his wife, 30 July [?Carlin]
20s. 3 September. Carlin.
20s. 27 October. Westminster.

1310/11 101/374/5.

f. 34^{r} 7s. 6d. to Richard Pilke, King's Waferer, receiving $7^{1}/2$d. per day for his wages, for the whole of the present, 4th (1310) year: namely, 365 days, during which time he was present in court 12 days.
30 November. 7th year (1313)

1310/11 E101/374/7. (Journal of the Wardrobe. paginated)

p. 5 5s. to the Clerk of the Pantry, for his office, by the hand of Ricard Pilke.

1311/12 E101/373/26. (Liber unde Respondebit)

Account of the Clerk of the Pantry.

f. 2^{r} 30s., by the hand of Ricard Pilke, concerning his 'office'.
3 September. Berwick-on-Tweed.
13s. 4d. by the hand of Ricard Pilke, King's Waferer, receiving the money for his 'office'. (i.e. work as Waferer).
19 September. Berwick-on-Tweed.

f. 2^{v} 20s. by the hand of Ricard Pilke, for his 'office', in cash; given to Elena, wife of the same Ricard.
14 October. Berwick-on-Tweed.

f. 3^{r} 4s. by the hand of William de Bosham, for the 'office' of Ricard Pilke, King's Waferer.
30 October. Windsor.

f. 4^{v} 5s. by the hand of Ricard Pilke, King's Waferer, for his 'office'.
17 May. York.

[All these entries mean that the Clerk of the Pantry was paying out money to Ricard for him to obtain the ingredients etc. for making wafers. They are not payments in respect of his wages.
His wife, Elena, evidently helped him in his 'office'].

1311/12 E101/374/19.

f. 8^{v} 20s. to [Ricard*] Pilke, King's Waferer and Elena, his wife, minstrels, for serving their wafers at the table of the two [young princes] and their household; and for making their minstrelsy in the presence of the two; and taking their leave to go to the lord King, who was in northern parts.
By gift [of the two] by the hand of J. de Weston.
24 June. Framlingham.

[*MS. has Willelmo, which must be a mistake.]

1311/12 MS. Cott. Nero. C.viii.
Ricardus Pylke, Waffrarius Regis.
f. 30v £7 10s. 0d., for money owing to him for his office in 1309.
To the same, for the same, for 1310- 117s. 7d.
To the same, for his wages, allocated to him on the Marshalcy Roll, in 1309 - 78s. 1½d.
To the same, for the same, for 1310 - 7s. 6d.
To the same, for his winter and summer outfits for 1309 and 1310 - £4.
Total: £21 13s. 2½d.
He received 21s. 8d. in squires' prests, in 1309.
To the same, 20s., given to him as the cost of his outfit in 1310.
Total disbursed to him: 46s. 8d.
And so, there are owing to him, according to his contract at London, 30 November 1313 - £19 6s. 6½d.
He has a bill.

1314 MS. Harley 315.
f. 49r An inventory of Jocalia remaining in the custody of John de Wakley 'now Keeper of the King's Wardrobe' (1309/10). There is a short list of gold and silver ewers, cups, spoons etc. and, on the last folio, on a ruled page, 4 entries, evidently payments for something (probably wages) of which the last is:
To Ricard Pilke, for the same, according to contract made with him, at London, the last day of November of the 7th year (1314) - 20s.

1314/15 E101/376/7 (a list of debita diversa)
[or later] f. 123r 60s. owing to Ricard Pilke, King's Waferer, for his outfits for the 8 and 9 Ed. II. (1314-16).

1316/17 MS. Cott. Nero. C.viii.
f. 10r 2 marks to Ricard Pilke, King's Waferer, for his winter outfit.
19 July. London.
f. 116r 20s. to Ricard Pilke, King's Waferer, for his summer outfit.
19 July. London.

1316/17 E101/373/26.

f. 26v 56s. 10 1/2d. to Ricard Pilke, who receives 7 1/2d. per day for his wages, for 365 days of the aforementioned leap year [so MS. ccclxv dies predictum annum bisextilem], during which time he was in Court for 91 days.
19 July. 10th year (1316/17). London.

1318/19 MS. Soc. of Antiq. 121.

f. 113r 20s. to Ricard Pilke, for his winter outfit.
2 November. (12 Ed. II). London.

[N.B. both Ricard and Brian are listed under serjeants of the Pantry and Butlery].

See BRIAN.

1320/21/23 Add. MSS. 9951. (Baldock's Journal)

f. 22r 40s. to Ricard Pilke, in compensation for a black horse of his, which was returned to the Almonry at Westminster on 14 May of the 16th year.
14 November (1323). London.

1324/5 CCR. 154.

Benedict de Shorne, fishmonger of London, acknowledged that he owed to Richard Pilke, Waferer, of London, 10 marks.

1325 CCR. 354.

John de Wroxhale acknowledged that he owed to Richard Pilk, citizen of London, £10.

PIPER (of the King)

1303 Add. MSS. 8835.

f. 42r

See KINGORN (JOHN DE)

PIPERS (of London)

1358/9 MS. Cott. Galba. E xiv.

f. 51v 10s. to 2 London pipers [fistulatores] for making their minstrelsy in the presence of the Lady Queen, on the feast of Easter and the 2 days following.
By gift of the same, by the hand of Edward Brouaret.
4 April.

POLIDOD (ROBERT)

1314/17 MS. Cott. Nero. C.viii. (The accounts of the Controllers of the King's Wardrobe. 1314/17).

f. 192r 18s. 7d. into the hand of Robert Polidod, King's minstrel, in part payment of 78s. 7d. owing to him for his wages in the war. [?Bannockburn], for his outfits and compensation for his horses
By a bill.
22 November.

1328 E101/383/4.

pp. 375/6 Listed among the squire minstrels of Ed. III's household:
Robertus Polidot.

1330 E101/385/4.

p. 381 Listed as one of the King's (Ed. III's) minstrels:
Robertus Polidode.

1335/8 MS. Cott. Nero. C.viii.

f. 226r 20s. to Robertus Polidod, minstrel in the King's household, for his outfit.

POVERETT

Minstrel of the Marshal of Champagne.

1290 C47/4/5.

f. 47r 20s. to Poverett, the minstrel of the Marshal of Champagne, who came to the wedding of Princess Joanna to Gilbert de Clare, earl of Gloucester on 30 April 1290; for making his minstrelsy at Westminster in the presence of the King.
By gift of the King on his departure.

THE KING'S BOYS

1271 Issue Rolls. 79

"£60 to Thomas de Pampelworth, clerk of Geoffrey de Picheford, Constable of Windsor Castle and Keeper of the King's (Hen. III's) Boys in the same castle, for the expenses of the boys aforesaid.

PUERI PRINCIPIS

The 5 boy trumpeters/choristers of Prince Edward, minstrels of the Prince's household.
They were: Richard the Rhymer, Crowder; Master Andrew; John Scot, trumpeter; Franceskin, nakerer; Roger de Forde, trumpeter.

1303 *E101/363/18*.
f. 5^{r} 8s. to Robert de Newentone, *nuncius*, sent on various occasions from London and Odiham to Windsor, to the constable of the Castle, to conduct the 5 boys there to Warnebourne(?), to the Court, for the Prince's chapel, to serve there over Christmas. Payment for 5 hackneys for carrying them; together with their expenses [incurred] between the said places.
Into his own hands; at Warnebourn.
24 December.

1306 *E101/369/6*.
Present at the Whitsun Feast.
Received 2s. each.

1305/6 *MS. Harley 5001*.
f. 32^{v} Boy minstrels/To *Ricard le Rimour, Magister Andrew, Janin Scot, Franceskin and Roger de Forde*, boy minstrels of the Prince's household, by his gift and grace, for the making of their gowns against the feast of Christmas, 12d. each, into their own hands.
21 December.

1306 *Add. MSS. 22923* and *MS. Harley 5001*. f. 40^{v}
f. 6^{r}
To Ricard le Rimour, going with letters of the Prince from Windsor to the Abbey of Shrewsbury, directing(?) him to stay at the Abbey for the purpose of learning the minstrelsy of the *Crwth*, 3s. by gift of the Prince for his expenses on his return.
7 April.

[See: i Letters of Edward, Prince of Wales, 1304/5. ed. Hilda Johnstone, p. 14.
ii Letters of the First Prince of Wales. ed. N. Hone. The Antiquary 31, 209.
iii Mrs Green, op.cit. vol.III. 47: a letter of the Prince to Sir John de London entreating him to "lend his clerk, who had taught his [i.e. the Prince's] children to sing, to his dearest sister, the countess of Hereford, to remain awhile in her chapel and to teach the children staying in the same chapel how to sing." [No reference given].

PURCHAS (THOMAS)

1314/17 MS. Cott. Nero. C.viii.
f. 192r £8 12s. 11d. into the hand of Thomas Purchaz, minstrel of the King's (Ed. II's) household, for money owed to him for his war-wages (?Bannockburn) and his outfits.
24 November; by a bill.

post 1328 MS. Cott. Galba. E iii. (probably Q. Philippa's Account)
f. 186r 7 ells (of yellow cloth and striped) and 1 lamb's fur, to Thomas Purchas, minstrel, for his summer outfit.

1335/8 MS. Cott. Nero. C.viii.
f. 226r 20s. to Thomas Purchace, for his outfit. [He was now a minstrel in the household of Ed. III].

PURLEY (JOHN)

1311/12 E101/374/19.
f. 8r 13s. 4d. to [King Druet and] John PERLE, trumpeter, minstrel of the lord Earl of Gloucester for making their minstrelsy in the presence of the two (young Princes, Thomas and Edmund).
By their gift, per Master John de Weston.
31 December. Chepstow.
[N.B. the spelling of Purley in the MS. There are innumerable examples in the MSS. of ...e being the equivalent of ...ey.]

See DRUET.

PYNKE

1289/90 Swinfield, 155.
"12d. to Pynke, the minstrel, at Colewell."

PYNKENYE (GUILLOT DE)

1290 E101/352/21. (Roll of money given to various people). 50s. to Guillot de Pynkenye, minstrel of the lord of Pynkenye, returning with his master, the aforesaid Sheriff [vicecomiti], from Court to his own parts. By gift of the King.

Q

QUEENHITHE (WILLIAM DE LA)

1307 E101/373/15.

f. 19r 20s. each to William de Quenheth, Janin the Trumpeter, Januche the Nakarer and Janin the Organist, minstrels of the King, for making their minstrelsies in the presence of the King, at Dumfries.
10 August. [Dumfries].

QUITACRE (RICARD DE)

1305/6 E101/369/11.
Harper of either the Countess Warenne or the Lady Despenser.

f. 96r £37 4s. 0d. given to Ricard de Quitacre, Ricard de Leyland, harpers, and divers other minstrels, making their minstrelsies in the presence of the King and other nobles, at Westminster, on the wedding-days of Johanna, daughter of the Comte de Baar, and Alienor, daughter of the Earl of Gloucester; that is to say, 20 May, on which day the Lady Johanna married the Earl Warenne, and 26 May, on which day the said Alienor married Lord Hugh le Despenser, the Younger, in the King's chapel at Westminster. The money was distributed at different times by various persons, in the house(hold) of Lord Otto de Grandison.
London.

1306 E101/369/6.
Present at the Whitsun Feast.
Ricardus de Quitacre, Citharista. Received 1/2 mark.
Richard de Whetacre, one of 'La Comune'.

RANCI (NICHOLAS DE)

Nicholas de Ranci. King's Minstrel (Ed. II).

1307 E101/373/15.

f. 7^{v} 1 mark, for his wages; into his own hands. 13 August. Lambeth.

RANULPH

King's trumpeter. (Ed. I)

1290 C47/4/4.

f. 26 [There are 2 pairs of trumpeters mentioned in this Wardrobe Book - Poncio de Caiark and Guielleme de Caiark - who were paid 60s. for their wages from 1 May to 16 July - and John and Ranulph. No note concerning their wages has been recorded. Probably the same as the two former].

See CAIARK.

RAULIN

Minstrel of the Earl Marshal [Hugh Bigod, earl of Norfolk].

1306 E101/369/6.

Present at the Whitsun Feast.
Received 3s. and 1 mark.

REGINALD (le Mentour)

A minstrel (? juggler) of John de Bourtetourte.

1306 E101/369/6

Present at the Whitsun Feast.
Received 12d.

REGINALD (the Waferer)

Prince's Waferer.

1302/3 E101/363/18.

f. 5^{r} 13s. 4d. to Reginald the Waferer, for a pair of irons, for his work; bought by him, for making wafers for the said Prince. 4 January.

f. 6v 4s. to Reginald the Waferer, sent from London to Blyth (Notts.) to the Court, with cloth and shoes, bought in London, by order of the Prince, for thirty Ash Wednesday poor folk; for the hire of a hackney to carry the cloth and shoes between the aforesaid places; for 4 days; receiving 12d. per day. And for the expenses for his horse and groom, for 6 days, during which he was going to and staying waiting at Court - 6s.
In the month of April. London.

f. 13r 40s. given to the Lord Edward, Prince of Wales, son of the King, at the town of St. John, of Perth, for his gambling with various soldiers there on the eve of St. John the Baptist. Given to him in cash, by the hand of Reginald the Waferer.

f. 25v [An interesting entry, throwing light on the different duties minstrels were expected to perform. It is entered under Nuncii. 'To Reginald, Waferer of the lord Prince, for carrying the Prince's letters under his Privy Seal...']

1302/3 E101/364/13.
f. 45v £4, by the hand of Reginald, the Prince's Waferer. Receiving cash from the said Master Walter (Reginald, Keeper of the Prince's Wardrobe), for an iron-grey horse sold to lord/master Grey de Pevercy, at Perth.
10 July.

REUE (ADAM DE)

1306 E101/369/6.
Present at the Whitsun Feast.
Styled 'Maistre'. Received 2 marks.

RICARD (the Guitarist)

1335/38 MS. Cott. Nero. C.viii.
f. 226r 20s. to Ricard the Guitarist [Ricardus Guttarer], minstrel in the household of Ed. III, for his outfit.

RICARD (the Harper)

1298 Gough. 184.
Richard the Harper, vallettus of Sir Walter de Beauchamp has a sorrel rouncy, valued at £10.

RICARD (of Carlisle)

1299/1300 LOG. 168. [f. 132]
6s. 8d. to Ricard, a harper of Carlisle, for coming before the King and making his minstrelsy.
By gift of the King at Carlisle.
14 November.

RICARD (the Harper)

Harper of Gilbert, earl of Gloucester.

1290 C47/4/5.
f. 47v 20s. for staying with the King at Havering-atte-Bower while other minstrels went to London, to perform at the Earl Marshal's wedding.
By gift of the King.

See JANIN, earl of Albemarle's minstrel.

1290 E101/352/12. (Private prests)
f. 17r To the Lady Queen, the King's consort, prest, conveyed to Janyn, the minstrel of the Earl Albemarle, Ricard *Harpator Comitis Gloucestrie* and Juglett, the minstrel of the Marshal of Champagne, 20s. each, because they stayed with the King and did not go to the Earl Marshal's wedding.

1290 E101/352/21. (Roll of money given to various people)
40s. to Ricard the harper of the Earl of Gloucester for staying with the King etc. (as above).
By gift of the King.
[24 June. Ricard was the harper of Princess Joanna's first husband, Gilbert de Clare]

1292/3 CPR. 19.
Letters for Ricard le Harpur, going with Gilbert de Clare, earl of Gloucester and Hertford, and Joan, his wife, to Ireland, nominating Robert le Vel and Simon de Higham their attorneys for 3 years.
1 June (1293). Westminster.

CPR. 20
Protection, with clause *volumus* for 2 years, for the following, going to Ireland with Gilbert de Clare, earl of Gloucester and Hertford:
[among them] Richard le Harpur

RICARD LE HARPOUR

Identity uncertain: perhaps the harper of Walter Beauchamp, Steward of the King's household.

1298 Gough. (Scotland in 1298)

p. 184 Ricard le Harpour, vallettus[Senescalli] has a sorrel rouncy, valued at £10.

1306 E101/369/6.

Present at the Whitsun Feast.

Received 40d.

1306/7 E101/370/16.

f. 11r (p. 61) 10s. in cash, given to Ricard le Harpeour, by Ricard de Woodhull.
24 April. Carlisle.

1306 E101/369/6.

Ricardus Citharista. Present at the Whitsun Feast.
Received 2s.

[Possibly a different person from the Ricard who received 40d. on the same (Latin) list but note entry E101/370/16, above. The Ricard there was with the King during his last days.]

RICARD LE HARPOUR (temp Ed. II)

1312 Bain III

p. 414 Ricardus le Harpour has a light bay horse. Valued at 6 marks.

p. 421 Ricardus le Harpour has a brown bay horse. Valued at 10 marks.
[?Two different persons].

RICARDUS LE HARPUR

1230 CPR. 359.

Protection to Ricard le Harpour, going overseas with the King. (Hen. III).
20 April. Portsmouth.

RICARD LE HARPUR

1260 King's Sergeant/minstrel.

CPR. 118.
Mandate to Hugh le Bygod, justiciary of England, to provide for the King's sergeants, Master Thomas, King's Surgeon and Master Richard le Harpur, who have served the King long and have not yet had whereof to sustain themselves in his service, to provide for each of them in £7 10s. yearly of land of wards or escheats.
15 March. St. Omer.
[Probably the same Ricard as in the previous entry].

RICARD LE TRUMPOUR

1314/18 E101/376/7.
f. 43v Ricard le Trumpour de Blida, squire/trumpeter of Ed. II.

See BLYTHE/BLIDA

f. 90v 20s. for his outfit.
3 April (1317/18). Stratford.

1319/20 MS. Soc. of Antiq. 120.
f. 165r 20s. for his winter outfit.
20 June. London.
f. 174v no issue of winter outfit, because he was not in Court.
25 May (?1318/19).

1310/11 E101/374/7.
p. 23 40s. to the Clerk of the [Kitchen] by the hand of Ricard le Trumpour, for fish.
20 November.

1319/20 MS. Soc. of Antiq. 121.
f. 129r Nothing for his summer outfit, because he was not in Court on Whitsunday.

RICARD (the Trumpeter)

1305/6 E101/368/12.
One of the trumpeters in the household of the two young princes, Thomas and Edmund.
Occurs, in name only, as Ricardus Trumpator, in the list of Minstrels of the Hall and Stable; and again, with his socius, Johannes in the issue of winter and summer clothing.

RICARD (vielle-player)

1332/3 E101/386/7.
f. 8r 12d. to a certain vielle-player, Ricard, for making his minstrelsies in the presence of Lady Eleanor. By gift of the lady, and by her order; into his own hands.
23 May. Rosyndale [Rosedale, Yorks.]

RICARDIN

King's [Ed. I's] vielle-player.

1290 C47/4/5.
f. 40r 20s. to Ricard, the vielle-player, for his winter outfit for the current year; into his own hands, per Master W. de Langton.

1290 E101/352/24. (King's and Queen's Household Account) Appears by name, Ricard Vidulator, in a list of household minstrels being issued their summer and winter outfits.

1290 C47/4/4.
f. 17r 20s. prest, to Ricardin, King's vielle-player, for his wages.
f. 33v [His name only, Ricard the vielle-player, because top of folio torn away].

1294/5 Fryde. 40
67s. 6d. wages for the whole year, namely 365 days, during which time he was in Court 108 days.
Winchelsea.

1296/7 Add. MSS. 7965.
f. 20r 10 marks for an iron-grey horse, bought from him and given to Ricard le Fissher, for draught-work in the long cart; given for duty at the Pantry, at Plympton.
17 July. Westminster.
f. 52r 50s. to Ricardin, the vielle-player, for making his minstrelsy in the presence of Princess Elizabeth and her husband, at their wedding.
f. 77v Ricardus vidulator/scutifer.
33s. for his wages from 20 August, on which day his horse was valued, to 19 November, both days included; 87 days, bar 4 at 12d. per day, 7^1/2d. from the Marshalcy and 4^1/2d. from the Wardrobe.
Ghent.

f. 126^{v} 20s. for his winter outfit.
f. 131^{v} 20s. for his summer outfit.

1300/1 Add. MSS. 7966.

f. 66^{v} 20 marks, given to a party of minstrels who entertained the King and Queen on Christmas Day and St. Stephen's Day (26 December). The money was given to Ricard, the vielle player, to be 'distributed and given' to the minstrels, on behalf of the King, 'each one according to his status' (unicuiusque iuxta suum statum exiget.)
28 December. Nottingham.

f. 165^{r} 24s. 5^{1}/2d. prest, to Ricard le Vilour, 'in parte panne' [?in the part payment for material or lengths of cloth, for his outfit.]

1305/6 CLL. Letter-book C.

p. 245 John Blound, the Mayor, issued a precept for the arrest of Ralph de Honilane, citizen and alderman of London, for debt. He could not be found. Even after a second search. Therefore, order given to evaluate his property. That, too, could not be found. No one could find any of his goods or chattels. After the extent, it was found that, "in the Vintry, in the parish of St. James, were two messuages of the yearly value of £18, from which must be subtracted 100s. annual rent, owing to Ricard le Vielour, 20s. annual rent to St. Giles Hospital and 40s. annually, for repairs..."
2 February 1305.

1307 E101/373/15.

f. 7^{r} 13s. 4d. to Ricard le Vilour, for his wages. Into his own hands.
3 October. Nottingham.

f. 7^{v} 10s. to Ricard le Vylour, for his wages. Into his own hands.
9 August. Lambeth.

1311/12 CLL Letter-book B.

p. 32 "...came Philip Lenfant, skinner, before the Chamberlain, in the presence of John de Wengrave and Henry de Durham, Aldermen, and acknowledged himself bound to Richardin le Vylour, in the sum of 20 marks; to be paid at mid-Lent..."
22 December.

p. 47 "...came Philip le[n]faunt and Richard Gentilcors, Skinners and acknowledged themselves bound to Richardin le Violour, in the sum of 10 marks, to be paid at Michaelmas..."
5 July.

1316/17 MS. Soc. of Antiq. 120.
f. 100v 40s. to Ricard, vielle-player, by gift of the lord King, as a help, to support his wife and children. Paid into his own hands.
13 June. Westminster.

1320/21 MS. Soc. of Antiq. 121.
f. 130r 1 mark to Ricard, vielle-player, for his summer outfit.
12 December. London.

1325/6 101/381/11
From a list of the King's household minstrels:
Ricard le Vieler.

See ROUNLO (RICARD)

RICARD (Earl of Lancaster's)

Vielle-player of Thomas of Lancaster.
Ricardus Vidulator Comitis Lancastrie.

1306 E101/369/6.
Present at the Whitsun Feast.
Received 5s.

RICARD (Watchman)

1306 Add. MSS. 2293 and MS. Harley 5001 - a copy of 2293
f. 6v 10s. each to Ricard the Watchman and Ricard de Burghardesle, Prince's Watchmen, for raising the alarm of fire to the Prince and other members of his household and for their help in extinguishig it and for evacuating in like manner divers people from the buildings and from the residence of the lord Prince.
17 April. Windsor.

f. 7v Ricard. Vigil Castri de Wyndesoure.
20s. for coming to the Prince's court at Byfleet (Surrey) by his order, and making his minstrelsy before the same lord (Prince) and other nobles there in his entourage.
By gift of the Prince, for his return to Windsor. Given to him in cash by J. Ingelard.
'In the month of May'. Byfleet.

1307 E101/357/15.
f. 27r 18s. owing to Ricard Vigil, at the end of the reign [of Ed. I].

RICARD (the Waferer)

1300/1 Apparently a Court Waferer, because his payment comes from the Wardrobe. Perhaps he was Ricard Pilke, later Waferer of Edward II.

E101/359/6.
f. 4v 6s. 8d. to Ricard the Waferer, prest, for his office (i.e. making wafers). Paid into his own hands.
(Sunday) 20 August. Osbernstone (Lanarks).
f. 14r 2s. and 13s. 4d. to Ricard the Waferer prest, for his wages. Paid into his own hands: 2s. at Donipace on 30 September and 13s. 4d. at the same place on 12 October.

RICHARD/orRICARD (le Harpur)

Perhaps the harper of Sir Thomas Multon.

1305 CPR. 337
Simple prohibition, until a year after Ascension, for 4 men, one of whom was Richard le Harpur, who were intending to go to Ireland with (Sir) Thomas de Multon.

RICHARDYN

King's Citole-player.

1326 MS. Soc. of Antiq. 122.
f. 49v (or, p. 50r) 20s. each paid to Henry Newsom, King's harper and Richardyn, King's Citole-player [Cytoler le Roi] who made their minstrelsies before the King and the Countess Marshal, who ate with the King today.
30 January. Heuyngham.

1306 E101/369/6.
Present at the Whitsun feast.
Received 2s.

See GALFRIDUS.

ROBERT (De Berneville)

1289 Minstrel of the King of France.

Add. MSS. 35294.
f. 9v 40s. by gift of the Queen.

See PHILIP

ROBERT THE FOOL

ROBERTUS FATUUS. Queen Eleanor's Court Fool.

1289 Add. MSS. 35294.
f. 4r 28s. for 12 ells of cloth, bought for the outfit of Robert the Fool. By the hand of the said William, the Queen's tailor.
6d. for removing the nap (pro retonsione) from the aforesaid cloth, for the outfit of the said Robert. 3s. for one fur of rabbits' pelts, bought for garnishing of the said Robert. By the hand of the said William [Cissor Regis].
f. 7v 3s. to the groom/page of Alianor de Saukeuyle, for cash on account [i.e. money borrowed] for Robert the Fool [lit. 'for cash given to him on account] for a game of dice; which the Queen ordered should be paid from her own [account] per Russelett.
Thursday. Quenington (Glos.)
f. 9r 2s. for a woollen pellisse [beta*] or cape, bought for the use of Robert the Fool; by the hand of Capeles, the Queen's preceptor.
Tuesday, Up-Lambourn (Berks.). 11 April.
f. 13r 40s. to Robert the Fool, going with the Count of Brittany. By gift of the Queen.
9 October. Tideswell (Derbyshire)
*beta lanata - lambskin

1311/12 MS. Cott. Nero. C.viii.
f. 83v 20s. to John de Mendlesham, groom (garcio) of Robert le Fol.
16 November. Westminster.

f. 85r 20s. to Robert le Fol, to buy himself a targe for performing [the sword and buckler dance] in the presence of the King. By the hand of Ricard de Watford.
9 February. York.

1317/18 Archaeologia xxvi. p. 334.
'10s. to Dulcia Withestaf, mother of Robert the King's [Ed. II's] Fool, coming to the King at Baldock. Of the King's gift.

ROBERT (the Harper)

1306 E101/369/6.
Harper of Nicholas de Culham, abbot of Abingdom, (ob. 1307).
Present at the Whitsun Feast.
Received 12d.

ROBERT (the Harper)

1312/13 E101/373/26.
A Court harper, probably Robert de Clough, but he is not called 'King's Harper' here.
f. 24r Robertus le Harpour: paid 7 1/2d. per day for his wages, for the aforesaid 365 days, during which time he was in Court for 30 days - 18s. 9d.
11 December. Westminster.

1311/1313 MS. Cott. Nero. C.viii.
King's Minstrel. Again, probably Robert de Clough.
f. 115v 20s. to Robert the Harper, for his winter outfit, according to the contract drawn up with him at Westminster.
11 December. 1312/13.
f. 121r Nothing to Robert le Harpour for his summer outfit, according to the contract drawn up with him at Westminster.
11 December. 1312/13.

ROBERT (mounted messenger)

1312 Bain III. 417
Robertus Messager has a sorrel piebald horse, with 3 white feet; valued at 14 marks.

ROBERT LE TABORER

1298 Gough. 45
Letter of protection for Robert the Taborer, who is with John de Warrene [Earl Warenne], while he is in Scotland.

ROBERT (le Trumpor)

1322 Cal. Chancery Warrants. I.530
Pardon granted to Robert le Trumpor, for being an adherent of Thomas of Lancaster.
10 May. York.

ROBERT (le Vilour)

1306 E101/369/6.
Present at the Whitsun Feast; one of 'la Comune' and therefore a minstrel belonging to one or other of the royal households or the household of a member of the royal family.

ROBERT (the Watchman)

Robert de Finchesley (Finchley), King's Watchman: references to him entered under various titles: Robertus Vigil; Robertus Vigil Regis; Robertus de Finchesle; Robertus le Geyte.

1302/3 E101/363/18.
f. 21^r 10s. to Robert, King's Watchman, for making his minstrelsy in the presence of the Prince. By gift of the Prince.
9 December (1302). Marlborough.

1302 E101/364/13.
f. 84^v Robertus Vigil. Prests, for his wages:

5s.	5 April.	Durham.
5s.	24 June.	Tynemouth.
5s.	9 July.	Tynemouth.
5s.	31 July.	Tynemouth.

[N.B. These places do not tally with the King's itinerary for 1302/3 or 1303/4. Edward I was at Tynemouth in September 1304].

1305 MS. Harley 152.
named as Vigil Regis on ff. 17^v, 19^r, 20^v.

1305/6 E101/368/27.
f. 21^v £6 16 10^1/2 to Robert de Fynchesle, receiving 4^1/2d. per day for his wages for the whole of the present 34th year; that is to say, for 365 days, because he was never absent (from Court).
f. 63^r 4 marks to Adam, the Watchman, Robert de Fynchesle, Geoffrey de Windsor, John de Staunton [The 4 King's Watchmen], 1 mark each, prest, for their wages. Into their own hands.
4 September. Newborough in Tyndale.

f. 63^v 5s. to each of the four, as above. Into their own hands.
24 August. Newborough in Tyndale.

f. 64^v 4s. prest for his wages. Into his own hands.
5 July. Thrapston.
1/2 mark, by the hand of Adam Skirewith.
1 November. Lanercost.

f. 68^v To Robert the Watchman, prests for his wages:
2s. 24 December. Amesbury.
5s. 20 January. Kingston Lacy.
3s. 5 February. Lyndhurst.
Total 10s.

f. 69^v To Robert de Fynchesle, prests, for his wages:
5s. 23 February. Wynton (Winchester)
5s. 22 March. Wynton "
5s. 10 May. Wynton "
Total 15s.

f. 70^v 2 marks to Robert de Finchesle, King's Watchman, for his winter outfit for the current year. Into his own hands.
23 February [?] Wynton [?] Warham.

1305 E101/369/11.
f. 203 his name entered for 5s. prest, for his wages, and then crossed out.

1306/7 E101/370/16.
f. 1^r 10s. for his wages, by the hand of John de Staunton.
25 November. Lanercost.

f. 3^v 10s. for his wages, by the hand of Adam de Skyrewith.
24 December. Lanercost.

f. 11^r 10s. for his wages, into his own hands.
24 April. Lanercost.

1318 Parl Writs. II 2. 130.
Pardon to Robertus le Geyte, for rebellious behaviour re the Despensers.
1 November.

ROBIN LE FOL

1290/1 This is Robertus Fatuus, the late Queen Eleanor's Fool.

C47/4/5.

f. 52r 60s. to Robin the Fool, being with the Count of Brittany and returning with his master to parts across the sea. By the hand of Walter de Sturton.
26 October. [Abergavenny]

1290 E101/352/21. (a roll)
40s. to Robin the Fool, going with the Count of Brittany, and departing with his master. By gift of the King.

ROBINET (le Tabourer)

1299/1300 E101/358/20. [a tattered and rubbed MS.]

f. 9r Money paid to Robinet the Taborer, for making his minstrelsy in the presence of the King at [Belsay; Northumberland] by gift of the King.
Dec[ember]

[The remainder of the MS. is illegible]

RODES (Janin de)

1302/3 A Flemish minstrel (organist).

E101/363/10.

f. 11v 10s. to Janin de Rodes, an organist, coming to England in the train of certain noblemen of Flanders, for making his minstrelsy in the presence of the King and Queen, at Ogerston.
25 March (1302). Ogerston (Hants.)

ROGER (a harper)

1210/12 Red. BK. of Exchequer. II. 540 (Sergeanties)
Rogerus Citharedus.
Roger the harper has 5 solidates for carrying the mantle while the King is in Cornwall.

[N.B. Peter fitz Oger has 40 solidates in Cabulion for a mantle of Gresenges, against the coming of the lord King into Cornwall]

ROGER (Keeper of the linen)

Roger le Mapparius

1311/12 E101/374/19. (Wardrobe Acct. of the 2 young princes)

f. 8r 3s. to Roger, the Mapparius, Philip de Windsor, and John de Dorchester, grooms/pages (garciones) of the household of the two [young princes, Thomas de Brotherton and Edmund de Woodstock], for making their minstrelsies in the presence of the same two. By gift of the two, per John de Weston. 28 October.

ROGER (the trumpeter)

King's Trumpeter.

1311/12 MS. Cott. Nero C.viii.

f. 87v 20s. by gift of the King. 29 January. York.

See DUZEDEYS, PETER

1314/17 f. 192v 60s. 3d. by the hand of Roger the Trumpeter, in part payment of £10 0s. 3d. owed to him for war-wages, livery and compensation for his horses. 23 January.

f. 193v Rogerus Trumpour Menestrallus hospicii Regis. £7 by the hand of Roger the Trumpeter, minstrel of the King's household, for money owing to him for wages, livery and compensation for his horses. By a bill. 23 February.

1314/15 E101/376/7.

f. 40r 37s. 4d. to Roger the Trumpeter and Arnald the Trumpeter, minstrels of the lord King, for playing (ludentibus) in the presence of the same lord King, between Woburn and Newport Pagnell. By gift of the King, being the cost of cloth and fur for them to have two outfits made for themselves. By the hand of Master Nicholas de Hugates, paying them the money at Lincoln. 1 September.

1316/17 MS. Soc. of Antiq. 120.

f. 100^v 40s. to a certain minstrel of the Count of Savoy, coming to the lord King, with the permission of his master and returning to him with letters of the lord King.
By gift of the lord King, by the hand of Roger the Trumpeter.
30 May. Westminster.

1319/20 MS. Soc. of Antiq. 121.

f. 117^r 20s. to Roger le Trumpour, for his livery; according to the contract drawn up with him at York.
26 October.

f. 129^r 20s. for his summer livery.
26 October. York.

1319/20 E101/378/4.

f. 22^r 48s. to Roger the Trumpeter for his wages for 48 days [11 August - 27 September, both days included] at 12d. per day, because he had had his horse valued.
4 February. Fulham.

1325/6 E101/381/11. (Fragments)
In a list of household officers/minstrels being issued clothing to accompany the King to France:
Roger le Trompour.

1328 E101/383/4.

pp. 375/6 Listed among the squire minstrels of Ed. III's household:
Roger le Trumpour.

1330 E101/385/4.

p. 381 As preceding:
Rogerus le Trumpour.

1335/8 MS. Cott. Nero. C.viii.

f. 226^r [a list of minstrels of Ed. III's household]
20s. to Roger the Trumpeter, for his livery.

ROGER (the Waferer)

1330 E101/385/4.

p. 381 In a list of minstrels of Ed. III's household:
Rogerus le Wafrer.

ROLAND (le Fartere)

1331 CCR. 187
To William Trussel, escheator this side Trent. Order not to intermeddle further with 40 acres of land in Hemmington, Arsk and Gosebek, and to restore the issues thereof, as the King learns by inquisition taken by Robert Selyman, his late escheator this side Trent, that the said 40 acres, [part] of the messuage and 99 acres of land in the towns aforesaid, that Roland le Fartere held of the King's progenitors by the service of making a leap, a whistle and a fart (saltum, siflum et pettum), were alienated long before the time of [legal] memory to divers men, which alienations King Henry, the son of the Empress Matilda, confirmed by his charter and that the justices late in eyre in Co. Suffolk, because it was presented before them that the said 40 acres were thus alienated and that the service aforesaid had been withdrawn for a long time, caused them to be arrented at 15s., with which sum the prior of Buttele, Ralph de Bockyng', and other tenants of the said 40 acres are charged, and that the 40 acres are worth yearly in all issues 13s. 4d., and that they were taken into the King's hands for the alienation aforesaid."

ROOS (Guillot de)

King's Vielle-player.

1285 E101/351/17. (Counter-roll of payments to members of the King's Household).

Sub Menestralli Regis.
Guillot vidulator.

1296/7 Add. MSS. 7965.
f. 52r 50s. to Guillot de Ros for playing before Princess Elizabeth and her husband (Count of Holland) at their wedding.
[8 January. Ipswich]

1296 CPR. 223.
Exemption, for life, to William de Ros, the King's minstrel, for his long service, from being put on assizes, juries or recognizances; also, that he be quit, for life, from any custody of the maritime parts, due from him by reason of his hands.
6 December. Nayland (Suffolk)

1299 CCR. 262, 351.

Order to the sheriff of Cambridge to deliver to William de Ros, the King's vielator, the chattels which Wyot de Keu stole from him...[[Wyot was subsequently hanged] which chattels were appraised at 6 marks 12s. 8d.

21 July. Chilton (Kent).

1304/5 E101/368/6.

f. 8r $^{1}/2$ mark to Gillot de Roos, prest, for his annual fee, which he receives from the Wardrobe. Into his own hands at Bamford.

8 December. [Gough has Amesbury].

[William seems to have been one of the few privileged servants to whom the King granted an annuity].

1306 E101/369/6.

Present at the Whitsun Feast.

Received 2/3 payments:

Guillot de Roos, vilour $^{1}/2$ mark [Latin]

Guillot de Roos. $^{1}/2$ mark and 40s. [French]

ROSE (Hugh de la)

1304/5 E101/368/6.

f. 12v Rose citharista. Prests, for his wages:

5s. into his own hands. 17 December. Sarum (Gough says Langford).

$^{1}/2$ mark. 8 January. Kingston Lacy.

5s. in cash, given to him by Peter de Brembre.

6 January. Kingston Lacy.

f. 13r 40s. to Hugo de la Rose; by the hand of William de Berkeley. B[rembre].

20s. prest, for his wages; by the hand of Master Gillot (William de Morley). The 4 King's Harpers at that time - William de Morley, John de Newenton, Hugh de la Rose and Adam de Clitheroe were paid together; 20s. each.

8 January. [Kingston Lacy]

1305 Cal. Fine Rolls. I.

p. 515 Hugh the Harper has made fine at the Exchequer in 40s. for entry into 12 acres and a rood of waste, in the forest of Ingelwoode, which the King granted him.
8 April. Westminster.

p. 523 Grant to Hugh le Harpour, for good service in the parts of Scotland and elsewhere, of 12 acres and a rood of waste in Ingelwood forest...in the place called Rawebankes, so that he may enclose the same with a small dyke and a low hedge, according to the forest assize and bring it back into cultivation. To him and his heirs of the King and his heirs, with free entry for all his animals and cattle, rendering yearly at the Exchequer, [at Michaelmas] 12s. 3d.
25 June. Lewes.

1305/6 E101/368/27.

f. 20^{v} £5 16s. 10½d. to Hugh de la Rose, receiving 7½d. per day for his wages, for the whole of the current year; that is to say; for 365 days minus 178 days when he was absent (from duty).
23 February. London.

f. 63^{v} 5s. each to Adam de Clitheroe and Hugh de la Rose, King's Harpers, prests [for their wages]; by the hand of Adam.
24 August. Newborough in Tyndale.

f. 66^{v} Prests, for his wages:
5s. into his own hands. 17 December. Say.
½ mark. 8 January. Kingston Lacy.
5s. in cash, given to him by Peter de Brembre. 6 January. Kingston Lacy.
Total: 16s. 8d.

f. 67^{r} 20s. each to the 4 King's Harpers, William, John, Adam and Hugh, prests, for their wages; by the hand of William (Guillot).
2 January. Kingston Lacy.

1306 E101/369/6.
Present at the Whitsun Feast.
Received 2 marks.

1318 PW. II. 126.
Pardon to Hugo le Harper for rebellious behaviour re the Despensers.
22 October.
[Probably not Hugh de la Rose. In a list of pardons (PW. op. cit. 131) to the members of the household of Thomas of Lancaster there occurs: Hugo le Harpour de fformeby [Formby, Lancs.]

See HUGH (le Harpour) and HUGHETHUN.

ROUNLO (Ricard)

King's Vielle-player.

1290 E101/352/24 and C47/4/5 f. 40r
For his winter outfit and prest, for his wages; by the hand of Master William 20s. to Ricardin vielle-player [vidulator] de Langton. London.

1297 Add. MSS. 7965.
f. 139 A gold clasp, valued at 60s., given, by order of the King, through Ricard, the King's vielle-player, to King Adam, minstrel of the Count of Flanders.
[This minstrel was the famous Adinet le Roy].
8 November. Ghent.

1306 E101/369/6.
Present at the Whitsun Feast.
Received 1 mark.
Styled: Monsire Ricard le Vilour Rounlo.

RUE (Henry de)

1291 E101/352/21 and C.47/4/5 f. 5.
26s. 8d. to Henry de Rue, Waferer of the Countess of Gloucester, for coming to Court with his lady mistress and returning home with her; by gift of the King.
5 November.

SAGARD

1289/90 Wenlok. (Accounts)
p. 171 12d. given to a certain minstrel called Sagard, on the Feast of Holy Innocents. (28 December).
[On the second roll of the expenses of the Household of Abbot Walter, begun at Westminster, in the month of December, in the feast of the Birth of the Lord, 28 Ed. I.]

SAGARD (John)

1306 E101/369/6.
Present at the Whitsun Feast.
Received 12d.

SAGARD (William)

1301 Chesire in the Pipe Rolls. (edd. Miller and Stewart-Brown)
p. 195 (List of Receipts)
12s. from William Sagard, for fruit from the garden of Chester Castle. (See Menestrellorum Multitudo s.v.).

1303 CPR. 167.
Pardon, in consideration of service in Scotland, to William Sagard, for the death of Robert Aubray, son of John le Maszon of Weldon (Norf.)

1306/7 Add. MSS. 22923 and MS. Harley. 5001 (f. 40^{v} verbatim copy).
f. 6^{v} Willelmus Sagard, Croudarius.
13s. 4d. to William Sagard, crowder, coming to the Prince's Court at Windsor and making his minstrelsy in the presence of the lord Prince and other nobles there, in his train. By gift of the Prince, for his expenses on his return (home). Into his own hands.
17 April.

1306 E101/369/6.
Present at the Whitsun Feast.
Received 40d.

1307 CPR. 496.
Pardon to William Sagard of his outlawry before Sir John Bourtetourte and his fellow-justices, in the county of Northampton, when indicted of the death of Robert Aubray, son of John le Maszon of Weldon, he having been pardoned, 10 November 1303, for that death.

SANDWICH (Ricard de)

1296/7 Add. MSS. 7965.
Ricard vidulator de Sandwich.
f. 57r 20s. to Ricard, vielle-player of Sandwich, for playing before the King at Ghent on 6 September.
By gift of the King; by the hand of Ricard, the King's vielle-player [i.e. Ricard Rounlo].
7 September. Ghent.

SANZ MANIERE (William)

1306 Waferer of the Countess of Gloucester [Princess JOAN]
Present at the Whitsun Feast.
Received 1 mark.

1306/7 Add. MSS. 22923 and MS. Harley. 5001, f. 36v
f. 14v 20s. to Guilleme Sanz Maniere (Guillem saunz manoir) Waferer of the Countess of Gloucester, who came to the Prince's Court at Wetheral (Cumb.) and made his minstrelsy in the presence of the lord (Prince) and other nobles in his entourage there.
By gift of the Prince, for his expenses on his returning from Wetheral to his lady-mistress.
By the hand of W. de Boudon, who gave him the money on 15 February.

1306/7 E101/370/16.
f. 16v 40s. to Willelmus Sanz Manere, minstrel of the Countess of Gloucester, for making his minstrelsy in the presence of the King.
By gift of the King.
24 June. Carlisle.
[Princess Joan had died in April].

SAUTREOR (John le)

1275/6 CLL. Letter-book B. 261.
On Wednesday, 29 September, information was given to the Chamberlain and Sheriffs that John le Sautreor lay dead...in the house of William le Cuver...in the parish of St. Bride. The jurors find that his bed caught fire from a candle and that he was burnt whilst in a state of intoxication and in consequence died.

SAUTREOUR (William le)

Queen's Psaltery-player.
Guillot Menestrallus Regine.

1298 Cal. of Inquisitions II, 44, No. 186 and C. 145/74/No. 29.
On or about 1 August 3 of William's servants broke into his house by night and carried away goods to the value of £100.
[See Menestrellorum Multitudo 98ff.]

1299/1300 LQG.

p. 7 Sub Recepta).
27s. 11d. received from Master William de Chisoy, the Treasurer of the Queen's Wardrobe; money subtracted from the wages of Guillot le (MS. de) Psalterion, minstrel of the said Queen, which had been allocated [to him] in the Marshalcy Roll, in the time of the said Queen, by which he received a gift of hay and oats from the King's Marshalcy.

p. 95 3 of his horses being stabled, at the King's expense.

p. 161 £2 in compensation for his bay rouncy, with a star on its forehead; which was returned to the Almonry at Stamford (Lincs.) on the last day of April.
Paid into his own hands.
1 May. Stamford.

p. 162 £1 given to Guillot le Salterion, Queen's minstrel, [to reimburse him] for money which he owed Robert de Cotyngham, for a horse which he bought from him for more than 40s., which the said minstrel [spent] out of his own pocket to acquire the said horse.
12 May. Thetford (Suffolk).

1300/1 E101/684/62/3.
A quitclaim of a piece of land in Shropshire which William owned and which the Priory of (Much) Wenlock wanted to obtain. William quitclaimed it for £20, sterling. Seal, bearing William's portrait, attached.

1300/1 E101/359/5.

f. 1v £20, for money owing to him, by the hand of the Prior of Wenlock; a quitclaim of land.
Easter Monday, 3 April. Feckenham (Worcs.)

[See above]

1300/1 E101/360/10.

Membrane 1. Willelmus le Sautreour, is among the list of servants in the new Queen's (Margaret's) train when she and Prince Edward set out from Langley to join the King at Lincoln.
January 1301.

1302 Cal. Ancient Deeds II. (Rolls Ser.)

A.2050 Grant by Reginald de Walsingham to William the Minstrel (Istrio) of the Queen of England, of a tenement at Ebbegate, in St. Martin's Lane, in the parish of St. Laurence, Candelwick Strete.
15 May.

A.2068 The same, but in this he is called Guillot le Sautreour.

1302 CCR. 66.

John de Maunte acknowledges that he owes to William le Menestral, £10; to be levied, in default, of his lands and chattels in London.
Richard de Weyland acknowledges that he owes to William le Menestral, £40; to be levied, in default, of his lands and chattels in Suffolk.

1304 CLL. Letter-book C. 213.

p. 213 John le Lung, a goldsmith, imprisoned until he shall have paid to William le Sautreour, minstrel to the Lady Margaret, Queen of England, the sum of £40, due under recognizance.

p. 244 Settlement of the case and William's acquisition of 2 tenements and 10 shops in Cripplegate.

1306 E101/369/6.

Present at the Whitsun Feast.
Received 40s., which William de Morley, King's Harper, collected for him.

1306/7 E101/370/16.

f. 13v (p. 65) Deputed to pay 40s. to King Caupenny, John de Cressy and other minstrels, for performing miracle-plays before the Queen.
29 May. [Carlisle].

See CAUPENY.

1309 *Cal. of Inquisitions II*.
p. 16 No. 551. A yearly rent of 1 mark, out of a tenement in the city of London, which once belonged to Reymund de Burdeus; and a rent of £15s. 3d. conferred by Edward I on Guylot le Sautreour.

1309/10 *MS. Cott. Nero C. viii*. (Debts of the Queen's Household for 1309/10)
f. 15^{r} (16^{v}) 36s. 4d. (owing) to William le Sautreour. By a bill on the King's Wardrobe.
f. 38^{r} (39^{r}) 4s. 4^{1}/2d. for his wages for 1310/11. Paid 4 April 1312. London.

1310/11 *MS. Cott. Nero. C.viii*.
f. 149^{r} (150^{r}) Issues of livery to the squires of the Queen's household. William le Sautreour's name is crossed out; and written beside it: '*Cancellatus quia non fuit in Curia ad festum Pentecostes*'.
[Perhaps 1312].

1310/11 *E101/374/5*.
f. 33^{v} *Willelmus le Sautreour*.
To William the Psaltery-player, receiving 7^{1}/2d. per day for his wages, from 8 July, beginning of the 4th year (1310) to 7 July, the ending of the same year, both days included; for 365 days, during which time he was present in Court for 7 days.
4s, 4^{1}/2d. Queen's Wardrobe.
16 November (1311). Westminster.

1311/12 *MS. Cott. Nero. C.viii*.
f. 135^{v} 21s. 10^{1}/2d. to *Willelmus le Sautreour, scutifer hospicii supradicte* (i.e. squire of the Queen's household), who receives 7^{1}/2d. per day for his wages, from 8 July 1311 to 7 July 1312, both days included. 366 days (Leap year). Present in Court for 35 days.
13 July (1312). York.

1313 *CPR. 581*.
Protection until 1 August for William le Sautreour, who is going beyond seas with Isabella, Queen of England.
3 May. Westminster.

1313 *Foedera, II pars. I.212*.
Protection for John Drake, Willielmus le Sautreour, John Merlyn and others, going beyond seas with the Queen, in the train of Aymer de Valence.

1313/14 101/375/9. (Wardrobe Account of Queen Isabella)

p. 15r 15s. to William the Psaltery-player, squire of the Queen's household, paid 7½d. per day for his wages, from 8 July of the 7th year (1313) to 7 July of the same year, both days included; for 365 days, during which time he was present in Court for 24 days. According to the contract made in the Queen's Wardrobe, at York.
10 August. 1314.

1314 Cal. of Inquisitions 44. and C. 145/74. No. 29 (Latin text)
No. 186. Inquisition held concerning the robbery of William's house in Thames Street, in the Parish of All Hallows the Less, by his servants, Roger and Thomas de Keneby and Hugh, son of Michael Picard on 1 August 1298. Goods to the value of £100 carried off. [16 years after the robbery! Hugh Picard was still at large see CLL. Letter-book B. p. 32. He was alive in 1311, borrowing money (£40) from John de Cherleton, mercer. 21 December.]

1314/15 E101/376/7. (sub. Roba)

f. 93r William one of 12 squires of the Queen's household, who received 'nihil' for their outfits, because they were 'out of Court' on Christmas Day.

f. 124r 36s. 10½d. owing to him for his outfit for 1314.

1315 CCR. 311/12.
Enrolment of general release by Roger de Queneby to Guillot le Sautreor, minstrel, and to John le Grey, his son, saving any claim that he may have in the lands that were of the inheritance of Juliana, his wife, at Baldock (Herts).

[Refs. for William's long quarrel with Jordan Moraunt, King's Clerk, over the property of John Butterlye, late Keeper of the King's forest at Havering-atte-Bower. 1302. CPR. 48. 1303. CCR. 108; 1303 Cal. Chancery Warrants, 173; 1304 Ibid 206. 1304. CLL. Letter-book B 132, Letter-book E, 76; 1306. CPR. 420. 1307. CPR. 41, 44, 51, 86, 88, 147. 1308. CPR. 58, 60, 63, 200. 1309. CPR. 191. 247. 1310. CPR. 229, 233. Cal. Chancery Warrants, 269, 314, 513, 312. CPR. 427. 1313. CPR. 606. 1318. CPR. 298, 488. 1321. CPR. 28, 31, 57. 1322. CPR. 185, 192. 1323. CPR. 303.]

SAY (William de)

1305/6 E101/368/12.

Willelmus de Say, Waffrarius. [He was probably* Waferer to the 2 young Princes, Thomas and Edmund].

f. 4v 3s. 4d. to William de Say, Waferer, for staying in the household of the 2 sons of the King, to serve wafers to them, according to his office; and receiving licence from them to go to his own parts, because he was ill. In recompense to him for his work and service.
6 December. Windsor Castle.

*i.e. a Court waferer commissioned to be at the Castle to serve the Princes.

1310/11 E101/374/7.

p. 11 2s. to Thomas de Peusey, vallettus of the King, for a bow-case (furrellus, furellus) bought through him for a certain harper [MS. cithara] called Willekyn Sey, by order of the King.

SCARBOROUGH (Robert de)

1306 E101/369/6.

Present at the Whitsun Feast.
Received 12d.

SCOCIA (Jakett de)

1296/7 Add. MSS. 7965.

A King Herald. 'Jamie of Scotland'.

f. 52r 40s. to Jakettus de Scocia Rex, for performing at the wedding of Princess Elizabeth.

SCOT (John)

One of the Prince's boy Choristers/minstrels; later, King's (Ed. II's) Trumpeter.

1305/6 MS. Harley. 5001.

f. 32v Boy minstrels/To Ricard le Rimour, Master Andrew, Janin Scot, Franceskin and Roger de Forde, boy-minstrels of the Prince's household; by gift and grace of the same, to pay for the making of their outfits for Christmas Day; 12d. to each of them; into their own hands.
21 December.

1306 E101/369/6.

Present at the Whitsun Feast.
One of the 5 boys. Not mentioned by name.

See 5 Pueri Principis.

1305/6 MS. Harley. 5001.

f. 32^v Boy minstrels/To Ricard le Rimour, Master Andrew, Janin Scot, Franceskin and Roger de Forde, boy-minstrels of the Prince's household; by gift and grace of the same, to pay for the making of their outfits for Christmas Day; 12d. to each of them; into their own hands.
21 December.

1306 E101/369/6.
Present at the Whitsun Feast.
One of the 5 boys. Not mentioned by name.

See 5 Pueri Principis.

1310/11 E101/373/10.

f. 3^v 3s. each to John Scot, John de Kenynton, trumpeters, and Franciskin, nakerer, of the King, for their wages. By the hand of the said Franceskin.
29 March.

f. 5^v 2s. each to John Scot, John de Kenynton and Franciskin, nakerer, for their wages; into their own hands. [Clerk has - 12s.].
28 April.

1310/11 E101/374/5.

f. 91^r 3s. prest, for his wages. Into his own hands.
8 November. Berewick. [Berwick-on-Tweed].

1311/12 MS. Bodley Tanner 197. (John de Oxham's Wardrobe Book).

f. 50^r 3s. prest, for his wages, by the hand of "Fransekyn" the Nakerer.
29 March. Berwick-on-Tweed.
2s. for same.
28 April. Berwick-on-Tweed.

1311/12 E101/373/26.

f. 76^v 2s. prest, for his wages to Janin Skot [Trumpator Regis] Into his own hands.
20 June. Burstwick.

1318 PW. II div. ii 127.
Pardon to John Scot, for rebellious behaviour re the Despensers.
1 November.

SAY (William de)

1305/6 E101/368/12.
Willelmus de Say, Waffrarius. [He was probably* Waferer to the 2 young Princes, Thomas and Edmund].
f. 4^{v} 3s. 4d. to William de Say, Waferer, for staying in the household of the 2 sons of the King, to serve wafers to them, according to his office; and receiving licence from them to go to his own parts, because he was ill. In recompense to him for his work and service.
6 December. Windsor Castle.
*i.e. a Court waferer commissioned to be at the Castle to serve the Princes.

1310/11 E101/374/7.
p. 11 2s. to Thomas de Peusey, vallettus of the King, for a bow-case (furrellus, furellus) bought through him for a certain harper [MS. cithara] called Willekyn Sey, by order of the King.

SCARBOROUGH (Robert de)

1306 E101/369/6.
Present at the Whitsun Feast.
Received 12d.

SCOCIA (Jakett de)

1296/7 Add. MSS. 7965.
A King Herald. 'Jamie of Scotland'.
f. 52^{r} 40s. to Jakettus de Scocia Rex, for performing at the wedding of Princess Elizabeth.

SCOT (John)

One of the Prince's boy Choristers/minstrels; later, King's (Ed. II's) Trumpeter.

1319/20 E101/378/4.

f. 22r 48s. to John Scot, the Trumpeter, for his wages, from 11 August, on which day his horse was valued, to 27 September, both days included; for 48 days at 12d. per day.
4 February. Fulham.

1325 CPR. 161.

Grant for life to John le Scot, trompour, for his good service to the King, of a messuage, 8 acres of land and an acre of meadow in the town of Pontefract and Friston, late of William le Tabourer, a rebel, which have come into the King's hands by forfeiture, to hold without rendering anything to the King.
24 August. Langdon [Abbey, Kent].

1325 CPR. 168/9.

Letters of protection for persons 'going overseas with the King' (i.e. to France). Among them, John Scot, trompour.

1325/6 E101/381/11. (Fragments)

from a list of the King's household minstrels being issued outfits to go with the King to France:
Johann Scot, Troumpour.

1328 E101/383/4.

(pp. 375/6). Listed among the squire minstrels of the household of Ed. III:
Johannes Scot, Trumpour.

1330 E101/385/4.

(p. 381). As above: Johannes Scot.

1334 E101/387/9.

issued outfits and shoes.
Johannes Scot.

SEMTE

1307 (7 July-19 Nov.). E101/373/15.

f. 22r 10 marks to the damsel Semte, domicelle Semte and three other minstrels of lord Louis of France, and to lord/master Fotas de Serle, Constable of France, coming in the company of their 2 lords from France to London, to the King and returning to their own country; by the hand of Thomas de Pewsey, giving them the money at Sheen, on the same day.

SEYMOUR (Nigel)

1303/4 Add. MSS. 8835. f. 43^v
A Scottish trumpeter.

See BRIDE (Gilbert)
and CLYDESDALE (Andrew)

SIMON (the Messenger)

The mounted messenger of the Queen Mother, Eleanor of Provence.

1286 E101/351/26. (Roll of Robae).
Membrane 3.
No. 1712. 1 mark to Simon, the Queen's nuncius for his outfit for the current year.

1289 Add. MSS. 35294.
f. 5^v 6d. to Simon, the nuncius, going with letters of the Queen to...
24 November. Bindon (Dorset).
f. 6^v 8d. to Simon, the nuncius, bearing letters of the Queen to the Abbess of Cherwell.
28 January. [Westminster]

1289 Swinfield.
p. 149 2s. to Simon, the nuncius of the lady Alienor, Queen, mother of the King.

1290 CCR. 87.
Order to Geoffrey de Pycheford, Constable of Windsor Castle, to permit Simon the envoy of Queen Eleanor, the King's Consort, to fell 6 oaks, fit for timber, in the wood of Henry de Lacy, earl of Lincoln, at Asheridge (Bucks.) which is within the bounds of the forest of Windsor, and to permit him to carry them whither he will, quit of cheminage, as Henry has granted him 6 oaks in that wood. 18 June. Westminster.

1290 Wenlock. (Accounts)
p. 172 3s. given to Simon the cursor of the old Queen, on the Saturday next after the Conversion of St. Paul.
28 January.
[Here he is called cursor, which may indicate that he was a foot-messenger or 'runner' before he became a nuncius. There were 2 royal messengers called Simon: this one was Simon Attleigh; the other Simon Lowys. It is not always clear to which the entries refer.]
See below, 1294.

1294 <u>CPR. 81</u>.
Grant, for life, to Simon Leuwys for his long service as messenger of the King and of Eleanor, the late Queen Consort, of 3d. per day, at the Exchequer. (Vacated and cancelled).
18 July. Portsmouth.

1296/7 <u>Add. MSS. 7965</u>.

f. 40^r 37s. $10^1/2$d. to Simon, who was the <u>nuncius</u> of the Queen Mother, receiving $4^1/2$d. per day when he is in Court; for his wages from 20 November 1296 to 30 April, both days included; 162 days, during which time he was in Court 101 days.
Plympton.
to the same, 40s. $10^1/2$d. from 1 May to 18 August, both days included; 109 days, during which time he was not absent from Court.
Ghent.
Memorandum: that the said Simon received his wages from 18 August, on which day his horse was valued up to the end of the present [regnal] year. 12d. per day (because he was on campaign).

f. 75^r [Expenses of the Squires of the King's Household in Flanders] [80s.] to Simon, messenger of the Queen, mother of the King, for his wages from 18 August, on which day his horse was valued, to 19 November, both days included. 80 days at 12 per day.

[f. 108^r?] mentioned, as receiving his winter outfit: <u>Simon Lowys</u>, <u>Nuncius</u>.

1298 <u>Gough</u>. 210
<u>Simon le Messager</u> has a yellow rouncy, with a streak, (<u>cum lista</u>) valued at 6 marks.

1298 <u>CPR. 372</u>.
Grant, for life, to Simon Lowys, for his long service to the late Queen Consort, of the custody of the manor and park of Guildford, so that he answer and receive as much as Thomas de Candeure, deceased, who lately had custody of the same.
16 November. Finchale.

1299-1306 E101/357/15. (Debts of the Wardrobe)

f. 2^r £8 4s. 6d. [owing to] Simon who was the Nuncius of the Queen [mother] [i.e. Simon Attleigh]? 40s. 2d. [owing to] Simon le Messager [i.e. Simon Lowys]?

f. 23^r 40s. 2d. [owing to] Simon le Messager.

1299/1300 LOG.

p. 101 £2 14s. 4½d. to Simon, qui fuit nuncius Regine, for his wages, at 4½d. per day, from 20 November to 13 April, the first day included but not the last, on which day he left Court until the wishes of the King be known.

p. 322 20s. (or 1 li.) to Simon who was the Queen's messenger for his outfit for the whole of the current year, according to the contract drawn up with him at St. Edmunds.
10 May.

1305 E101/368/6.

f. 22^r To Simon Lowys, nuncius, carrying letters of the King to the earl and countess of Gloucester, 4s. for his expenses.
14 December.

1306 E101/369/6.
Present at the Whitsun Feast.
Received 2 marks.

1311/12 Cartulary of Holy Trinity.
No. 184. All Hallows, Barking. List of those paying rent; among them: Simon le Messager.

1313 CCR. 69.
To the prior and convent of Trinity Church, London. Request that they will grant to Simon le Messager, who long served the late King and is now blind, suitable maintenance for himself and a groom in food and clothing, to be received by him whether staying within or without the said house, making letters patent under the seal of their chapter concerning the grant for the same.
21 August. Windsor.

1316 CPR. 601.
Commission of oyer and terminer to John de Wengrave and Robert de Keleseye, touching persons who carried away the goods of Simon le Messager, at London.
23 December. Clipstone.

SINGERS 7 Women

1303/4 Add. MSS. 8835.

f. 42^{v} 3s. to seven women who met the King on the road between Uggeville and ?Gaskes, and sang to him in the way in which they were wont to do in the time of the Lord Alexander, lately King of the Scots.
By gift of the King.
May Uggeville.

SINGERS 4 Women

1332/3 E101/386/7. and Add. MSS. 38006.

f. 7^{r} 13s. 4d. to four women of Lescluses, for singing in the presence of the Lady Alianora. 3s. 4d. to each of them, by gift of the same lady there.

f. 8^{r} (Add. MSS.) By the hand of the treasurer.
7 May. Lescluses.

SISSONS (Gerard de)

1314/15 E101/376/7.

f. 125^{v} 26s. 8d. owing to Gerard de Sissons, valet of the Queen's Chamber, for his outfits for 8 Ed. II.

SKIRMESOUR (John le)

1299 LOG. 273. (sub. Vadia Nautarum)

£4 18s. 0d. to John [l]e [Topham has read de] Skirmesour, for his wages and those of his 26 companions; from 24 July to 6 August, both days included. For 14 days.

SKIRMISHOUR (Walter le)

1306 E101/369/6.

Present with his brother [to play at sword and buckler], at the Whitsun Feast.
Received 3s. each.

SKIRMISSOUR (William le)

1294 Fryde. 148

£6 to Lord Walter de Beauchamp, Steward [of the King], prest, for his wages for the month of January, by the hand of Willelmus Leskirmissour, his valet.
Aberconway.

1298 Gough. 31

Letters of protection for Willelmus le Skirmisour, who is with the King, in the train of Walter de Beauchamp, Steward of the King's Household.

1298 Gough. 183
Willelmus le Skyrmeseur, valet of Lord Walter de Beauchamp, has a black rouncy with a star on its forehead, valued at 16 marks.

SKYREWITH (Adam de)

King's Watchman.

1285 E101/351/17. (Counter-roll of domestic payments to members of the King's Household).
Listed among the King's Minstrels, and bracketed with John de Berkyng and John de Wyndesore, as Vigiles Regis.
Adam [Sc. Skyrewith]

1289 CCR.
p. 54 Adam le Gayte of Skyrewith and Joan his wife came before the King on Friday, the feast of St. Calixtus (14 October) and sought to replevy their land in Binyngton and Leverton, which was taken into the King's hands for their default against Matilda, late the wife of John Tulle of Boston. This is signified to the justice of the bench.
p. 515 Henry de Whyteby acknowledges that he owes to Adam de Skyrewith 9 marks, to be levied in default of payment, of his lands and chattels in Co. Cumberland.
8 September. Berwick-on-Tweed.

1290 C47/4/5.
f. 38r 2 marks to Adam Squirewyt, Vigilator Regis, for his outfits for the whole of the year.
5 February.

1294/5 Fryde. 41
£6 16s. 10 1/2d. His wages at 4 1/2d. per day for the whole year (365 days) because he was never absent from Court.
London.
[Non pacatur et nichil habuit de prestito]

1296/7 Add. MSS. 7965.

f. 56r 40s. to Adam Skyrewith, in compensation for his brown bay rouncy.
20 July. Berwick-on-Tweed.

f. 79v 56s. 3 1/2d. to Adam de Skyrewhit, King's Watchman, his horse having been valued in the said war in Flanders, for his wages from ?24 day of August, on which day his horse was valued, to the said 19 November, both days included, for 94 days, bar 4; receiving as heretofore, 12d. per day, out of which 4 1/2d. per day is allocated to him in the Marshalcy Roll and here (at Court) 7 1/2d. per day. Into his own hands.
26 March. Westminster.

f. 127r [20s.] for his winter outfit.

1298 Gough. 34
Letters of protection to Adam le Gayte, who will be setting out with the King [for Falkirk].

1299 CCR. 319
To the abbot and convent of Croyland. Request that they will admit into their house Adam de Skyrewith who has long and faithfully served the King and whom the King is sending to them and that they will find him for life the necessaries of life, making to him letters patent under the seal of their chapter granting the same to him.
[The abbot, up to 1305, was Richard Croyland, native of the town.]

1299/1300 LOG. 323.
1307 2 marks to Adam Vigil, for his outfits for the whole of the current year, according to the contract made with him at Westminster.
25 September in the first year of the reign of King Edward, son of Edward I.

c. 1300 E101/371/8. (Part I) fragments.

frag. 16 Adam le Geyte - 5s.

frag. 42 6 marks to Adam de Skyrewyth, for a horse bought [from him] for the use of Elias de Wodeburgh.

frag. 48 1/2 mark for his wage. (See JOHN THE TRUMPETER.)

frag. 101 10s. for his wages.

1300/1 <u>E101/359/5</u>.

f. 2r £4 18s. 3d. to Adam de Skirewith, for his wages, in a letter of quitclaim made to him concerning the farm of the manor of Tilbay (Northumb.)

1302/3 <u>E101/363/18</u>

f. 22r 6s. to Adam <u>Vigil</u>, who is ill and is going home, on the advice of the Prince.

[The entry is somewhat cryptic, but, since Adam's native town, Skirewith, was not all that far from Newcastle-on-Tyne, it looks as though he was being sent home to get well. Skirewith is in Cumberland, not far from Penrith.]

1302/3 <u>Add. MSS. 35292</u>.

f. 28r and <u>passim</u> numerous payments of wages.

1302/3 <u>E101/364/13</u>.

f. 80r 5s. 2d. to Adam the Watchman by the hand of Agnes atte Wode, of Winchfield, for money that she owed him.

1303 <u>CPR. 123</u>.

Grant to Adam de Skyrewith, King's watchman, in succession to a former grant to him of his custody of the lands of John de Dauthorp, in Alneburgh, now deceased, in the county of Cumberland, an idiot from birth, to hold for the life of the said idiot - of the custody of the lands late of the said idiot in the town of Alneburgh, and Dauthorp, Co. York, which should fall by hereditary right to William Berchet, nephew, and one of the heirs of the said idiot, but who, as appears by an inquisition made by Master Richard de Havering, King's Clerk, Escheator this side Trent, is also an idiot; to hold for the life of the said William or until he returns to sanity.

11 March. Westminster.

1303/4 <u>Add. MSS. 8835</u>.

(1307) f. 68r £8 12 6d. for his wages, when his horse was valued in the Scottish War, from 20 November to 21 August, both days included. 276 days of this leap year (1307) receiving 12d. per day etc.

25 September 1 Ed. II (1307). Westminster.

f. 114v 2 marks for his outfits for the whole of the current year (1307) 25 September. Westminster.

1304/5 <u>E101/368/6</u>.

f. 12r Prests, for his wages:

3s. 29 November. Osney (Oxon.)
3s. 19 December. Ringwood.
4s. 24 December. Kingston Lacy.

1305 <u>Cal. Fine Rolls</u>. 530/1

Grant for life to the King's servant, Adam le Gayte, of all the lands in Tilbeye, Co. Northumberland, which he held before, of the King at the King's will, at the rent of £4 18s. 3d. at the Exchequer, yearly, as he used to render.

5 November. Westminster.

1305/6 <u>E101/368/27</u>.

f. 20 £6 16 10 1/2d. to Adam Skyrewith, Watchman, receiving 4 1/2d. per day, for his wages, for the whole of the current year; 365 days, because he was never absent from Court.

25 September. Westminster.

f. 58v Prests, for his wages:

16s. 4d. 20 June. London.
10s. 7 June. Westminster.
13s. 4d. 22 June. London.
1/2 mark. 1 November. Lanercost.

f. 63r 5s. prest, for his wages.

24 August. Newborough in Tyndale.

1 mark, prest, for his wages.

4 September. Newborough in Tyndale.

f. 66r Prests, for his wages:

3s. 29 November (1305) Oseney.
3s. 19 December. Ringwood.
4s. 24 December. Kingston Lacy.

[cf. E101/368/6 f. 12r above]

f. 68r Prests, for his wages:

5s. 25 January. 'Werdeforde'.
5s. 26 February. Itchen Stoke.
5s. 10 May. Winchester.

Added in margin: 2 marks, to the same, in cash, given to him for his winter outfit.

7 February. Wareham.

f. 70r Adam Skyrewyt. 2 marks, prest, for his wages.

6 February. Wareham.

1306 <u>E101/369/6</u>.

Present at the Whitsun Feast, although not mentioned by name.

Received 1/2 mark.

1306/7 E101/370/16.

f. 1r (p. 41) 10s. [for his wages] 25 November. Lanercost.

f. 3v (p. 46) 10s. 24 December. Lanercost.

f. 11v (p. 61) 10s. by the hand of Robert Finchesley. 24 April. [Carlisle]

f. 16r 5s. ?14 June.

1306/7 E101/357/15. (Debts of the Wardrobe)

f. 17r £13 10s. (owing to) Adam the Watchman (Adam Vigil).

f. 21r £17 14s. 4d. Adam de Skyrewyth.

1306/7 E101/364/13.

f. 24v £6 16s. 10d. for his wages, for the whole of the current year, at 4 1/2d. per day, during which time he was never absent. 25 September. Westminster.

f. 80r 6s. 2d. for his wages, by the hand of Agnes atte Wynchefeld, for money which she owed him.

f. 82v 6s. 8d. prest, for his wages. 17 October. Dundee. 10s. 9 November. Dunfermline.

(See WINDSOR, Alexander de)

1313/18 Add. MSS. 34610.

pp. 47-74 (bis) Adam de Skyrewith. Tally for moneys concerning the farm of certain lands in the manor of Tylbay.

[These entries probably refer to 2 Adams; father and son].

SPAIN (John of)

1319/20 E101/378/4.
f. 1r 2s. 4d. to John de Ispannia, groom (vallettus) of the King's Chamber; for his summer shoes.

SPANG (John)

1188 Giraldus Camb. De rebus a se gestis (Rolls Ser. I. 77. Cap. xix)
John Spang, Court fool of Rhys ap Gruffydd, Prince of South Wales.

This is the only reference to a Court Fool in a Welsh Court which I have come across so far. I base the fact that he was such on Giraldus' description of him as being one "qui simulata stultitia et lingua dicaci magnum curiae solatium praestare solet." Geraldus is, as usual, boasting about himself. He says that the crowd was "valde moti" by the preaching of Archbishop Baldwin and himself. The Fool turns to Rhys and says 'You ought to send away this archdeacon relative of yours, because he has sent off to the crusade today a hundred or more of your men; and if he had preached in Welsh, I believe that you wouldn't have one left out of the whole of your great gathering.

STAUNTON (John de)

King's Watchman.

c. 1300 E101/371/8. (Part I) Fragments.
frag. 16 - John de Staunton - 5s.
frag. 41 - 10s.
frag. 48 - 1/2 mark, for his wages.

1304/5 E101/368/6.
f. 12v Johannes de Staunton, Vigil Regis.
Prests, for his wages:
3s. 19 December. Ringwood.
4s. 24 December. Kingston Lacy.

1305 E101/369/11.
f. 202v 1/2 mark to John de Staunton, prest, for his wages. By the hand of Adam (de) Skyrewith, at Lanercost.
1 November. Lanercost.
f. 203v The names of the King's Watchmen recorded thus:
Johanni de Stanton. Hugoni de Lincoln.
Roberto de Fynchesle. Galfrido de Wyndesore.
5s. to each, prest, for their wages.
24 August. Newborough in Tyndale.
[Robert's name crossed out].
also, f. 203r 1 mark, prest, for his wages. Into his own hands.
4 September. Newborough in Tyndale.

1305 <u>MS. Harley 152</u>.
ff. 17^{v}, 19^{r}, 20^{v}. The names of the King's Watchmen: John de Stanton, Robert de Fynchesle, Geoffrey de Windsor and Hugh de Lincoln.

1305/6 <u>E101/369/11</u>.
f. 100^{r} 1/2 mark to John de Staunton, King's Watchman, to buy himself various things (<u>diversa instrumenta</u>). By gift of the King. Into his own hands.
8 February. Lytchett Maltravers (Dorset)
f. 100^{v} 14s. to John de Stannton (or Staunton), to buy himself an outfit [or, in this instance, a gown?]. By gift of the King; into his own hands.
18 April [Winchester].

1305/6 <u>E101/368/27</u>.
Prests, for his wages:
f. 60^{r} 10s. 7 June. Westminster.
4s. 5 July. Thrapston.
£4 13s. 4d. by the hand of John de Okham, for money which he owed him on recognizance, in the Wardrobe.
1/2 mark. 1 November. Lanercost. per A de Skyrewith.
f. 63^{r} 1 mark. 4 September. Newburgh in Tyndale.
f. 63^{v} 5s. 24 August. Newburgh in Tyndale.
f. 66^{v} 3s. 19 December. Ringwood.
4s. 24 December. Kingston Lacy.
f. 68^{r} 5s. 25 January. Werdford.
5s. 26 February. Itchen Stoke.
4s. 29 April. Winchester.
5s. 10 May. Winchester.

1306 <u>E101/369/6</u>.
Present at the Whitsun Feast, but not mentioned by name. Received 1/2 mark.

1306/7 <u>E101/369/16</u>.
Prests, for his wages:
f. 26^{v} 10s. 25 November. Lanercost.
10s. 24 December. Lanercost.
10s. 4 February. Lanercost.
10s. by the hand of Robert de Fynchesle.
24 April. Carlisle.
5s. 21 June. Carlisle.
1/2 mark. 4 July. Kirkandrews.

1306/7 E101/370/16.

f. 1r 10s. for his wages. 22 November. Lanercost.
f. 3v 10s. for his wages. 24 December. Lanercost.
f. 11r 10s. for his wages, by the hand of Robert de Fynchesle, 24 April. Lanercost [?Carlisle].
f. 16r 5s. 13 June.

1307 E101/357/15. (Debts of the Wardrobe)

f. 13r [Owing to] John the Watchman - 8s. 11d.
f. 24r Johannes Vigil - £13 8s. 7d.

1311/12 E101/373/26.

f. 71v Prests, for his wages:
5s. 20 June. Burstwick.
1/2 mark. 2 July. 'Albehawe'
5s. 21 April. Newcastle.
6s. 8d. in cash, given to him per Master Roger Wengesfeld. 5 February. York.

1313 Foedera. II. part I. 212.

Letters of protection for those going overseas with the King and Queen, in the train of Aymer de Valence: among them, Magister Johannes de Staunton. 3 May. Westminster.

1319/20 E101/373/26.

f. 27r £6 13s. 1 1/2d. to John de Staunton, King's Watchman, receiving 4 1/2d. per day for his wages, from 8 July, the beginning of the current year, to 7 July, the last day of the same year, both days included; for 366 days, the aforesaid being Leap Year; except 11 days, during which he was absent.
8 July. London.

1320/21 MS. Cott. Nero. C.viii.

f. 116r 20s. to John de Staunton, Watchman, for his outfits for the whole of the current year, according to the contract drawn up with him at London, on 8 July of the 14th year.

STOURTON (Walter de)

King's Harper.

1289/90 Swinfield. 163.

20s. given to Walter de Sterton, harper.
By gift of bishop Swinfield.
Westminster.

1290 <u>C47/4/5</u>. <u>Walter de Storton, harpator Regis</u>.

f. 48r — £100 given to Walter de Storton, King's Harper, for 426 minstrels, English as well as foreign, on behalf of John, son of the Duke of Brabant, on the occasion of his marriage to Princess Margaret.
8 July. Westminster.
£40 to Walter de Sturton, for bringing 19 minstrels from various parts of England, on behalf of the King, to Westminster, after the wedding of the lady Margaret, his daughter.
12 July. [Westminster]

f. 49r — 40s. to John de Celling, minstrel of the Count of Holland, going from Court to his own country in the train of his lord.
By gift of King, by the hand of Walter de Sturton.
11 August. [Westminster.]

f. 52r — 60s. to Robin le Fol, who was with the Count of Britanny and who was returning overseas with his master; by gift of the King, by the hand of Walter de Sturton.
26 October. Abergavenny.

1290 <u>E101/352/12</u>.

f. 15v — 40s. private prest, paid to Juliana, wife of Walter de Storton; by the hand of Robynett de Rye, her/his grandson/nephew (<u>nepos</u>).
30 January.

1290-2 <u>Botfield</u>. 135.
40s. to Walter de Sturtone*, 'for things bought from him for the Queen's use'; by the hand of R[obert] de Bures, at that time Keeper of the Queen's Wardrobe.

*[There were two men of this name at Court; one was King's Harper and the other King's Chamberlain. This and the following entries from Fryde's <u>Book of Prests</u> seem to refer to the Chamberlain].

1294/5 <u>Fryde</u>.

p. 49 — £11 4s. $4^1/2$d. to him as his wages for the year 1294/5, during which time he was in Court 359 days and absent 6. London.

p. 169 — 60s. for his wages.
23 April. Llanfaes (Anglesey).

p. 170 — 60s. for his wages.
2 June. Cardigan.

p. 179 — 100s. for his wages.
19 October. Westminster.

p. 199 The King gave a length of cloth (one pannus) for placing over the body of Michael de Stortone. [? a relative]. 29 January. Aberconway.

1296/7 Add. MSS. 7965.

f. 56r 40s. to Walter de Sturtone, in compensation for his iron-grey horse, returned to the Almonry at Castle Acre (Norfolk) in February. Into his own hands there. 22 July. Westminster.

f. 123v In a list of servants of the King's Chamber: De Camera Regis 20s. to Walter de Sturton for his winter outfit. Into his own hands, at Castle Acre.

1299 CCR. 299.

Henry de Grey acknowledged that he owed £100 to Maud, late the wife of Walter de Sturton; to be levied, in default of payment, of his lands and chattels in the county of Devon.

SUTOR (Roger)

post 1328 MS. Cott. Galba E iii. (Temp. Ed. III)

[This was thought to be a wardrobe account of Eleanor of Castile, because, in the table of contents of the complete MS. No. 13 is entitled Compotus Garderobae Alienorae Reginae uxoris Edwardi Primi; but this table is written in a later hand. A modern note affixed to the fly-leaf of the MS. ascribes it to the reign of Ed. III and suggests that the account is Queen Philippa's.]

f. 188v Minstrels/To Master Robert the Fool, for the making of a gown (roba) of striped cloth of Ypres - 12 ells. 1 lamb's fur; 2 budge furs 1 budge cap

/to Roger Sutor, 'master' 'guardian' or 'keeper' of the said Robert, for the making of a gown for himself of the same cloth - 6 ells, 3 quarters. 1 lamb's fur.

[Roger and Robert evidently wore the same colours, but Master Robert the fool had more fur and twice the yardage of cloth].

See ROBERT THE FOOL.

SWANSEA (John de)

1303/4 Add. MSS. 8835.

f. 44v Court minstrel, making his minstrelsy, with other Court minstrels in the presence of the Lady Mary, the King's daughter. [? October. Burstwick (Yorks)].

See DRUET.

1311/12 E101/373/26 (Liber unde Respondebit)

f. 16v Johannes de Swaneseye. [?Wages]

SWYLINGTON (Adam de)

1306 E101/369/6.

Citharista. Present at the Whitsun Feast. Received 2s. [Perhaps the harper of Sir Adam de Swillington (Yorks) ob. 1328].

T

T(homas?)

1287 Documents illustrating the Rule of Walter de Wenlock, abbot of Westminster. ed. Barbara F. Harvey. (Camden Soc. 4th Series; Vol. 2 1965) p. 52. Writ of Walter the abbot to his auditors. Dated 1287 'and 2s. given to T. the harper of the King's Chancellor. [The Chancellor was one of Ed. I's closest friends, Robert Burnell, bishop of Bath and Wells.]

TABARIE (Jakemin de)

1302/3 E101/364/13. f.98v

A squire/minstrel of the Queen's (Margaret's) Household.

f. 98v Prests, for his wages:

30s.	23 June.	St. John de Perth.
20s.	2 August.	Aberbrothock (Forfarshire)
30s.	3 September.	Banff.
40s.	17 October.	Dundee.
5s.	9 November.	Dunfermline.

1305/6 E101/368/27.

f. 30s. Prest, for his wages, for preparing a room for the Queen at Lanercost. 5 October. [Lanercost].

TABORER (Audham)

1306 E101/369/6.
The Tabourer of La Dame de Audham
Present at the Whitsun Feast.
Received 1 mark.

TABORER (John le)

1300/1 Add. MSS. 7966.
f. 166v 16s. for his issue of cloth for his outfit.

1303/4 Add. MSS. 8835.
f. 40v Johannes le Tabourer, sometarius vesselle de Elemosina.
4s. 8d. for his shoes. March ?St. Andrews.

TABORER (Peter le)

Probably taborer of Sir John de Vescy.

1278 CCR.
p. 512 Enrolment of a grant by John de Vescy [Ward of Peter of Savoy, the Queen's uncle and close friend of Ed. I] to Peter le Taborer, for life, of 100 marks yearly of land in his manor of Chatton, Northumberland, rendering therefor a clove yearly. He also grants to Peter for life common of turbary and of heath (bruere) in the said manor and 20 cartloads of brushwood yearly in John's woods in the manor, except for John's park.
7 November. Westminster.

1279 CCR.
p. 563 Peter le Taborer acknowledges that he owes to John de Vescy 578 marks; to be levied, in default of payment, of his lands and chattels in the county of Northumberland.
26 April. Westminster.

1288/96 CCR. 16
By this time Peter was dead. Sir John died s.p. 1288/9, aged 44. Peter's son, William, and his widow, Christiana, held the lands which had been enfeoffed to them by John, and after John's death, were assigned to Isabella [his widow?] in dower.

TABORER (William le)

1325 CPR. 161.
Probably Thomas of Lancaster's taborer. Ed. II gave his lands in Pontefract and Friston to his trumpeter, John Scot.

See SCOT (John).

TAILLOUR (Ralph)

1335/8 MS. Cott. Nero. C.viii. (at f. 200, a Wardrobe Account 9-11 Ed. III)
In a list of minstrels of the Royal household:
Radulphus Taillour.

TANTALOUN (de)

1289/90 Swinfield.
p. 155 (footnote): "One gentleman in the King's band of musicians rejoiced in the high-sounding title of De Tantaloun. This makes no mystery of the instrument on which he continued to delight or stun the monarch's ears; though a castle in East Lothian, in pronunciation, nearly approaches to this name."

TEGWARET (Crowder)

1303 E101/363/18.
f. 18r Tequareth le Crouther. 10s. for his shoes for the year.

1306 E101/369/6.
One of the 'Comune'. A Welsh crowder in the Prince's household.
Present at the Whitsun Feast.
Among the Welsh soldiers who served with the King in Flanders in 1297 was one from North Wales called Tegwaret ap Llewelyn. In 1298, CPR, 335, a safe conduct was issued for him to return to England.

TEYSAUNT (John)
King's Herald

1330 E101/385/4. (p. 381)
Listed among the minstrels of Ed. III's household but not called a herald, here:
Johannes Teyssaunt.

1332/3 E101/386/7. (An acct. of the expenses of Princess Eleanor, sister of Ed. III).

f. 4v [ ] to Hanekin de Gaunt, clothier of Bruges [Bourges] for 2 lengths of striped 'squires' cloth, bought from him by order of the Lady Alienor and given to divers squires and minstrels by the same lady: namely, to Teaysaunte, Herald of the lord King of England, Pametto de Recte, squire of the lady Queen, Robert de Hacle, King's sergeant-at-arms, being in the train of the said Lady...

f. 7v £20 to divers minstrels for making their minstrelsies in the presence of the Lady Countess on the day of her marriage [Princess Eleanor of Woodstock. b. 18 June 1318; married, May 1332 Reginald Count of Gelderland; died 22 April 1355.]
By gift of the same; by the hand of Le Teysaunte.
23 May.
40s. to John Teysaunt going from the parts of Germany to the lord King of England. By gift of the Lady Eleanor, as a help towards his expenses in going thither. Into his own hands.
17 May.

1335/8 MS. Cott. Nero. C.viii.

f. 226r Listed among minstrels of the Royal Household:
Johannes Teissaunt.
20s. for his outfit.

THOMAS (le Fol)

Court Fool.

1296/7 Add. MSS. 7965.

f. 29v Thomas fatuus. 13s. 4d. for his expenses in going with William de Lonbrugge, from St. Edmunds "in Kancia" to Lord Edward. the King's son, leading a courser (cursarius) and 2 greyhounds (leporarii) from the King.
November.

f. 52r Thomas le Fol. 50s. for making his minstrelsy before the Princess Elizabeth and her husband at their wedding.
8 February. Ipswich.

f. 127r 20s. for his outfit.

THOMAS (le Harper)

1290/1 Harper of Earl Warenne.

E101/352/21. (Roll of payments)
40s. to Thomas, le Harpour of the Earl Warenne, for playing his harp in the presence of the King.
By gift of the King.
27 September.

1291 C. 47/4/5.
f. 51v 40s. to Thomas le Harpour of Earl Warenne, for playing his harp in the presence of the King at Macclesfield.
By gift of the King, on his departure from Court.
30 April.

THOMAS (Citole-player)

King's minstrel.

1314/17- MS. Cott. Nero. C.viii.
f. 192v £4 5s. 10½d. to Thomas Citoler, in part-payment of £8 5s. 10½d. owing to him.
By a bill.
23 January.
f. 195v 40s. to Thomas Citoler, menestrallus Regis, in part payment of £8 5s. 10½d. owed to him.
By a bill.
21 July [?1318/19].
f. 196v 40s. to Thomas the Citole-player, King's minstrel, in part payment of £8 5s. 10½d. owed to him for his war-wages, his outfits and compensation for his horses.
By a bill.
15 April [?1319].
1335/8 f. 226r Thomas Citoler [now a minstrel in the household of Ed. III] 20s. for his outfit.

E101/385/4. (p. 381).
Thomas Cytoler, [in a list of minstrels of the household of Ed. III].

THOMAS (Vielle-player)

1300/1 E101/360/10. (Expenses of the Prince's journey, with Queen Margaret, from King's Langley to Lincoln. January 1301)
Membrane 1. In a list of the Prince's servants, who went with them:
Thomas le Vilur.

1306/7 E101/357/15.

f. 24r £4 11s. 4d. owing to Thomas Vidulator, at the end of the reign.

1307 E101/373/15.

f. 7r 13s. 4d. for his wages. Into his own hands. 2 October. Nottingham.

1311/12 E101/373/26.

f. 70r 10s. prest, for his wages. 20 June. Burstwick.

1325/6 E101/381/11.

In a list of household officers being issued livery to go with the King to France: among the minstrels:
Thomas le Vilur.

1328 E101/383/4 and E101/383/11. (pp. 375/6)

Listed among the squire/minstrels of Ed. III's household, and receiving the King's livery:
Thomas le Velhour.

THOMASIN (Vielle-player)

Prince's Vielle-player. [Perhaps the same person as Thomas, above].

1302/3 E101/363/18.

f. 21v 12s. to Thomasin le Vilour, for playing to the Prince with John Garsie and John de Catalonia, trumpeters, and John, the Nakerer, at Newbattle (Edinburgh) on Trinity Sunday. By gift of the Prince, to buy himself a black silk cloak.
Sunday, 2 June.

[N.B. The King was also there].

1306 E101/369/6.

Present at the Whitsun feast. Styled: Thomasin Vilour Monsire le Prince.
Received 1 mark.

1307 E101/373/15.

f. 7v 10s. to Thomasin le Vilour, for his wages. Into his own hands.
9 August. Lambeth.

THOMELIN (Vielle-player)

1296/7 Add. MSS. 7965.

f. 52r Thomelin vidulator. 20s. for performing at the wedding of Princess Elizabeth.

THOMELIN (de Tunly (Glos.))

1297 Add. MSS. 7965.
f. 52r Among the minstrels present at the wedding of Princess Elizabeth to the Count of Holland: 20s. to Thomelin vidulator.

1306 E101/369/6.
Thomelin de Thounleie.
Present at the Whitsun Feast.
Received 1 mark.

1321 P.W. 166.
Among the followers of the Earl of Hereford; granted pardon for 'pursuing' the Despensers.
Thomas de Tounleye.
20 August. Westminster.

TICKHILL (Ricard de)

1302/3 E101/363/18.
f. 21v 13s. 4d. to Ricard de Tickhull, trumpator, for making his minstrelsy in the presence of the Prince at Clipstone (Notts), staying there 3 days, in March.
By gift of the Prince.
28 March. Clipstone.

TOUR [John de la] [Janin]

One of the trumpeters of Henry de Beaumont.

1306 E101/369/6.
Present at the Whitsun Feast.
Janin de La Tour.
Received 1 mark.

1310/11 E101/373/10.
f. 7v Johannes de la Tour, trumpator domini Henrici de Bello Monte.
20s. into his own hands; by gift of the King.
14 July.

TREACHANT (William)

Royal herald.

1303/4 Add. MSS. 8835.

f. 42r Willelmus Treachant, haraldus.
20s. to William Treachant, herald, for making his minstrelsy in the presence of the King. Into his own hands; by gift of the King.
1 January (Feast of the Circumcision)
Dunfermline.

TRENTHAM (John de)

Royal harper.

1306 E101/369/6.
Present at the Whitsun Feast.
Johannes de Trenham, Citharista.
Received 2s.

1312 CPR. 494.
Pardon, at the instance of James Daudele, King's yeoman, and kinsman, to John le Harper of Trentham, for the death of Adam de Grymmeshagh.
15 September. Westminster.

1328 CCR.

p. 365 To the abbot and convent of Muchelneye. Request they will admit into their house John de Trentham, the King's harper (citherator) who has long served the King (Ed. III) and his father, and that they will grant to him by letters patent the same allowance as John le Fougheler, deceased, had therein by the late King's (Ed. II) request, certifying the King of their proceedings by the bearer.
24 February. York.

[They refused].

p. 567 To the prior and convent of Bath. Request that they will admit into their house John de Trentham, the King's harper, whom the King is sending to them, in consideration of his good services to him and that they will grant to him by their letters patent such allowance as John le Convers, deceased, had in their house by the late King's request, writing back by the bearer hereof an account of their proceedings in this matter.
15 August. Gloucester.

TRISTREM (Richard)

1324 CCR.
An order to Thomas de Dunstaple to deliver to Richard Tristrem, harpour, his horse, price 20 marks, as the King has received complaint from him that whereas he was at the bridge of Burton [on Trent] on the King's service, and ought to have returned thence to his own parts, by the King's licence, certain malefactors assaulted him at Trentham and took and carried away the said horse, which came, it is said, into the hands of Geoffrey Detheyt, from whose custody the aforesaid Thomas took it for the King's use, in the name of 'Wayf', when he was Keeper of the King's manor of Beaurepayr.

By the King.
8 March. Westminster.

TRUMELL

1319/20 Add. MSS. 17632.
f. 35^{v} Two French minstrels; minstrels of the French King, who were evidently staying at Court over Whitsun were given new clothes for the Pentecost Festivities:
Trumell: *$3^{1}/2$ ells, coloured silk, $3^{1}/2$ ells, striped and 1 lamb's fur. [*de dicta serica*].
Tusset: $3^{1}/2$ ells, coloured silk, $3^{1}/2$ ells, striped and 1 lamb's fur.
*7 ells of silk *de dicta [serica]*.

TRUMPETERS (Anonymous)

1290 E101/352/24. (Household Account of King and Queen)
In a list of minstrels being issued winter and summer livery/outfits:
2 King's Trumpeters.

1296/7 Add. MSS. 7965.
f. 52^{r} 20s. each to two trumpeters of the King, for performing at the wedding of Princess Elizabeth.

c. 1300 E101/371/8. (Pt. I).
fragment 41. 20s. *quibusdam trumpatoribus*.

1302/3 E101/363/18.
f. 10 26s. for making 4 pennoncells of beaten gold, with the Prince's arms on them, for the Prince's trumpeters; and for painting and fringes.

1306 E101/369/6.
2 trumpeters of the young Prince; Thomas of Brotherton (then 5 years old).
Present at the Whitsun Feast. Received 1 mark.
[These were William and John].

1305/6 E101/368/12.
f. 4v 20s. to Martinet the Taborer, William and John, the trumpeters, minstrels of the two [young Princes: Thomas of Brotherton and Edmund of Woodstock.] for making their minstrelsy in their presence on the Eve and Day of Epiphany.
By gift of the 2 [young] lords.
5/6 January. Windsor Castle.

1306 E101/369/6.
Two trumpeters of the Earl of Hereford.
Present at the Whitsun Feast.
Received 1 mark each.

1306 E101/369/6.
Two trumpeters of the Earl of Lancaster.
Present at the Whitsun Feast.
Received 1 mark each.

1306 E101/369/6.
Two trumpeters of Lord John de Segrave.
Present at the Whitsun Feast.
Received 1/2 mark each.

TUDER AP CAUDEL

Trumpeter of Ed. II.

1307/8 Add. MSS. 35093.
f. 1r 10s. for his shoes.
10 July.

TUSSET

1319 Add. MSS. 17632.
See TRUMELL.

U

UGHTRED
or/HUGHTRED

1296 Ughtred le Harpour; prob. domestic harper of William de Moravia.
Rotuli Scotiae I. 28
Restoration of his lands and goods by the King.
10 September. Berwick-on-Tweed.

1297 CPR.
Grant to Ughtred le Harper to restore to him a messuage with its appurtenances in Berwick, in the neighbourhood called Sutecesgate, and a parcel of land, with its appurtenances in Fyskeresgate, which Ughtred held before the King overcame John de Bailliol and took the town.
23 July. Westminster.

V

VALA (John)

1319/20 MS. Soc. of Antiq. 121.
f. 130r 1 mark to Johann Vala for his summer outfit.
14 April. London.

1330 E101/385/4.
p. 381 In a list of minstrels of the household of Ed. III:
Johannes Vala.

VALA (Jerome)
King's minstrel; citole-player.

1312/13 E101/375/8.
f. 29v £4 6s. 8d. to Jirome Vala le Cetoler [menestrallus Regis, in margin] and his companion [fellow citoler, socius] Thomas Dynys, by gift of the King, the price of 2 hackneys, bought from William Blaunkepayn and William le Taverner of Canterbury and given to them. 11s. to the same, the price of 2 saddles, bought at Canterbury and given to them.
Total: £4 17s. 8d.
20 May. Canterbury.

1325/6 E101/381/11.
In a list of the King's household minstrels:
Yomi Vala.

VASCONIA (Ralph de)

c. 1300 E101/371/8. (Part I)
fragment 121.
10s. to Radulphus le Trompour de Vasconia, on his returning to Spain; to help toward his expenses. [perhaps the same person as Ralph the Trumpeter].

VESCY (John or Jacke de)

1306 E101/369/6.
Present at the Whitsun Feast.
One of La Comune.
[Probably minstrel of the dowager Lady Isabella de Vescy, sister of Henry de Beaumont]

VIELLE-PLAYER (Fiennes)

1285/6 E101/352/4.
Membrane 3.
No 2015 And 1 cup, (silver gilt, worked with enamel, with foot and cover) of the weight of 2 marks less 4d.; value 40s. given by the King to the vielle-player of Sir W. de Fenes.
11 December.
[William de Fiennes, King's banneret].

VIELLE-PLAYER (Wake)

1306 E101/369/6.
Present at the Whitsun Feast.
Vielle-player of Lady de Wake,
Received 5s.

VIELLE-PLAYERS (anonymous)

1332/3 E101/386/7.
f. 7r 12d. to divers vielle-players, for making their minstrelsies before the Cross at the North door in the church of St. Paul, London. By gift of the Lady Alienor there; by the hand of the Treasurer, on the last day of April.

VIELLES (Guillotin de)

1306/7 E101/370/16.
f. 2v (p. 44) 40s. to Guillotin de Vielles, minstrel of the Lord de Rocheford, coming into England in the train of the Duc de Brie.
13 December. Lanercost.

VIGILES (anonymous)
King's Watchmen in the Tower.

1262 CPR. 73
Mandate to the Constable of the Tower that he should, without delay, add 2 more watchmen to the 2 already there.
By the King.
9 June. Canterbury.

VISAGE

1296/7 Add. MSS. 7965.
f. 52r 20s. for making his minstrelsy before the Lady Elizabeth on her wedding-day.

See GRISCOTE and MAGOTE.

VITALIS (Vielle-player)

1198/9 Book of Fees, II. Appendix 1339
Gloucester.
The land of Moses, the Jew, was confiscated by the lord King; and Vitalis the Vielle-player has it, on the authority of the lord King John; its value is half a mark.

VOLAUNT (William)

1360 Issue Rolls, 171.
£40 to William Volaunt, King of heralds and minstrels, being at Smythfield, at the last tournament there; in money, paid to them, of the King's gift.

VYELET (Walter)

1210 Rotuli de Liberate ac de Misis et Praestitis. Regnante Johanne [ed. T. Duffus Hardy. 1844]
Rotulus de Prestito, 12 John.
p. 230 1 mark to Walter Vyelet, Vielle-player, at Bridgenorth.
p. 242 1 mark, by the King to Wiolet, the vielle-player.
p. 244 1 mark to Vyolet, the vielle-player.
p. 246 1 mark to Vielet, the vielle-player at Ipswich.

VYELE (William)

1290 C47/4/5.

f. 49r 40s. to William Vyele, vielle-player of Count Artaud, (Guillehm Vyele vidulator comitis Artaud), returning from the Court, with his master, to County Richmond.
By gift of the King.
3 September. Rockingham.

1290 E101/352/21. (Roll)
As above, with alteration: vidulator Comitis Britanniae which makes more sense.

VYELUR (William le)

1264 CPR. 321.
Pardon to William le Vyelur of Estlegh for the death of Simon le Vyelur his son, upon trustworthy testimony that he killed him by misadventure.
[May not be minstrels].

W

WAFERER (Prince's)

1296/7 Add. MSS. 7965.

f. 52r 10s. to the Waferer of the King's son, for performing at the wedding of Princess Elizabeth [Waffrarius filii Regis]

WALTER (Despenser)

1298 Gough. 188 (Roll of horses)
Walter, vielle-player, vallettus of Sir Hugh Despenser, has a bay rouncy with one white foot; valued at 25 marks.
Killed at Falkirk.

WALTER (fitz Walter)

1290 E101/352/12.

f. 11v 13s. 4d. to Walter, vielle-player, of Lord Robert fitz Walter, prest [for his wages]
9 August.

WALTER (trumpeter)

1306 E101/369/6.
Present at the Whitsun feast.
One of La Comune.

WALTER (trumpeter) (Arundel)

1320/1 Add. MSS. 9951.
f. 21r One of the trumpeters of the Earl of Arundel.

See CORBET (William)

WALWAN
Mounted messenger of King John.

1229 CCR. 169
The King to his barons of the Exchequer, greeting. Know that we have granted to Master Odo, our coachman (carectarius) the gift of 2d. which Walwan, one-time mounted messenger of lord King John, which he was want to receive every day by the hand of the sheriff of Essex, as alms from us; and we therefore order you to see to it that the aforesaid gift be given to the said Odo, as aforesaid.
Teste Rege (Hen III)
Windsor. 24 April.

WATCHMEN (Royal)

1296/7 Add. MSS. 7965.
f. 52r 10s. each to 4 of the King's and the King's son's Watchmen, for performing [or being on duty] at the wedding of Princess Elizabeth.

1306 E101/369/6.
4 King's Watchmen, present at the Whitsun Feast. Received 1/2 mark each.
[They would have been 4 of the following: Adam de Skyrewith, John de Staunton, Robert de Fynchesley, Hugh de Lincoln, Geoffrey de Windsor, Alexander de Windsor, Richard de Windsor, whom see under each name]

WATCHMEN (of Ed. III)

1330 E101/385/4. (p 381)
Listed as King's Vigiles:
Radulphus le Geyte,
Johannes Hardyng.
Willelmus Hardyng.

WEARDUS (Horn blower)

1328 E101/383/4. (pp. 375/6)
In a list of squire minstrels of Ed. III's household:
Weardus le Corner.

WELSH (crowders and trumpeters)
anonymous

1290 C47/4/5.

f. 48^{v} 5s. each to 2 Welsh trumpeters, coming to the King, for the weddings of the 2 daughters of the King - Johanna and Margaret and returning to their own country.
By gift of the King.
5s. each to 2 Welsh crowders, as above.
3s. 4d. each to 2 grooms (boys) of the said trumpeters and crowders, as above.
By gift of the King.
20 July. Westminster.

1290 E101/352/21. (Roll)
As above, but with no reference to the grooms.
25 July.

WERINTONE (Adam de)

1306 E101/369/6.
Present at the Whitsun Feast.
Received 2 marks.
[Werintone - Warrington, Lancs.]

WHISSH (Henry)

1314/17 MS. Cott. Nero. C.viii.
Squire/minstrel of the King's household. His name occurs in a long list of payments to King's Minstrels:

f. 192^{r} £8 10s. 0d. into the hand of Henry Whissh (Henricus Whissh), squire of the household of the Lord King, for money owed to him for his war-wages and his outfit.
11 December. By a bill.

1335/8 f. 226^{r} Henricus Whyssh, minstrel in the King's (Ed. III's) household. 20s. for his outfit.

1330 E101/385/4. (p. 381)
In a list of minstrels of the household of Ed. III:
Henricus Wysshe.

post 1328 MS. Cott. Galba E.iii.
f. 186^{r} 7 ells and 1 lamb's fur for Henricus Whiss, menestrallus, for his summer outfit; for having an outfit made of yellow cloth and striped samite, against the Day of Revelation.

WILLIAM (acrobat)

1312/13 E101/375/8.

f. 14v Willelmus le Saltor. [Saltator]
3s. to William the acrobat and his companions, for making their vaults at Surflete, on the return of the King through it.
By gift of the King; by the hand of Merlin de Cene, who gave them the money, by order of the King, on the same day there.
8 July. Surflete.

WILLIAM (Champagne)

1311/12 MS. Cott. Nero. C.viii.

f. 84v Guillelmus menestrallus Comitis Campanie.
40s. to William, minstrel of the Count of Champagne, for making his minstrelsy in the presence of the King.
By gift of the King.
23 February. York.

WILLIAM (Le Harpur')

1212 Book of Fees. I. 151.
Nottingham and Derby.
In Wiston, below the same manor, 4 and a half bovates of land which were want in old time to answer for 10s.; which King Henry (Hen. I) the grandfather of lord King John gave to one William Le Harpur, rendering 16d. a year, and his heirs still hold it.

WILLIAM (Sutherland)

1302/3 Add. MSS. 35292.

f. 11r 1/2 mark to William, minstrel of the Earl of Sutherland, for making his minstrelsy before the King.
By gift of the King.
2 October. 'Gartonothe'. (Morayshire)

WILLIAM (harper)

1298/9 CPR. 372
Pardon to William, the harper of Askumo, for the rape of Matilda, wife of Simon Dornesheved.

WILLIAM (organist)

1313/16 Add. MSS. 34610.
Vol. 5, p. 4. 55s. 4d. given, in cash, to William the Organist. [Willelmus Organiste. ?King's organist]; by the hand of the Chamberlain of Scotland.
[This MS. has been transcribed from an original roll, Liberatio Facta Ingelardo de Warde, Keeper of the King's Wardrobe.

WILLIAM (taborer)

1323/4 Abbrevatio Rot. Orig., 272.
Willelmus le Taburer.
probably taborer of Thomas of Lancaster.
Deprived of his lands by Ed. II after the battle of Boroughbridge: They were given to John Scot, King's Trumpeter.

See JOHN the trumpeter.

WILLIAM (trumpeter)

King's and Prince's Trumpeter.
1299/1300 Add. MSS. 35291.
f. 159v Willelmus Trumpator.
Prest, for his wages.

1300/1 E101/360/10.
Membrane I. One of the trumpeters who accompanied Prince Edward and Queen Margaret, when they went from Langley, in January 1301, to join the King at Lincoln.
[Probably the Gillot, who figures as Prince's Trumpeter at the Whitsun Feast.]

1305/6 E101/368/12.
f. 4v 20s. to Martinet Willelmus Trumparius and John, his fellow-trumpeter for making their minstrelsy in the presence of the 2 [young] princes, on the Eve and Day of Epiphany (5/6 January)
Windsor Castle.

See MARTINET.

1306 E101/369/6. Gillot, Trumpour Monsire le Prince.
Present at the Whitsun Feast.
Received 1 mark.

1306/7 E101/357/15.
f. 13v 32s. 3d. owing to him at the end of the reign.

1307/8 E101/373/15. (Wardrobe Book of Ed. II)
f. 5r for his wages:

10s.	25 July.	Carlin.
6s. 8d.	29 July.	Carlisle.
10s.	27 August.	Comenoke'.
6s. 8d.	26 September.	Clipston (Notts.)

13s. 4d. by the hand of Master W. de Melton, 18 October. Hamslape.

1310/11 E101/374/5.
f. 34v Willelmus Trompour.
45s. 9d. to William the Trumpeter, receiving 4 1/2d. per day for his wages for the whole of the current year (1310), for 365 days, during which time he was present in Court for 122 days by the contract made with his wife, Margery.
6 May. Westminster [1315].

1311/12 MS. Cott. Nero. C.viii.
f. 116r Willelmus le Trumpur; King's minstrel.
20s. for his winter outfit, according to the contract drawn up with him at London.
5 February. 1315/16.

1315/16 E101/373/26.
f. 26r 3s. to William the Trumpeter, receiving 4 1/2d. per day for his wages, for the whole of the current year, that is, for 366 days of the aforesaid leap year, during which time he was in Court for 8 days.
5 February. London.

1322 Foedera. II 375.
Pardon, re Thomas of Lancaster, to Willelmus le Trumpour.

WILLIAM (Vielle-player)

1254 CPR. 376.
Protection, with clause volumus, for the following, who are going with the queen, to the King (Hen. III) in Gascony, for so long as they are there on the King's service: William le Vilur.
8 May. Westminster.

WINDSOR (Alexander de)

King's Watchman.

1296/7 Add. MSS. 7965.
f. 127r [20s] for his winter outfit.

1299/1300 Add. MSS. 35291.
f. 155r prest, for his wages.

c. 1300 E101/371/8. Pt. I.
fragment 101. 10s. to Alexander de Wyndesore, for his wages.

1300/1 E101/359/5. (fragment of a Wardrobe account)
f. 7v Alexander de Windesore, Vigil Regis...

1302/3 E101/364/13.
f. 78v Prests, for his wages:

1/2 mark.	9 April.	Lenton.
1/2 mark.	18 March.	London.
1/2 mark.	30 June.	St. John de Perth.

f. 80r 5s. 2d. to Alexander, the Watchman, by the hand of Agnes atte Wode, of Winchfield, for money that she owed him.
f. 82r 6s. 8d. prest, for his wages.
17 October. Dundee.
f. 82v 10s. each to Alexander de Windsor, Adam de Skyrewith and Geoffrey de Windsor; prests, for their wages.
Bracketed together and called Vigiles Regis.
9 November. Dunfermline.

WINDSOR (Geoffrey de)

King's Watchman.

c. 1300 E101/371/8. Pt. I.
frag. 16 Galfridus de Wyndelsore - 5s.
frag. 41 Galfridus de Windesoure - 10s.
frag. 48 1/2 mark for his wages.

1300/1 E101/359/5.
f. 3r 1 mark, for his expenses.
[20 April] Worcester.

1302/3 Add. MSS. 35292.
f. 28r and passim. Payments of wages. Too frequent to quote.

1303/3 E101/364/13.

f. 82^{v} 10s. prest, for his wages.
9 November. Dunfermline.

1304/5 E101/368/6.

f. 12^{r} Prests, for his wages:

3s.	19 December.	Ringwood.
4s.	24 December.	Kingston Lacy.

1305 MS. Harley 152.

f. 17^{v} named as Vigil Regis.

1305/6 E101/369/11.

f. 203^{r} 1 mark, prest, for his wages.
4 September. Newborough (Northumberland).

f. 203^{v} 5s. prest, for his wages.
24 August. [Newborough].

1305/6 E101/368/27.

f. 60^{r} Prests, for his wages:

	10s.	7 June.	Westminster.
	4s.	5 July.	Thrapston (into his own hands)
	1/2 mark.	1 November.	Lanercost. (by the hand of Adam Skyrewith).
f. 63^{r}	1 mark.	4 September.	Newborough in Tyndale.
f. 63^{v}	5s.	24 August.	Newborough in Tyndale.
f. 66^{r}	3s.	26 November.	Abingdon.
	3s.	19 December.	Ringwood.
	4s.	24 December.	Kingston Lacy.
f. 68^{r}	5s.	25 January.	'Werdford'.
	5s.	26 February.	Itchen Stoke.
	10s.	18 March.	Winchester.
f. 70^{r}	2 marks.	6 February.	Wareham.

1306 E101/369/6.

Probably one of the 4 Watchmen present at the Whitsun Feast.
Received 1/2 mark.

1306/7 E101/369/16.
Prests, for his wages:
f. 26^v 10s. by the hand of John de Stanton.
25 November. Lanercost.
10s. by the hand of Adam Skyrewith.
24 December. Lanercost.
10s. 4 February. Lanercost.
10s. by the hand of Robert de Fynchesle.
24 April. Carlisle.
5s. by the hand of John de Staunton.
21 June. Carlisle.
1/2 mark. 4 July. Kirkandrews.

1306/7 E101/370/16.
f. 1^r (p. 41) 10s. for his wages.
25 November. Lanercost.
f. 3^v 10s. by the hand of Adam Skyrewith.
24 December. Lanercost.

WINDSOR (John de)

King's Watchman.

1285 E101/351/17.
Listed as one of the King's minstrels.

See ADAM and BERKYNG (John de)

1290 C47/4/5.
Johann de Wyndesoure, Vigilator Regis.
f. 38^r 2 marks for his outfit for the whole year.
5 February.

1294/5 Fryde.
p. 53 £6 16s. 10 1/2d. for his wages, at 4 1/2d. per day, for 365 days; for he was never absent from Court.

1299/1300 Add. MSS. 35291.
f. 155^r prest, for his wages.

WINDSOR (Philip de)

1311/12 E101/374/19.
Philippus de Wyndesoures, groom (garcio) of the household of the 2 young princes.
f. 8^r 12d. for making his minstrelsy in the presence of the 2 princes.

See ROGER (Mapparius)

WINTON (Robert de)

1305 Add. MSS. 37656. (Wardrobe Book of Thomas de Brotherton)

Robertus de Winton, Waffrarius.

f. 1r 2s. to Robert de Winton, Waferer, serving the sons of the King and the Lady Maria, their sister, nun of Amesbury, at table, with his wafers.
By gift of the 2 (princes).
22 August. Ludgershall.

WYCOMBE (Nicholas de)

1311/12 MS. Cott. Nero. C.viii.
King's Watchman.
f. 196r Nicolaus de Wycombe.

See Harding (William).

WODEROVE (Roger)

1296/7 Add. MSS. 7965.
f. 111v King's mounted Messenger.

WODEROVE (William) (trumpeter)

1306 E101/369/6.
Willelmus Woderove, Trumpator.
Present at the Whitsun Feast. Received 2s.

WOODSTOCK (Walter de)

1294/5 Fryde.

p. 83
6s. 8d. for his little expenses, when going out of Court to fish.
21 June. Worcester.

p. 86 6s. 8d. for going out of Court from Worcester to fish in the fish-pond there; because William piscator was ill.

p. 90 6s. 8d. for money paid by him to various runners (cokini, 'kitchen-boys') night and day, for the King.
26 August. Westminster.

1296/7 Add. MSS. 7965.
f. 33v (Here he is styled Walterus de Wodestoke, subianitor Regis. Money paid by him to various mounted messengers and runners.

1300/1 E101/359/6.

3s., prest, for his expenses when going to Linlithgow to fish.

f. 8r half a mark, for his wages.

12 October. Dunipace.

1302/3 E101/363/10.

f. 13r 4s. to little Walter of Woodstock (paruo Waltero de Wodestoke) for carrying letters of the King to Lord Ralph de Monthemer, earl of Gloucester. For his expenses.

1303 E101/364/13.

f. 59v 4s. 8d. for his winter and summer shoes for the current year.

28 May. Roxburgh.

1306 E101.369/6.

Present at the Whitsun Feast.

See GAUTERON LE PETIT.

1306/7 E101/370/16.

f. 7r (p. 53) 4s. 3d. prest, for repairing the ditch and making hedges around Lanercost Priory.

12 February. Lanercost.

3s. 9d. for making a ditch at Lanercost.

14 February. Lanercost.

f. 7v (p. 54) 1 mark for his outfit and shoes.

16 February. Lanercost.

1311/12 E101/373/26.

f. 90r in moneys paid out by the Cofferer, by the hand of Walter de Woodstock, 12s. 2d. 'in preparacione'.

YEUANN

1307 E101/373/15.
{ f. 14v { f. 15v 4s. to Ieuan and Ithel, Welsh trumpeters, retained on wages of 2d. per day each, by special order of the King (Ed. II).
f. 17v 2s. 4d. to Ieuan and Ithel, trumpeters, retained on wages of 2d. per day each, during the period 26 August to 1 September.
f. 19r 40s. to Ieuan and Ithel, Welsh trumpeters, for making their minstrelsy in the presence of the Lord King, at a certain banquet which the Earl of Cornwall [Gaveston] held at... By gift and grace of the King, by the hand of William le Gascoign.

YORK (Gilbert de)

1300/1 Add. MSS. 7966A.
f. 66r To Gilbert of York and William Hatheway vielle-players, for making their minstrelsy in the presence of the King.
By gift of the King, namely, 13s. 4d. to the aforesaid Gilbert and 6s. 8d. to the aforesaid William; into their own hands.
2 April. Evesham.

E101/359/5. (Fragment of a Wardrobe Acct. Journal)
f. 1v 1 mark to Gilbert of York and 1/2 mark to William of Hatheway [de Hathewy], vielle-players, Easter Sunday (2 April) [Evesham].

YORK (Robert de)

1302/3 E101/364/13.
f. 80v Robertus de Eboracum, Trumpator.
King's Trumpeter.
Prests, for his wages:

13s. 4d.	9 July.	St. John de Perth.
10s.	8 August.	Brechin.
5s.	9 November.	Dunfermline.

1303/4 Add. MSS. 8835.
f. 44r 50s given to Robert of York, trumpeter, by J. de Drokenesford, for him to buy trumpets for himself and his fellow-trumpeter; the money given to him at Newcastle-on-Tyne, on his setting out for London to get them; and for his expenses in returning to the King.
29 January [Newcastle-on-Tyne].

YORK (Robinet de) (Taborer)

1300/1 Add. MSS. 7966A.
f. 68^v 6s. 8d. to Robinet(t) the Taborer, of York, for making his minstrelsy in the presence of the King.
By gift of the King at ?Doneye.
8 December.

YPRES (Alvin de)

1296/7 Add. MSS. 7965.
f. 57^v 10s. each to Robinet(t) de Ipre and Alvinius de Ipre, minstrels of Ypres, for making their minstrelsies in the presence of the King at Ghent. By gift of the King.
5 November. Ghent.

YPRES (Robinet de)

1296/7 Add. MSS. 7965.
f. 57^v as preceding.

YTHEL

1307 E101/373/15.
Welsh trumpeter.

See YEUANN.